THE SUDDEN DISAPPEAR- ANCE OF SEETHA

ANDREA GUNRAJ

VINTAGE CANADA

VINTAGE CANADA EDITION, 2010

Published in Canada by Vintage Canada, a division of Random House of Canada
Limited, Toronto, in 2010. Originally published in hardcover in Canada by
Alfred A. Knopf Canada, a division of Random House of Canada Limited,
Toronto, in 2009. Distributed by Random House of Canada Limited, Toronto.

Vintage Canada with colophon is a registered trademark.

www.randomhouse.ca

LIBRARY AND ARCHIVES CANADA CATALOGUING IN PUBLICATION

Gunraj, Andrea, 1978–
      The sudden disappearance of Seetha / Andrea Gunraj.

ISBN 978-0-307-39698-3

      I. Title.

PS8613.U58S93 2010   C813'.6   C2009-906720-X

Book design by CS Richardson

Printed and bound in the United States of America

10 9 8 7 6 5 4 3 2 1

For my mother, Genet Gunraj
1944–2004

Now we see but a poor reflection as in a mirror;
then we shall see face to face.
(1 Corinthians 13:12a)

He take my baby. Terror burned through her. She rushed from room to room, the calm of sleep jolted from her eyes. She checked inside the musty closet, behind the chest, under the kitchen table, the bushes in the backyard. All she found were scuttling cockroaches and dry leaves and dust. *Not my child, my little Seetha* . . .

The blood pulsed through her head. She stumbled out of the front door to get Lenda, the only person she could think of running to now. Fear hardened in her throat. *How could I do dis, how could I let dis happen?* The scar on her shoulder throbbed.

He had taken her child and it would be impossible to get her back. *I should-a known he would do dis, I should-a left dis town long time* . . . The knife that had cut into her three years ago in the rainforest of Seetha's birth was ripping her open once again. She had stood her ground in front of the two men, breathing the fumes from the burning school, refusing to let them claim her baby. She may have been threatened and wounded, but that time, thanks to her peculiar power, she had escaped with her daughter. *How could I let dis happen?*

"It ain't your fault, Neela. We just need to get de girl back." *Get her back?* She watched helplessly as Lenda rushed about, doing what any loyal friend would do, enlisting the town of Marasaw in the hopeful search. *They won't find her,* she thought, aching to tell Lenda, *and there's nothing I can do to get her back.* Neela's connection with Seetha was gone; all that remained was a sickening void of white noise. In the coming months, she begged her powers to arise in her and bring her daughter back to her arms. But the powers, stubborn and single-minded as she, had a will of their own—they were part of her but hardly subject to her.

As the search intensified, Marasaw's rumour war began. People on one side of the argument said it was better that the girl was taken as a child too young to remember being lifted from her mother's cot. *It's a blessing in disguise, man, at least de girl won't know to cry for her mommy!* Those on the other side believed it worse to have been taken at three years old, because at that age, memories do form. Over fried plantain and curried fish, they predicted that dreams of kidnap would haunt Seetha. *Dat girl gon' develop serious problems, you know, she might go mad . . . She gon' fear travelling and darkness, even sleep! . . . Ow, poor thing, it gon' prevent her from developing properly . . . A child needs her mother, yes, but a mother who can't protect her? What good is dat?*

What Neela didn't know was that she had started this argument, that the dying remnant of her childhood powers had ignited the controversy. She had never really understood her magic and how it came to her, worked as it pleased and reaped the consequences that it did, passed down from generation to generation, never failing to surface, never skipping a beat.

PART ONE

Neela's abilities had first manifested themselves when she was ten and her brother, Navi, was twelve. Navi was the smart child, known throughout the neighbourhood for his ability to add, subtract, multiply and divide faster and better than any other twelve-year-old, and probably better than anyone else in Marasaw. He would pace around his grandmother's rickety wooden house in grey school shorts and an undershirt, using whatever he came upon to test his mathematical speed and accuracy. *Twenty-seven and twelve tin cup is thirty-nine tin cup! A hundred and three by six tea towel is six hundred and eighteen tea towel!* Neela's grandmother, only in her early forties when Neela and Navi were near puberty, encouraged her grandson's domestic calculation rampages. She challenged him to problem-solve questions: "If I throw seventy-seven black-eye pea in dis pot and boil it for forty-nine days, and spill two quart-a water straining de peas out, but forget de fire on and almost burn down de town by eleven o'clock, how much peas left?"

In his younger days, Navi would stare at the sandy floor-boards and, after some reflection, whisper, *Seventy-five?* But these days he had learned better. "De same amount you start with, Granny."

"Ah Navi-boy," she sighed, with an artificial old-lady voice, "you too quick for your old granny."

While the whole neighbourhood prophesied about Navi's future as a banker or engineer, thrilled that their modest town should possess a boy of such talent, Neela's prospects were rarely discussed. They were hardly noticed in light of her brother and this manifested itself in bodily form—she grew skinnier, shorter and more awkward than he. She tried to do mathematics like her brother, but she would pass household objects and forget to put them into equations. Even when she made a painful effort to do so, she was never as daring, as acrobatic, as Navi. *Nine and four channa is twelve . . . no, thirteen channa . . .* She was aware of how silly she sounded coming up with those lacklustre sums. "Alright girl, dat's good," was as much of a confirmation as Granny could muster, flipping and oiling roti on the stove. "Must follow your brother's example when he wins de contest."

The famous Children's Mathematical Challenge, or the CMC, as the students had nicknamed it, had been initiated by a foreign diplomat who had come to the country. Dismayed at the lack of competitions between schools, he had originally founded the Student Spelling Challenge. He had laboured to get headmasters from towns all over the country to send their most talented spellers to the competition, but his excitement hadn't ignited the country's imagination. It was only years later that the diplomat's son, convinced that arithmetic, not English, was the world's common language, transformed it into a popular math competition.

Navi was Marasaw Elementary School's natural choice. After the headmaster announced that Navi would attend the CMC in the capital city, adult townsfolk took credit for the boy's brilliance. *I taught de boy for four years,* his teacher told the other teachers. *He takes after my family, you know,* his grandmother informed her neighbours. *It's his name we raise to heaven in prayer, man,* his Sunday school teacher confirmed. But deep down, they knew Navi's uncanny skills didn't come from any of them—it wasn't clear how he achieved his spectacular sums, but they knew full well that he didn't need anything from them to know that *three by six hundred and seven papaw is one thousand eight hundred and twenty-one papaw.*

Still, Navi was generous in his acceptance of the honour. "It's my family, my neighbours, my school and all de good citizens of Marasaw dat made dis happen. Without them teaching and guiding me, I would not even be able to spell seee-emmm-see," he declared in a speech to the whole school, for which he received applause made insincere by his classmates' secret jealousy and overly sincere by his teachers' delight. "Will you join me now, fine students and teachers of Marasaw Elementary," he said in conclusion, "to sing our school's most beautiful anthem? For I am going to dis Challenge only for you." More than two hundred children, sweating in uniforms cuffed by green and orange bands, stood up noisily.

But Neela didn't sing. She had no choice in attending the assembly, but she had the choice of whether or not to sing. As the others belted out the school's anthem in that off-key, half-shouting way they always did, Neela mouthed the words, pretending to take heaving breaths between stanzas. She had started such little feats of rebellion the afternoon her granny and brother sat at the kitchen table to write his acceptance speech. Her anger had begun to seethe against Navi's lofty accomplishments, and she knew that the time had come for her to act. *I done with being his copycat, done being his hand-puppet.* Her underground revolt might go unnoticed, but she didn't need anyone's attentions. She would still strive to poison the enthusiasm swirling around Navi and his mathematics. *He gon' be sorry, real sorry . . .*

"Hey, girl," a classmate with puffy ponytails whispered from behind her, between verses three and four, "you so *lucky* to have a brother like dat!" Neela pretended to be too absorbed in her singing to hear the compliment.

Neela attempted to throw a tantrum, whining to continue playing outside with her friends, but her grandmother would have none of it. "Get your tail in here and help you brother finish packing de bags!" Granny commanded. So Neela kept silent when the three of them took a taxi to the dock at the edge of town. She sucked in her *Look over there!* when, as their ferry started across the river, a large orange bird that had captured a squirmy fish in its beak perched on a post and stretched out its wings. She held her tongue and clamped her teeth when they arrived on the other side and descended from the boat along wobbling wood planks, dizzy with noontime sun and confused by shouts of family meeting family, *Eh boy, eh girl, we over here!* Navi's vocal calculations extended to their surroundings while they awaited a minibus—palm trees and expansive bushes, taxi drivers bullying customers, a girl selling ginger beer, stacks of bleached crates acting as chairs. Passengers packed into a lime green van and held tight as it whipped down crowded city streets, blasting everything in its path with a horn rigged to sound like a siren. But, wedged between old women and their plastic bags, Neela refused to affirm her grandmother's reflection: "Dis driver a madman, I tell you . . ."

It was the first time that Neela had visited the capital and stayed as a hotel guest. Even though her Marasaw hometown of aged houses and elderly neighbours was only a mile across the river, it seemed terribly unsophisticated in comparison to the city. Never again would she be as mesmerized as she was this time—all the colourfully dressed ladies, shops constructed with bricks, humming mopeds and taxis, poor children jumping in puddles of brown water. It was so animated, so celebratory, even in its most mundane elements. As they walked by the sprawling outdoor market, Neela envisioned the Big Top described in her *Royal English Reader for Students* textbook. *Mighty lions jump through flaming hoops while seals balance balls and clowns tickle everyone's fancy,* she recalled when they passed a crowd cheering a jester; he manoeuvred his homemade marionette to flirt with bashful little girls.

That evening, Navi applied arithmetic to everything in the hotel room, more impressive than ever dividing and multiplying the pillows and sheets. "Neel babylove," Granny said, "whole day you quiet. What happen, ba-ba, you sleepy? Go to sleep."

"Yes, Granny," she answered, too genuinely tired to go through her nightly *Ow Granny, a little longer, nah* routine.

Granny rubbed her hand over a folded blanket on the bed. "See how nice these hotels does be? Watch how pretty dis blanket is. You must enjoy de place while you here—feel it, nah?" she asked, hoping to engage Neela's interest. "Now hear, children, both-a you," Granny said, over *twelve hundred and sixty beds minus four hundred and thirty beds,* "must call me 'Mommy' when we out tomorrow, you understand? Nav? Hear, Neela?"

"Yes, Mommy," they replied with equally distracted voices. As Navi became more lavish in his calculations, Neela sank lower into the despair of her brother's sure victory at the contest. Grudgingly, she acknowledged that her silent campaign had made no impact on his spirits or abilities. He spent the night dreaming of stars and planets and moons to add and subtract— he had the strange gift of calm. Although she had seen no results, Neela was too stubborn to abandon her protest. She brought the soundless demonstration into the bustling hotel auditorium the next morning. Navi and dozens of other uni-formed children were lined up on stage in velvet-backed chairs, restlessly awaiting the opening speech.

"Ladies and gentlemen, family and friends, students and educators, thank you for being with us today as we mark our thirty-seventh annual Children's Mathematical Challenge. This is a truly marvellous event of higher learning that I look forward to every year," the diplomat's son said, cloaked in a woollen suit at the polished wood podium. "As you are well aware, the fifty fine boys and girls before you have been selected as your country's most promising young mathematicians."

"Shhh, boy, hear de man, nah?" a man sitting behind Neela and her grandmother whispered to his whimpering toddler son. "Watch your sister up there, she over there, you see? Dat man talking about her when he say 'mathematician,' eh? Aw, she bright bad, yes? Hummm?"

Neela frowned to herself. She knew that the man's attempt to console the boy on the basis of his sister's overbearing accomplishments would make the child more upset, more impatient in his own ordinariness.

"There is nothing more satisfying than seeing children carry the torch of mathematics into the future," the diplomat's son continued, wiping moisture from his forehead with an embroidered handkerchief. "You should be proud of your sons and daughters. Many of them will take what they discover here and, no doubt, will grow to forge a noteworthy legacy for your country. They will bring their childhood success into adult excellence."

"You hear dat?" a woman a few seats away said in a scathing growl toward her two shrinking daughters. "Y'all play-playing whole time at school, and look where your brother is." One girl stared at her shoes while the other concentrated on smoothing her skirt over her knees. "You hear me, you ungrateful pickney?"

A current of warmth rose through Neela, vicarious anger and shame accumulating under her cheeks and ears.

"Y'all think life is easy but it ain't so. Your brother work hard and if you keep play-playing, he gon' leave you behind. See how quick y'all become nothing." Neela watched the girls avoid eye contact with their mother, knowing that she would interpret it as encouragement to continue.

"It's one thing if y'all was succeeding in your classes. Then you could do all your wicked heart desires. You could run all over de square and I'd let you go along your way. I'd keep my mouth shut. But how you girls carry on, must ready yourself for failure. Don't come to me, 'Mommy, why you didn't tell us how hard it would be? Why you didn't show us de way?' Because I done tell you, I done show you . . ."

Applause drowned her out, forcing Neela's attention back to the diplomat's son. "I expect your very best today, boys and girls, as we begin our Challenge. As you know, our rules are simple—contestants who provide correct answers will move forward. The contestant who completes the competition without an error will be declared the winner. I wish you the best of luck, children, we all do." More applause rang through the auditorium. "And good luck in all your future endeavours."

The Children's Mathematical Challenge started with simple arithmetic questions posed to each competitor by a panel of judges. Although instructed to hold their applause until the end of each round, family members of children who answered correctly—*De answer is four hundred and eighteen, Honourable Judges*—responded with infectious clapping and commentary. *Yes! Dat's right, child, correct!* But by eleven o'clock, after the first of three rounds had closed and errors had purged more than half of the competitors, the audience was edgy. The judges' questions became more compounded—*Contestant, what is four thousand and thirty-seven by sixty-two minus five hundred and nine?* Answers no longer snapped out immediately, and delay tactics emerged. Some children asked for questions to be repeated—and other children stopped in the middle of their calculations to fulfill an urgent need to buckle loose shoes. Contenders no longer approached the podium bouncy and self-assured, hoping that humbled steps would translate into more cautious calculations.

Yet Navi didn't share this hesitation. Although his grandmother sat stiffly in her seat, squeezing Neela's hand whenever the words *Navi Keetham, please address de Honourable Panel* were sounded, Navi himself was just fine.

"Ah, your brother's something else, Neela." Granny sighed as her grandson, the strongest competitor in the CMC, strolled back to his chair after a particularly complex sum. "You hear what he say, love? You hear your brother give de correct answer? And he didn't break a sweat!" Only now aware that Neela had been silent the whole morning, Granny bent her neck so her eyes would meet her granddaughter's.

"Yes, Mommy, I hear."

"Oh, Neela," Granny said, straightening herself and wrapping an arm around Neela's shoulders, "you nervous for Navi, nah? Ow, don't worry yourself, he gon' do good."

Neela grasped onto the misguided comfort, knowing that it was fleeting. She pressed her ear to her grandmother's chest, into the heavily flowered material of her best and least-worn dress. "Mommy, if all these people praying for they own children to win, but only one is to win, how come everybody think their prayer gon' be answered?"

Her grandmother grinned. "Well, Neela, you asking a hard thing now, girl! Why you want to get trap up in dis kind-a hard question? You mus'-ee need some senna to move your belly and pass it away . . ."

"No, Granny!" Neela said, having difficulty restraining laughter whenever her grandmother reduced all ills to the need to take laxatives. "I mean, Mommy."

"Looks like I gon' got to get you some good castor oil when we reach home, nah?"

"No! Answer me! Please?"

Granny drew a large, thoughtful breath. "Baby, I can't really tell you," she said, fingering two skinny gold bangles on her wrist, twisting them to reveal their patterned sides. Neela watched how they glided over a well-known streak of dark scars on her arm, scars and gold looking as shiny as each other in the auditorium's lighting. "Maybe it's wrong for them to pray for they own children. Maybe they should pray for de right one to win and be at peace with it. Or maybe it ain't right to pray for dis kind-a thing at all. I don't know, Neela."

"You praying for Navi?" she probed, passing her forefinger over the texture of her grandmother's bangles and watching them slide back down over the scars.

"Well, all dat being said, of course I'm praying for your brother. I can't help but pray with all my heart dat he'll win."

Neela looked to the podium and a lanky, unsteady girl. Her school uniform was similar to Neela's, only it included a white hat with a neat navy blue bow to the side.

"Contestant, what is seventeen hundred and thirty-six by forty-eight plus ninety-three?"

Body motionless, the girl's eyes flickered to her father and little brother, right behind Neela and her grandmother.

"It's okay, girl, take your time and think it through," the father whispered in his daughter's direction. Neela found herself thinking that perhaps this tall girl was the right child to win, even though Granny was praying so earnestly for Navi. *You can get it, you can get dis answer, girl,* she thought to herself, on an impulse.

The girl shifted her weight from one elongated leg to another. "Can you please repeat de question, Honourable Judge?" she requested.

"What is seventeen hundred and thirty-six by forty-eight plus ninety-three, contestant?"

She scratched the back of her neck, causing her hat's front rim to bob up and down at the audience. "Come on, you know dis!" her father whispered urgently. The girl watched him, fear of elimination distorting her expression into a grimace. *Don't worry with your daddy,* Neela silently consoled,

*just think carefully. Think about de numbers, don't worry with
anybody else.*

The girl opened her mouth rashly but snapped it shut
again, letting her sightline pause at her shoes. She straightened
her back. "Please answer de question, contestant," a judge
instructed unsympathetically. *Don't worry with him, either,*
Neela thought, *you gon' be fine.*

"Oh no, looks like she gon' lose dis one," Granny murmured, feeling uneasy for the girl's father. *Uh-uh, I think you
can get dis answer, girl, I know you gon' get it,* confirmed Neela.
You close, I can see you close . . .

"Answer de question, please," another judge ordered, irritated, and the girl lifted her head. She squinted. *You can do it,
girl, you might be de right one to win!* The girl opened her eyes
wide with knowledge. *Yes! You got it!*

"De answer is eighty-three thousand, four hundred and
twenty-one, Honourable Judges."

"Very good, contestant. You may take your seat."

Everyone cheered for the tall girl, her father most of all; he
leaped to his feet and clapped his hands high above his chest—
Dat's my child, my daughter!—while she skipped to her seat and
enjoyed back-patting from contestants around her. Neela
smiled without reservation for the first time that day.

Neela started to encourage every contestant in the same way,
save one. She spoke to them with growing confidence as they
took their place at the podium, inwardly telling them, *You could
be de one to win, you can get de correct answer, your family too-too
frightened you gon' lose but I believe you can win.* And they were

thirsty for it, soaking in her bountiful support while struggling through increasingly difficult questions. She prompted the others not in panic of their failures, but in apprehension about her brother's success. Her faith was certain in a way that those children had never known from wishful parents, grandparents, aunties and uncles. It was safe, lavished equally upon them all.

But, unbeknownst to him, Navi was at a severe disadvantage at the end of the third and final round, when only he and one contestant remained in the challenge. A sharp scratch of doubt ran through his body as he was called to the front of the stage. He noticed that his grandmother and sister had come forward on their seats and were staring at him. He pushed aside his uncertainty and recomposed himself on the way to the podium, legs straight and eyes fixed on the judges' platform.

You was sure of yourself till now, nah? He heard himself think. "Contestant, what is twelve thousand and forty-two and eight hundred and sixty-five, minus six hundred and seventy-seven divided by five?" Navi suspended his senses to process the numbers.

Alright, let's see if you can get dis one, he thought. Twelve thousand and forty-two and eight hundred and sixty five is twelve thousand nine hundred and seven. Subtract six hundred and seventy-seven? *Were those de right numbers?* Yes. *You sure?* Yes . . . I think . . . *You ain't sure. Don't tell me you forgetting de question so fast.* Twelve thousand and forty-two, add eight hundred and sixty-five, minus six hundred and seventy-seven. Yes. Dat does sound right. *Or is it six thousand and seventy-seven? Or seven thousand and sixty-six? They barely read de thing and it's slipping from you.* No, I'm alright, I got de right numbers. Twelve thousand and forty-two. Eight thousand and sixty-five. Six hundred and seventy-seven . . . wait. Something don't seem right. Twelve thousand and forty-two . . . eight thousand and . . . or is it eight hundred . . . *It's all starting to get mix up, boy.* "Honourable Judge," Navi asked, "would you please repeat de question?"

The judge observed him over spectacles that rested low on the tip of his nose. By this point in the day, he was tired of repeating himself. "What is twelve thousand and forty-two and eight hundred and sixty-five, minus six hundred and seventy-seven divided by five," he replied.

Alright, dat's it—twelve thousand and forty-two, eight hundred and sixty-five, six hundred and seventy-seven. *You a-hundred percent sure?* Um-hum, de first piece equals twelve thousand nine hundred and seven; dat number minus six hundred and seventy-seven is twelve thousand two hundred and thirty. And dat's divisible by five, so . . . *But dat can't be right.* Yes, it is, twelve thousand and forty-two minus eight hundred and sixty-five, minus six thousand and seventy-five . . . is six thousand eight hundred and thirty. So how did I get twelve thousand two hundred and thirty de first time? *Hum. Getting confused again.* First I'm to subtract, then add, then divide. Or add, then subtract . . . or subtract both times and divide? *You mean dis simple question's too hard for you to calculate? Come nah, man. What a disappointment you turning out to be.*

He looked to the judges with artificial hope that they might speak his question once more, but the judge with the spectacles gave him nothing. "Please answer promptly, contestant," he said flatly when their gazes met. Navi was aware that bewilderment had infested his expression. Amongst the layers of auditorium seats, he located his family again. One of them had predictably anxious eyes and furrowed brows. The other had a face of pure stone.

I thought you was better than dis. Six thousand eight hundred and thirty . . . *Dat calculation just don't sound right.* Is it adding both times and dividing by five? Or adding and subtracting, and then dividing? *You can't remember de numbers or what to do. Looks like you ain't as clever as you thought.* Twelve thousand and forty-two, eight hundred and seventy-seven . . . six hundred and sixty-five?

"Answer de question now." *You hear de judge, you can't stall no more.* Six thousand eight hundred and thirty divided by five is one thousand three-hundred and sixty-six. *Time run out.* Dat must be de answer. *It's all you can offer them now . . .*

"Contestant, answer de question."

"One thousand three-hundred and sixty-six, Honourable Judges," Navi answered, as if his grandmother had tricked him with a math problem about peas in a pot.

"Incorrect. De answer is two thousand four hundred and forty-six. You have been eliminated from de competition."

Granny remained rigid, unable to let go of Neela's hand. Navi returned to his chair robotically, too numb to perceive the audience excitedly applauding the winner—they had fused into a mass of disjointed faces. He could hardly comprehend that he had gotten so far and lost. That's why he didn't expect to tell himself such a thing when he sat down, a thought so contrary to what he had blindly assumed ever since he had been chosen to compete—*Maybe I was wrong all along, maybe I wasn't de right one to win.*

~

The tall girl accepted the first place cash prize and a large trophy for her headmaster to display at her school, while Navi accepted a bronze plaque emblazoned with *Second Place.* Granny proudly positioned the plaque in her rickety cabinet, between the Her Majesty's collector plate and a yellowing regal dolly with a lavender ball gown. She would point to it every time visitors came by—rather than impressing them, it led to a further question. *What happen, Sugee, why de boy didn't win first place?* Even when visitors fought the temptation to pose such a thing aloud, Navi was guarded against their flash of puzzlement over his second-place status, the very confusion he felt when he glanced at the plaque himself.

He didn't take it with him years later when he left the country, and he certainly didn't reply to the part of his grandmother's letters that read, *I polish your award every week, when I open the cabinet to dust the plates . . .* He completely disregarded the plaque when he became the first from his country to fill an impressive overseas government position. But he would never forget that look on his sister's face before he made an inexplicable error at the Children's Mathematical Challenge.

CHAPTER 2

A large brown-paper-wrapped box arrived at Marasaw's post office. Its bulkiness slowed Granny's journey home that evening. Navi and Neela stood on the front porch bickering about its contents, continuing their unending quarrel in the absence of an adult referee. They had earnestly anticipated it since morning time, when the postman walked by their house with a shout to their grandmother—*Sugee-girl, must drop by on your way home dis afternoon, you get a parcel from your daughter!*

"She's in a different country, Neela," Navi said, twisting his face in contempt of her naivety. "How she gon' find tamarind balls to buy?"

They peered down the straight road, hands clutching the front porch's weathered railing. "Maybe they got our kind-a candy over there. You don't know nothing about what they got."

"They got their own candy and their own everything. Why Mommy gon' give us what we can get here? She gon' send us things you can only find over there."

Annoyed by her brother's voice, Neela kissed her teeth stiffly and stared harder. "So?"

"So nothing. All I mean is dat you can't expect to get what you want. You gon' got to take what she send." Navi rested his elbows on the porch railing and realized that the sunset was just beginning to tint the sky. "So, what you want?"

She made a show of tucking her arm close to her body to ensure it wouldn't accidentally touch her brother's. "I ain't care," she mumbled, chewing a hangnail irritably, thinking, *Dis boy only want to humbug me* . . . "What you want?"

He shrugged. "It don't matter. Well, I guess a book. Or a telescope."

She coughed a cynical laugh. "How Mommy gon' send us a telescope? Dat's plenty money, you know! You gon' be lucky if you even get a book!"

"Well, she knows I like astronomy," he answered defensively, only mildly convincing himself that it was possible.

"How she gon' know dat?"

"Granny told her . . ."

"When?"

"Last time on de phone!"

Neela rolled her eyes. "Even if Granny told her, Mommy won't remember something so stupid like dat . . ."

"How you know?" Navi argued. "You don't know nothing about Mommy. You was only a baby when she left . . ."

"You wasn't a big man yourself . . ."

"I was older then you!"

Neela suddenly jerked from her spot and scuttled into the

house. Navi squinted to discover the speck of his grandmother labouring down the road, her striped dress only a smudge of colour in his eyes. She was kicking up dust and favouring her left side.

They flopped on opposite seats at the kitchen table. Navi wiped perspiration from his neck and Neela instinctively adjusted her ponytail. They remained mute but regularly caught each other's eyes.

"Children?" Granny called from outside the front door. She dropped her laundry bags and flicked her ground-down sandals on the stoop. "You in de house?"

"Uh, yes Granny." Navi controlled the pace of his words, knowing that rushing through them would betray his grand expectations. "We in de kitchen waiting for you."

Neela blasted a glare at him, mouthing, *Why you say dat?* through wrinkled lips. Realizing his error, he answered her with a sheepish grimace.

Granny placed the parcel in the middle of the table. "It looks like it come through okay." She smiled. "Your mommy gon' be glad to know." Neela tried to focus on her grand-mother's happy face, but she was too attracted to the package's paper and tape and string. She hunched toward it while Navi feigned indifference by rubbing his eye. "Well, it's not Christmas Day yet. But I think we can open it now in any event. Might got something dat could spoil."

The two children trapped their hands under their bottoms while Granny took her time unwrapping the brown paper; they bubbled in a stream of restless conversation. *You think it break, Granny? It come a far way, whatever it is, it mus'-ee break . . . We can fix it though, yeah? I good at fixing, don't worry, Granny . . . Yeah, don't worry with it, we don't got to throw it away, it don't matter what state de thing in . . .* The emergence of two smaller packages in poinsettia-pattern paper silenced them both. Neela and Navi had never gotten individual gifts from their mother in the past and they were astounded by the simple idea of not having to share.

Navi abandoned his pretense and tore into his present. "An art kit!" he exclaimed, lifting a glossy box with two delighted blond-haired boys on its cover. Several colourful tubes were displayed in its plastic window, forced in place by twists of wire. He flipped over the box and read what his mother had scribbled over the kit's instructions: *Navi, you are very bright and I want you to learn how to do the fine art of the masters that I read about in school. Please ask Granny to send me something you make. All my love.* "It's got all kind-a brushes, Granny, and plenty colour pencil, and different-different fancy paper, and . . ."

Neela couldn't stand it. She attacked her gift, anticipating the discovery of an astronomy kit—*I gon' see de whole universe and Navi gon' bawl!* But her grin smeared when she realized that she was holding a skipping rope, a rainbow-swirled rubber bouncing ball, and two wooden paddles, laid out in the box's window to appear as if they were more than they were. She turned the box on an angle and expected to hear something else rattling underneath.

"Oh, you get three different toys, lucky girl!" Granny said

cheerfully, inspecting the striped tube beads that had been strung across the rope. "It's a good quality jump rope."

Perplexed, Neela searched her gift to read what her mother's hopes and intentions were; perhaps her words could transform the rope and ball and paddles into something important, something meaningful. Yet all she could find was *Neela, I hope you enjoy your new toys, all my love.* She glanced at Navi to see him methodically lining up the paint tubes across the table, captivated and whispering their fanciful names to himself. She wanted to ask her grandmother what she could possibly craft to send to her mother from this present—*Dear Mommy, did you know that I skipped and paddled ball today?*— but she knew not to. And both Neela and Navi knew not to harass their grandmother, not after she had extracted her daughter's Christmas card from the bottom of the package and found her face covered by unforeseen tears.

~

Merry Christmas, the cover read in grandiose golden script, etched over a grey-blue scene. It was a softened image of a small town's main street during a snowfall; shop windows glowed warm yellow through gleaming white snowflakes. Inside, the initial message was elaborated upon by calligraphy: *Wishing you the best of joy and love this season.*

Mira had returned the card to the slot after checking its price, discouraged by its serious tone. She eyed another—this cover had a cartoon reindeer leaning coolly in sunglasses and a leather jacket, two hooves resting on each other as if it were crossing its arms. A caption over the reindeer's head wondered, *Y'know what's worse than having to fly Santa's sleigh after he's eaten a million cookies?* Mira kissed her teeth and snappishly retrieved the card she had first considered. Another customer pondering the aisle's countless holiday greetings furrowed his brow at her gestures.

When the card had been tucked into a safe enclosure in her purse, Mira pulled on her gloves and hat and steeled herself to return outside. The corner store's door was stiff; wind was buttressing it shut and a mound of snow collected at its bottom. She gripped her purse strap, hugging it close, and pinched her scarf against her neck. She didn't dare lift her head to challenge the blowing snow, but concentrated on her unstable steps and regretted that she didn't own a real pair of boots.

Upon arriving at her apartment on the seventeenth floor, she shook melting ice from her coat and wiped her shoes clean. She couldn't stand seeing slush and salty water ooze into the carpet, even if it was already discoloured and emitted a stale cigarette odour. She plugged the kettle in and sat on a mattress that functioned as her table, couch, and bed, wrapping herself in a comforter and shivering until the water boiled. Remembering her purchase, she retrieved the Christmas card and peeked inside with serious doubts.

Wishing you the best of joy and love this season. It didn't seem right. She surveyed the cover again and noticed something she hadn't seen in the store—a fluffy grey cat peered into the snowy watercolour sky from a window. The more she examined the image, the more she spotted new details: a tree by the cobblestone street carried two chipmunks, Ye Old Christmas Shoppe sold porcelain cherubs, a lamppost served as the base for a bluebird's nest. At the back of the card, near the Royal Seal logo, a squirrel smiled and clutched an acorn. These little elements made her feel more at ease. Although its words were stoic, the card had tender features that would uncover themselves, if the receiver would only seek them.

Dear Mommy, Navi and Neela, she wrote, having to redraw letters as the pen was slow to release ink, *I hope you have a very Merry Christmas. I miss you very much.*

She ached over what to say next, how much to reveal, how to communicate without worrying them. She found herself in this position too many times.

I want to come home and see you soon.

Love, Mira

She squeezed "ALL MY" in small block lettering before the word "Love." She looked her message over, concerned about how it flowed with the preprinted greeting; she slipped the card into the envelope, pulling it back out as if she were the one who had retrieved it from the post office. *I want to come home and see you soon. ALL MY Love, Mira . . .* She shook her pen to ensure that it would flow without sputtering, as if there was no hesitation between what she had written before and what she was about to add, as if she had been able to jot it in all ease and confidence. Under the place she had signed her name, Mira wrote *Mommy,* in brackets.

Navi stalled, begging to spend more time with his art kit, but Neela was eager to follow Granny to Mr. Jenhard's house. He was the only neighbour nearby who could afford a telephone. There was such demand from Marasaw's citizens that Mr. Jenhard had drawn a bold cardboard sign for his front window—*Local $2.00 a minute, overseas $4.00 a minute + user fees*—and had taken to raising his rates at popular occasions of the year. He would hem and haw when townsfolk questioned his exorbitant costs, stammering about how expensive it was to maintain a line. *De man is robbing us, plain and simple,* old-lady neighbours had already asserted, and the others agreed with their grievances, *You right, auntie, is a sin what he's doing . . .* But even as they doubted Mr. Jenhard's motivations each time they carried on conversations under his hovering gaze, there were few alternatives.

"We can't talk too long, Mira," Granny said, "but we want to say thank you for de lovely card and gifts. You can catch a moment now?" She could hear a little child clamouring and misbehaving in the background.

"Yes, Mommy, I can use their phone for a while." The line crackled with every word Mira spoke, and Granny frowned at Mr. Jenhard's poor upkeep. She vowed not to come back, knowing that her promise would be broken guiltlessly at the next opportunity. "Don't want to take advantage, though."

"No, girl. I always tell you, you mustn't push them people's kindness." Granny took mothering seriously, even if she could only maintain a silhouette of it—by now, it had been distilled into adages and proverbs.

"Hold on."

Granny could hear Mira cup her hand over the mouthpiece and scold the whining child—*Stop it, or I gon' tell your parents how you fret with me whole day.*

"Sorry for dat, dis boy always gets on bad when I don't give him full attention. He's de hardest one to deal with out-a them all. De children with you?"

"They anxious to say hello." Granny passed the receiver to Navi and Neela and they both grasped it tightly, yanking to get their ear closer than the other. Mr. Jenhard watched nervously and signalled—*Careful with de cord!*

"Mommy?" Navi asked, timid.

"Hi, baby."

"It's me," Neela piped in, attempting to elbow her brother over. Her grandmother rocked her head at an insistent angle and shook her finger to get her to stop.

"Hi, darling. Y'all alright? You being good? You eating your food? Helping your grandmother with de housework?"

"Yes Mommy," they answered in unison.

"And doing your studies?"

"Yes Mommy."

Navi strained his neck toward the mouthpiece. "Thank you for de art kit. It's de nicest art kit I ever see."

"And I love de toys, Mommy. Love them. Thank you for sending them to me," Neela snapped.

"I'm glad, children. And you gon' send me a painting, right?"

Navi beamed smug at his sister's pout. "I gon' send you de best picture I paint," he chirped. "And you can put it up wherever you want . . ."

"And, and I gon' send you one too, Mommy," Neela blurted, "I gon' send you de most prettiest picture I can make, it gon' be so nice and bright . . ." She made one last effort to wrestle the phone away, but her brother brawled back; before Mr. Jenhard could lurch over and ban them permanently, Granny swatted the receiver and clenched it between the two of them with a stern hand.

"Dat's very good, children. You must share with one another, hear?"

They snarled at each other from the corners of their eyes. "Yes Mommy."

Granny reclaimed the receiver. "You doing good, Mira?"

"Yes Mommy, I'm alright."

"De children and I are waiting to see you. When you gon' come back?" She had asked the same question each time they had spoken since Mira had left nearly ten years ago—and she was always given the same answer.

"I can't leave right now, Mommy. But soon. Must tell de children I gon' get to see them soon."

When she had first decided to leave, Mira had held high hopes that she would either return to Marasaw with money or find a place for herself and her family in the new country. "When I see you again, things gon' be better," she had assured them. "You know it's too hard to find good-paying jobs here."

But her mother had been unconvinced from the very

morning Mira signed up with the employment agency in the capital city. She had glared into her dhal pot and stirred. "But you gon' pick up and leave just so? Leave de children and me on our own?"

"Mommy, you know it does take long to get to go. I got to try and see what happens, or I might not get de chance again. I gon' send for you and de children to come too."

"It ain't easy over there, you know. Can't just go and come as you please . . ."

"Yes, Mommy, I know."

" . . . and they gon' throw you out if you don't do things right. They does throw people out, you know, it don't mean nothing to them if you been there for plenty years."

"I know."

"And they nah gon' worry with you. It ain't like here where you got your family and your neighbours. You starting from scratch over there, yeah?"

"But Miss Pami sister gone up and they say she been making good money."

"I know of plenty others with a different story, girl."

Despite her mother's warnings, Mira had used all of her money to apply overseas. Since her mother had taken care of children and she had two young ones herself, the man at the employment agency declared her an *in-home child-care provider* on the form without hesitation. He coached Mira on the right answers to give everyone she would have to speak to. "You gon' got to pay extra for these," he said, holding some official yellow documents in front of her.

Mira's eyes narrowed. "But you didn't tell me . . ."

He chucked the sheets carelessly to the desk. "You can't go without these papers. They gon' throw you out before you even reach."

"But I done tell you, I ain't got no more money . . ."

"Then you wasting your time and you wasting your money already." The man shrugged. He pulled a file from a tottering pile on the floor and leafed through it casually. "De application won't go through properly, dat's all," he said, as if speaking to himself.

Mira glared at the greying clusters of hair raked across his bald head; she was indignant but hardly knew how to express such feelings.

"There's plenty more you gon' need to pay fee for, and if you ain't willing to find de money, you might as well stop now."

She grappled with a response. When she had first entered the agency, Mira had been determined not to pay for anything more—her mother had warned her about how these people worked, how they kept demanding money long past the time their services ended. She could hardly afford the initial application, let alone the endless documents they insisted upon. But as the man absorbed himself in someone else's papers, the prospect of going back to Marasaw and staying there forever made her shrivel.

"I . . . I can't pay now," she said, voice waning, "but I gon' get some money together and send it to you. You can arrange dat, right?"

"Well then. What you got for collateral?"

Mira had felt pressed to leave home ever since the father of her children had disappeared. She had met him when she was sixteen and had soon become pregnant with Navi. She had hastily embraced the idea that they would marry, but when she had given birth to Neela two years later, he had simply left town and never returned. She had done everything to appear as if she wasn't grieving his absence, wasn't shocked, horribly disenchanted, by his abandonment—after all, Marasaw's women had long foreseen the man's departure in their matter-of-fact soothsaying. She readily joined her mother in cooking, cleaning, and comforting children throughout the town.

Yet work was always more scarce than need and Mira didn't hesitate when, just a year after Neela was born, the overseas employment agency sent a letter informing her that her application had gone through. "I gon' go for a short time and I gon' send you all de money I get. You won't be with de children alone for long, alright?"

But her mother refused to even set eyes upon the agency's letter in Mira's grasp. "It ain't de children dat worry me, girl. You still my only child."

Mira justified her desire to leave with dreams of a steady job and a chance to save money for her children. In truth, she longed to escape Marasaw and the rumours that had gathered in a squall around her ever since her belly had rounded with the first baby. *You see what happen here? She thinks de man gon' marry her . . . If he didn't marry her already, why he gon' bother now?* the neighbourhood women noted to each other with lowered voices. And it only intensified with time. *Watch dis. She get his two pick'ney—two!—and de man just pick up and gone . . . What you mean, he left her for true? . . . He got brothers in de city, you know. Mus'-ee gone to them, escaping de trouble he create here . . . Ow, girl, I does feel sorry for poor Sugee, she bear her daughter's troubles quiet-quiet . . .*

Mira wasn't surprised, even when the women used her as an example to scold their budding girl-children, the ones who wore brassieres at ten or were under siege of menstruation before their friends. *Mustn't run with them boys, understand? You gon' get in a mess like dat girl down de street, you want dat?* She fully expected her neighbours' sputtering as they avoided the topic of Neela and Navi's father when she was standing in front of them.

Still, it weighed heavily. There had been a time when she was so bright, so loud, so at ease in Marasaw. She would beg her friends to desert their homework and relax with her, lounging throughout the town, getting into mischief, being brash and carefree. But after she had the babies of a man who refused to marry or at least stay with her, she was overtaken by shy awkwardness, uncertain about completing her high school classes or visiting the market or even speaking without her mother's presence to cushion her. And Mira changed how she was with her mother, too—she had been silly and talkative with her, quick to get into fierce arguments about day-to-day affairs, but she locked that away after Navi was born. It was a self-imposed timidity, one she thought necessary to demonstrate a kind of self-punishment.

She didn't anticipate that it would become so isolating and spiritless. It wasn't long before she didn't have to force the quietness upon herself—the apprehension transformed from a manufactured trait to a natural state. She knew she wouldn't be able to survive in her hometown much longer.

~~~

Navi had hidden his art kit at the very top of the kitchen pantry, behind his grandmother's collection of empty mismatched jars. But it wasn't too long before Neela poked around the house's hidden corners thoroughly enough. "You think you clever, eh boy?" she mocked from their bedroom doorway, bouncing her hips and waving a perfect, unopened paint tube. No matter where he buried them, she always managed to excavate his treasures.

He launched from his reclining pose on the bed. "Give it back!" he pounced, but she snapped the tube behind her back before he could get close. "It's mine, stop it," he said with staccato exhalations dotting each word, "you gon' squeeze it and make de paint waste, Neela!"

"Why you hide your kit from me?"

"Why you care?" Navi curved his lips into a satisfied smirk, recognizing that he had the upper hand.

"I don't."

"Yes you do. You jealous 'cause Mommy sent you a girly jump rope and she sent me a whole art kit. You can't help but be jealous." He waltzed back to his homework, assured that as much as Neela hated that he had got the kit, she longed for the thing too much to ruin it. "And you might *wish* to send Mommy a painting, but she really only want one from me. She knows I can do de *real* art and you don't got de talent to do *nothing*."

Neela dropped her eyes to the Fire Orange paint tube, feeling suddenly soft toward it. "But I gon' send something for her too . . ."

"What? Skips on a rope? Bounces of a ball?" Navi didn't raise his head from his scribbled math calculations.

"No, I making a picture too, Mommy told us to share!"

He watched her coldly. "How she can tell us what to do? She ain't here. I already tell you, you ain't using nothing from my kit. You can touch it all you want, Neela, but you can never use it."

She wanted to dig her nails into the tube's silvery surface until the cap popped off and fire orange squirted on the floor in a messy blaze. Surely he would howl. But she couldn't bring herself to assault it like that, something so flawless, so desirable. "Dat ain't fair," she grumbled instead.

It was rare to stumble upon something to dangle over his sister's head, and whenever Navi did, he exploited it to its fullest. "So. I ain't care." He scratched his pencil over the page, pretending to record brilliant thoughts. "You ain't never using my Christmas present."

He expected her to lash out or cry for their grandmother, but she simply strolled to his bedside and dropped the tube on the notebook propped on his bent legs. It rolled unevenly to his stomach. "Then I hope it don't ever get through," she said calmly.

"What?"

"Your precious little painting. I hope it never arrive to Mommy. No matter what you do." She folded her arms and watched him with callous, penetrating eyes.

Nervousness crept in from the edges of Navi's hair but he shook it off. "And what you can do about it?"

By now, Neela had her back to him. "You gon' see . . ." She nodded on the way out of the bedroom.

Just a few weeks later, Navi had created what he and his grandmother declared to be an exceptionally beautiful painting, a bird with multicoloured wings soaring over a mountainous rainforest backdrop. When they had wrapped and taped the envelope meticulously, Granny scrounged her last bit of stamp money and headed to the post office. But Neela concentrated on her grandmother's shape shrinking down the road as she skipped near the trench with her red-white-and-blue rope. *I hope it don't get through,* she grinned to herself, jumping faster and higher with the scrumptious thought, *and I hope none-a them get through. Just watch, Navi-boy. . .*

By the time they could afford the expense of another call, Navi had mailed three pieces of art that all failed to arrive to Mira. "It's too bad," Mira said to her children while they grappled with each other for the telephone. "I don't know what's happening with de mail service these days. It's not usually dat bad. Must try to send a next one for me, okay, Nav?"

"I gon' try," he answered sourly. He knew that his grandmother wouldn't allow this to continue forever; she was already fretting about the wasted postage.

"Mommy," Neela shot in, "I been skipping every day, you know. All de girls love my nice jump rope and say I jump best."

"Really? I happy to hear, Neel. Dat's very good, I proud-a-you. Keep trying your hardest, yes?"

Puckering her lips, Neela savoured the sound of her mother's encouragement—it echoed satisfyingly in her ears long after being spoken.

"Children, put your grandmother on, okay?"

"What happen?" Granny said, shooing Neela and Navi as they bellyached to talk with Mira some more. *You children,* Mr. Jenhard said, frowning from his watchdog stool by the living-room window, *don't make sport near my telephone!*

"You get anything more from de agency?"

Granny hesitated to answer. "Yes, a few things . . . not plenty though . . ."

"I gon' send more money in a few days, alright Mommy? I gon' get paid soon and I gon' send it and they gon' stop bothering you, I promise . . ."

"Mustn't worry with them, girl. I tell you, once they get a little something from you, they keep coming back for more. You can't really stop them no matter how much you pay. Dat's how they does stay."

"But de house sign over to them!" Mira exclaimed. "What if they try to take it from you? What you and de children gon' do?"

Granny tried not to reveal the worry she had nursed ever since she received the first notice in the mail that her daughter owed the agency. She knew that neither of them could afford to pay, not even if they pooled their resources. "It gon' be alright. They can't take nothing more than what they already took from me." She sighed. "We want to see you, Mira. When you gon' visit?"

"I hope soon." Mira didn't consider revealing to her mother that it would be too risky for her to attempt to leave the country. She knew her sloppy counterfeit immigration papers wouldn't allow it.

Mr. Jenhard pointed at the telephone to indicate that Granny's call would end soon—with his mounting profits, he had installed a timer to prevent conversations from bulging beyond their allotted paid time. *Got to give de phone a little rest between calls,* he explained to his fed-up customers, *and you know how these damn Marasaw people love to talk* . . . "But Mira," Granny ventured, "you happy over there? Truly happy, in your soul?" She wouldn't normally ask such a question, but she was abruptly compelled.

Mira fumbled. "I . . . I okay, I doing okay. Can't complain . . . de people I work for treat me nice and pay me regular, give me a place to live, so at least I got something . . . other people here don't even got dat, you know . . . you can't really complain . . ." Her voice failed and they remained silent for a while, attending to the comforting filler of background static.

"Yes, girl. I know. But tell me. Are you really happy without your family?"

A blaring dial tone overtook the conversation before Mira could form a response. Granny almost cursed Mr. Jenhard's conniving phone aloud, but noticing Neela and Navi's saddened postures, she delicately placed the receiver down.

The three walked home without a word, and once they arrived, the children knew to creep off and leave their grandmother in peace. Neela went to the backyard to scan the ground for a final handful of pebbles. Ever since Navi had denied her his kit, she had been pursuing a vengeful search for artistic talents of her own—*It don't matter dat Mommy don't want my painting. It don't matter if Navi gon' keep de kit to himself. My art gon' beat his art and he can't stop me. And I gon' make a better painting than he could ever make, my own way, for my own granny, it gon' put de boy to shame!* She took her time walking home from school along the same dirt road, studying the skyline where blues met greens, attentive to subtleties of colour surrounding her. She observed how some houses appeared dangerously top-heavy on their stilts and how, when she unfocused her eyes, her perspective shifted and dense background foliage seemed to float within reach. She collected all sorts of materials along the way, including a studded gold earring she had been so lucky to find lying astray on the road.

Neela crept inside and scooped her collection from under the bed, ignoring Navi and his homework. She hurried out again with a near-empty jar of cassareep and several newspaper-wrapped bundles, laying them on the grass from largest to smallest. She opened them gingerly—twigs, dried leaves, seeds, handfuls of reddish dust. In an effort to smooth a weathered sheet of plywood she had been saving, she applied a dried sea sponge to it, the closest thing she could find to sandpaper. Even though its surface was no smoother than it had been before the sponge was scraped across it, she felt more prepared for the next phase of her masterpiece. She poured a dribble of cassareep on the wood and used a scrap of newspaper to spread it across the surface.

This blank canvas ignited her creativity—she rested on her knees to sprinkle, dab and position the seeds, twigs, leaves and dust onto the cassareep. With a perfectionism adopted only for this moment, she shifted her materials to the left and right with a sliver of wood. After a stretch of meticulous work, she pulled the earring from its hiding place in her shoe and pushed it into the canvas.

Her creation was a natural landscape of texture and colour, an evocative abstraction—crushed leaves hinted of thick forests, twigs implied towering trees, shades of red dust suggested old hills; even the cassareep gleamed through, sunlight slapping choppy rivers. The gold earring was the most suggestive element, and much to her delight, it conveyed nostalgia of the sun, the moon and infinite flecks of nighttime lights, all in one moment. She propped the canvas against a young banana tree and quietly returned to the house.

But no steps were ever too soft for her grandmother. "Neela, where you been dis whole time?" she fussed. "Come and help me with dinner. I can't do all these things alone, girl. Y'all got to learn to do these things yourself sometime too because when I dead and gone, what gon' happen with you and your brother? Hum?" Granny was always demanding after phone calls to Mira, but Neela was so pleased by the prospect of unveiling her art that she didn't mind. She gladly stirred the pot and rolled the roti in anticipation of revealing her new-found talent.

"You know, it's good for you to learn to take care in de kitchen," her grandmother said, more peaceful with the passage of time. "I don't know how I been raising you two on my own, girl. If your mommy was here, she would-a been able to teach you cooking and thing . . . you know, your mommy can cook good. Handle herself well in de kitchen. And your grandfather—he was a good man, love children, boy! If he was alive, y'all would-a learn so many things from him too. But you didn't even get de chance to know him."

"Yes I do, I know him," Neela corrected.

"What you mean?"

"I talk with him when I sleeping. See him like he used to be."

She stopped rubbing salt on skinny fish strips for the stew. "Oh yes? What did he look like?"

"Ah . . . he had tall boots, like them cowboy kind-a boots. Curly-curly hair grease up nice with Brylcreem. Long bushy beard too, like . . . like Santa Claus!"

Granny laughed at the strange vision.

"And Grandpa would wear a big cowboy hat, and on his shoes them spinning star metals."

"You talking about spurs?" she asked, pushing hair from her forehead with the back of her hand, careful to keep her oiled fingertips pointed away.

"Yeah, spurs shining and spinning." Her grandfather's imaginary spurs made Neela remember the gold earring she had stuck into her canvas. "Granny, I got something to show you from de backyard! Can I show you? Please?"

Her grandmother saw how eager she was and became curious. "Alright, go quick and come back. De roti ain't done rolling."

Neela sped into the yard, once again impressed by the memory of her masterpiece. But when she arrived at the foot of the banana tree, a goopy piece of wood collapsed in syrup and dead leaves and drowned ants had taken its place. Her first impulse was to scramble and sweep the materials back into their positions, as if she could reassemble its splendour through haste. But she knew better. Her creation was gone. As she kneeled before the mess, the only thing left intact was that lost earring, still gleaming gold into her watering eyes.

Neela wiggled it out, spat and wiped it clean of cassareep with the hem of her skirt. She curled a fist around it to save the little that remained of her masterpiece.

"How did you do it?" Navi burst from behind, making her jump. "How did you stop de mail from going through?"

She saw the alternating flashes of bitterness and bafflement in his face. "Leave me alone," she said, hoping to return to the kitchen before her grandmother marched outside to find her.

But he blocked her path. "I don't know how you've been doing it, but I know it's you. You causing de mail to not reach Mommy."

"I didn't do nothing. I didn't touch your things, and Granny never sent me to de post office . . ."

"No, no, dat's not it." He knew that she didn't interfere with Granny's post office trips. He suspected something more profound but couldn't imagine what, after silently stewing in their bedroom for the past few weeks. "You hoped my paintings wouldn't get through and they didn't. Three times in a row. It's you who made de mail get lost and I don't know how . . . but I know you did. You would do something like dat, I know it."

She shook her head at his sureness and batted the mosquitoes that always appeared at dusk. "Navi, how can I possibly do dat? How can I make what you put in de mail go or not go anywhere? How can you, with all your brains and marks, think I could do anything like dat?"

She shoved him with her shoulder and stormed off to the front yard indignant, but she wasn't truly angry—she just didn't have a passable answer that either of them could understand or believe, and she knew that, no matter what she did, her brother was the artist. She became aware of the earring once more, felt its metal edges imprinting itself in the folds of her hand. Instead of hiding it in a sock and keeping it her secret treasure as she had originally planned, she tossed it into the trench and resigned herself to losing it forever.

My little children. Mira sat on the bed in her frigid bachelor apartment and stared at the blank paper for a while before writing another word. She looked at the phone and felt her mother's question in her head. *I miss you both so much. Navi, do you remember how I used to sing to you when you were a baby? You probably can't. But I used to sing the hymns your grandmother sang when she cooked. I bet she didn't think I was paying attention, but I was. I learned every word. I hope your grandmother still sings and I hope you listen and learn. They're good to keep in your heart as you grow. I think those songs might have made you into the bright little boy you are.*

Neela, I used to pray over my stomach when you were in there. I put my hand on my belly and stood out on the porch every night, praying that I would have a girl. I asked that you would be a very special child. When I was a child, I was very special. Nobody else knew, not even your grandmother, but I could do incredible things sometimes, unbelievable things that I can't even describe to you now. It was amazing, Neela. But I didn't do much good with it and after I met your father, things started to change. It went from me and now I'm not special at all. I prayed for you because I wanted you to be what I was, to do better than I did.

Children, I'm sorry. I'm far from you. I can't picture what you look like. I have to look at the photos your grandmother sends me to see you. What kind of mother can't see her own children's faces in her heart? But I can't, not even when I try my hardest. I am so sorry. Please forgive me.

I want you to care for each other. I want you to protect one another because I can't do it for you. I worry that you aren't doing that, children. Your parents should show you how to do it and we're not showing you anything. You don't have a father and I'm not a good mother. I didn't want it to be like this for you. Please believe me.

I know I shouldn't ask for favours from you. But Navi and Neela, please, can you have mercy on me and take care of each other? If you did that, then I could have peace.

She laid her pen aside without signing her name, no intention of mailing the letter. She brought the paper to the balcony window and pressed it to her chest, words facing inward. She scanned the night sky. City sights obscured her view, but she patiently fixed her eyes upward until tiny points of starlight sparkled through.

CHAPTER 3

At fourteen, Neela was still yearning for a talent to rival Navi's. Like all of her mysterious abilities, one came upon her unannounced and uncontrollable, materializing when a classmate pulled off her hat and dashed away giggling. Neela chased her so rapid and wild that she not only knocked her opponent down, but tripped over her as well. *Girl fight! Fight, fight, fight!* the boys egged them on, but they lost interest when Neela staggered to her feet, hat in hand, apologetically helping the other girl up. "Neela, man, I thought I was fast," her schoolmate laughed, brushing soil from the front of her uniform, "but you too-too good!"

She discovered that she was indeed fast, so uncannily swift that barriers broke when she moved her legs. She began to race her friends, bullying them until they were forced to agree to her terms, even if the sun was too hot for running. She took these impromptu contests very seriously, irritable when her girlfriends became distracted by conversations or congregations of curious boys. "Don't worry with them jackasses!" she ordered, snapping them back into line. Neela would inevitably win, but she could never be sure if she was victorious because she was the fastest or because her friends didn't really try. She once called out, "Faster, faster!" during a race, hoping that it would make them put more effort in their legs. But they only griped in return.

"What you mean, faster?" one girl responded, purposefully slowing to a jog in protest. "I going as fast as I can!"

Neela came to the conclusion that she would have to do something much bolder to determine if running was her true gift.

"You crazy," Shami exclaimed. "Bust in de head. Mad!"

Lenda agreed. "You want to race Kangee? He and his boys are ignorant bad, you know. He ain't gon' be easy on you."

The three were walking home from school together, slurping on snow cones that Neela had purchased with change stolen from her grandmother's sardine-tin piggy bank.

"I don't want him to be easy on me. Y'all don't even try to run but dat boy gon' put his whole heart and soul into making me look bad, especially if he and his friends hate me." She took a bite from the top of her cone, where the syrup had soaked down and left a naked mound of ice. "He ain't gon' win, though," she snickered.

Lenda kissed her teeth. "Dis girl mad for true. He's a *boy,* you can't outrun him. You see them play cricket?"

"She's right, listen to her," Shami said sternly. "They can bust up de field easy-easy. You can't outrun them boys, especially Kangee."

"And why not? You yourself done tell me I fast!"

"Yes, you fast, Neel," Shami replied, "for a *girl*. Right, Len?"

Lenda was busy wiping an expanding blue syrup stain from the front of her skirt. She nodded distractedly, whispering to herself, *My mother gon' cut my tail when she sees dis mess . . .*

Neela stopped and put a hand on her hip to demonstrate her deep sense of insult. "What you mean?"

"All I'm saying is dat they know how to run, dat's what boys does do. You should know, man, you got a brother," Shami answered.

"My brother can't run for nothing. And he can't run faster than me."

"How you know, you ever race him?"

"No. But I know. Navi could never win a race against me. He's got brains, yes, but he don't got the strength to beat me. And there ain't nothing he can do about it."

"Yes, alright then." Shami rolled her eyes. "But even if you could win against your brother, Kangee is still faster than de other boys. And he won't care if he makes a fool of you in front-a de whole school. See how bad he does carry on?"

"Good-looking, though!" Lenda piped in, making Shami grin mischievously.

"I good-looking too, eh sweetie?" an old man remarked from the shade of a bar's broken porch, drinking Shawlster brand beer as the girls passed. "What you say, honeybunch?"

They snarled. Lenda made an especially disgusted face.

"Maybe a hundred years ago, when you wasn't a stinky-dirty old man!"

The three burst out laughing and skittered away as the old man cursed their backs. Neela made sure to outrun her friends, even then.

As usual, Neela strolled to school with Lenda and Shami, meeting other girls along the way and carrying on boisterous conversation at the side of the road. Cool dawn breezes steadily tapered at this hour, giving way to unmoving humidity. The girls fanned their necks by swinging notebooks in exaggerated, big-lady movements; their banter and growing laughter forced goats to stop chewing trash and shuffle in the dust to make way. Neela was most confident on these occasions, especially when she used the opportunity to be the noisiest and most outrageous of them all. *Neel, you bad!* her friends squealed when she mocked their classmates from afar and did impressions of teachers, *You gon' get us in big trouble!* But their giggles only gratified and encouraged her.

"Eh-eh, what's wrong with you?" one girl scoffed at a boy who, attempting to pass the group on his bicycle, pushed them dangerously close to the trench's gritty brown water. Instead of returning their scorn with a retort, he curled his top lip and hung his tongue out.

"Nastiness!" Lenda said as the others cut their eyes and warped their faces.

"Can smell de stink breath from here!" Shami complained. She half-smiled at the boy's flirty mockery. "Close your mouth, nah!"

But they got their revenge—with his grasp released from the handlebars, the boy was too consumed with the girls to notice a lazy goat in his path. *Watch, watch!* They pointed in amusement, making him panic and swerve into the trench with a muddy splash.

They were still delighted about the mishap when they arrived at school, but Neela's attention had shifted elsewhere. She grabbed Shami and Lenda, gripping tight and twisting when they resisted.

"Ow!" Lenda protested. "Why you so rough!"

"Come on, don't worry." She dragged them across the schoolyard to the boys' side, a place for wrestling and posturing and play-fighting.

"What's wrong with you, Neela? I tell you no!" Shami said.

"Oh no, not dis!" Lenda tried to pull back to the girls' area.

"Come on!" Neela demanded, tugging them both hard. She noticed that Kangee had planted himself in the middle of a crowd and terrorized a short boy with curly hair.

"Eh, mix-boy, kinky-hair! What, he don't speak?" he badgered. The curly-haired boy bent his head at an angle that revealed the reddish sheen of his spiralling locks, matching the redness of his cheeks and ears. Neela held Lenda and Shami hostage beside her and melted into the mass. "How come he's suddenly dumb? Eh? Your mommy and daddy quick to do it outside of they own, but they can't teach you to answer when somebody's talking to you?"

Those nearest to Kangee jeered along with his rhetorical questions, but the boys at the edge of the circle watched on, quiet.

"Why de boy letting dat fool bully him?" Neela whispered.

"Neela, let's go, before he sees us," Shami muttered nervously. "Len, come on."

Lenda stretched her neck to get a view between the backs of the boys' heads. "Oh no, his freckles are getting dark-dark," she noted. "Dat's how you can tell a mixed-boy feel shame, you know! Uh-uh, it's bad . . ."

Kangee poked the boy's shoulder with two fingers, causing his arm to twitch and ricochet back into place. The boy stiffened his hands into fists and made his muscles rigid to portray an indignant response, but his subtle shivers assured Kangee that he was blighted by fear, and malleable. "You ugly bad, you know? Pure spots on your skin. How you look so?" He seized a handful of rich brown-red hair and yanked firmly. The boy lost his already unsteady footing; stiffness dissolving, the sting made him tumble to his knees.

"Picking on dis little boy and pulling his hair don't mean nothing, you know," Neela proclaimed, both Lenda and Shami hushing her frantically. "What can he do to you, really? He small as ever and, funny thing, look how you humbugging him instead of all de other strong-boys. What's dis?"

Kangee's eyes flashed up in bewilderment. Realizing that he was being tested, he lost fascination in his prey. "Who's talking nonsense to me?" he asked in Neela's direction, causing the whole crowd to turn toward her. The curly-haired boy picked himself up and scurried off, embarrassed by the ordeal, and relieved.

"You might think you big and bad, but you ain't prove nothing to me," she continued, unfazed by the crowd's stare. "Instead of picking on people all de time, why don't you prove you big and bad?"

"I gone!" Shami declared, but now Lenda held her from leaving.

"Stupid girl," Kangee sputtered.

Neela shrugged. "Dat's all you can say?" She put on a high-pitched voice. "What happen, you *dumb?* Your parents nah teach you to answer? You *talkie-talkie* before, what happen now? Eh?" Everyone giggled at the mockery and even Kangee's friends puckered their mouths to hold snorts in. Lenda cackled in full enjoyment of the exchange, but Shami only sulked and turned away.

"You asking for trouble, girl!" he said.

"Neela, not 'girl,' Neeelaaa," she enunciated. "You understand de Enggglish dat I am speakinnng, or do you need some-baaady to explain it to yoooou?" They laughed again, and this time even Shami had to press her smile with her fingertips.

Flustered, Kangee elbowed through the crowd. "You best watch yourself, you hear me, it don't matter dat you a girl, I gon' lick you down just de same, you gon' be so sorry you ever talk to me . . ."

Neela made a brushing gesture with the back of her hand. "Alright Kangee, calm yourself. You want put me in my place?

Race me tomorrow, here in de yard after school. They say you run fast. Well, prove yourself tomorrow, nah?"

Everyone chattered about it in class through eager whispers and scribbled notes. *Y'all hear about de big race tomorrow? Girl versus boy, eh, girl versus boy!* It bubbled in elaborate arguments at lunchtime, boiling over to flood the whole school. The race clearly represented something more significant than Neela's simple challenge to Kangee. *I rooting for Neela, she standing up for de girls . . . No, man! A girl can't beat a boy, she's too weak. Kangee gon' win easy, man . . . How you know about who gon' win? Women are stronger than men, they give all you worthless boys life . . . And what kind-a thing are you bringing up now!*

"Please, please, pleeease, Neel!" Lenda begged on the walk home. "You have to beat Kangee, all-a-we counting on it now!" Their group of girlfriends had ballooned to dozens this afternoon, and everyone babbled in agreement. Neela strode at the front of the assembly.

"I gon' have to do Marrel's poetry assignment next week if you lose! You can't lose!" one girl pleaded.

"But you gon' do Marrel's assignment in any event, because you love him and want to marry him and raise his babies," Lenda responded, sparking teasing from the others.

Shami was taking it very seriously. "Neel, hear me. It's not just about you proving to Kangee dat you can run. It's all de girls and you. All them boys gon' continue to think they better than us if you lose."

"I won't lose. Kangee is full of big-talk but talk don't mean nothing to me. You watch."

"Dat's my girl!" Lenda affirmed with a clap of her hands.

"Look." Neela turned to survey her entourage. "I gon' race y'all right now. Who want to try? You ready?" She tossed her books to the side of the road and assumed a pre-sprint stance as the others gathered near and did the same. "On de count-a three. One . . . two . . ."

Neela shot off and left her competitors stationary. *Cheat! Cheat!* they objected, hooting and cheering.

After lying awake in bed for hours, Neela dreamed she was running through a jungle so fast that her bare feet kicked into the air and leaped in expanded arcs. Soon she broke into the netted foliage, launching herself over treetops and soaring into the sky. She split through the atmosphere and tore it apart; plunging deep into the ocean, she splashed back out and skimmed over its clear surface, gliding smoothly, bouncing off the edges of enormous foaming waves. It felt as if she were running for many days and nights on end, conquering fanciful, mysterious landscapes with her bounds and transcending distance, time and fatigue. When she awoke the next morning, immersed in a solid beam of Marasaw sunshine, she was panting and refreshed and stuffed with self-assurance.

Her midnight imaginings had felt so supernaturally real that she hardly cared when her brother tried to discourage her before they left for school. "I see how dat Kangee boy does behave," Navi said, tussling with the stuck zipper on his uniform pants. "He won't let you win and he gon' make you look foolish."

Neela buckled her shoes and grabbed her bookbag, flinging it over her back. "Just because you feel to wee-wee your panties when you see him don't mean I frightened, Navi."

"I ain't afraid-a him!" He bit his lip and made his fingertips white with all the effort he put into closing his zipper.

"Then how come I'm racing him and you just playing with yourself?" She clacked the front door and jogged out to the road before her brother could respond.

Neela was charged throughout the school day, especially when supporters buzzed about her—*Run him down, run him down, Neela-girl, Neela-girl! Win for de girls!* Almost every student went out to the far end of the schoolyard that afternoon, where grass turned into unkempt bush and the sun was hazy shining through brown tree leaves. Girls kept together, playing with each other's hair and getting annoyed when boys snuck over to punch a shoulder and scamper away. The boys segregated themselves in a section of the yard as well; to show off and irritate the girls all the more, they exaggerated their jostling and recreated kung fu movie fight scenes.

Kangee and Neela hid in the middle of their own packs of friends, who were busy preparing their star athletes for the race. Lenda worked on getting Neela's hair into a ponytail; she grumbled because she didn't have a comb.

"Must look straight ahead, don't watch de people around you, don't worry with Kangee either, hear? Knowing him, he

gon' try to distract you," Shami advised to Neela's sombre nodding. "He might try to trick you and make you slow down . . ."

"Stop move-moving you head or your pony gon' be twist-
up!" Lenda scolded, hassled by Neela's knotted black hair.

One of Kangee's friends, Jaroon Begwan, approached
Shami with a grin. "What y'all doing so long?" he asked,
crossing his fingers into each other and resting his palms on
the top of his head. "When are y'all going to be ready? She
don't have to have nice hairstyle to lose de race, you know."

Shami scowled and narrowed her eyes. "Shut your mouth.
What you want, her hair to lick Kangee in de face when she's
passing him by?" She flicked her head away dismissively
while Neela's friends snickered.

He chuckled. "Hear dis rudeness now! Alright, we gon'
see who get shame just now." He looked to Neela's serious
expression and winked; her face got warm and her eyes
skipped to the ground. "Well, good luck, Neela-girl. If any
of you girls can win against Kangee, it's certainly you . . ."
He strolled back to the boys, humming to himself.

Lenda looped Neela's lock through the elastic band one last
time. "Let we go!"

Rules took a great deal of debate to establish, but they
decided to mark the finish line with a boy and girl standing
across from each other. Since they couldn't agree to who
would call the start of the race, Neela's and Kangee's friends
settled on calling it together. The two competitors took their
positions, legs apart and arms up, posed in action as if they had
been frozen halfway through another race.

"You gon' be sorry, girl," Kangee muttered to his opponent without looking at her directly.

Neela grunted. "You just watch who gon' be sorry at de end of all dis." But she felt a nervous sting in her belly for the first time since she had goaded him into racing her. Abruptly, she felt like spurning the attention she had so clung to and fostered. *If he wins, I gon' look foolish in front de whole class. They gon' all watch me lose.* There were many witnesses, and what bothered her most were the girls—they were relying so heavily on her to win.

"You best watch yourself," he answered.

Neela bent forward and hardened herself. She doubted that her brother would have abandoned his haven, the library, to stand with the crowd, but she knew the branching path of school rumours too well. *Navi gon' say he was right all along.*

Lenda approached the competitors and cupped her hands around her mouth. "Ready?" she called. The audience cheered, gathering tightly around the area. "Not too close, give them space, come on!"

"Kangee, you need to watch your boasting," Neela threatened with a harsh whisper. "Dat big-man talk gon' make you fall."

"Ready to call it out?" Lenda signalled to Kangee's boys and Neela's girls.

Kangee sneered. "You shouldn't talk back. Your mother didn't teach you properly, little girl? Or was she too busy whoring around town?"

Their friends shouted in unison: *Ready!*

"Shut up. Don't talk about my mother."

Steady!

"You shut up. Bitch."

Go!

They burst off frantically, step in step. The spectators were so thunderous that their voices swarmed in Neela's ears—*Go, go, go! Run! Faster! Faster!* they screeched, some clamping their eyes to scream louder. Kangee lengthened his stride. *Run, run! He's passing you!* the girls cried. Neela crouched lower to build her speed, alarming the boys. *She's winning! Go! Go!* First one pressed into the lead, then the other.

But as she ran at the pace of a cracking whip, Neela felt an elbow stab in the side of her stomach. She lurched off course and a fist heaved into her neck. She winced and folded, toppling hard and spinning violently, uncontrollably, over the grass. *Cheater! No fair!* she heard the girls yell as she rolled. She knew what had happened—Kangee had sabotaged her run when he realized that he might not beat her. Stung by anger, she lunged a hand out, grabbing whatever she could find; she clasped onto his ankle and wrenched as hard as she could.

Kangee hurtled to the grass in front of her. *She cheat! See? She cheat!* hollered the boys. "You pull me down!" Kangee howled.

"You push me down first!" Neela yelled back, stumbling to her feet and yanking her wild ponytail out of her eyes. "You was losing and you push me down! I would-a win!"

Kangee leaped up, ready to battle. "You was losing! I was ahead-a you!"

"You lie! And you push me down!" The girls fought alongside Neela—*Lie! Bold-face lie! Can't stand de girl winning!*—while the boys stood by Kangee—*She was losing and she fall down first! Kangee win! Boys win!* "Liar! You lie!" Neela spat at him again.

"I was winning when you fall, so I win!"

"I didn't fall, you push me down! It's not fair!"

But Kangee had already made up his mind, already rewritten what had happened. The boys agreed with it only to aggravate the girls, first declaring victory to taunt them but quickly believing in it themselves. *Boys win, boys win, girls lose! Girls lose!*

"No!" Neela insisted. "It ain't fair! Race me again! Race again!"

But haughty Kangee wouldn't have it. "I win! I de fastest, I win!" he repeated, drowning her out. Enraged, she stomped off and left her schoolmates in the yard; they were already moving on to their own conversations, less and less bothered by the race's outcome. "Go home, you lose!" Kangee called. "Loser!"

Lenda and Shami ran behind her. "Neel! Neel, wait!" Shami exclaimed. "Neela!" They pulled at her arms to make her stop but she continued storming away, teeth fastened and eyes clouded by tears.

"Neela, Kangee's a liar! He pushed you down, we all saw dat, even de boys saw it, they just being ignorant!" Lenda explained.

"No! They don't see! They think he won and they convinced I lose! They don't even care about it!" she shouted. "It ain't fair!" She jerked away from them and ran, ignoring their pleas for her to come back.

Neela cried as she rushed home and continued sniffling in bed. All of her insolence and valour had gotten her nowhere—no one would take her running seriously and she was no closer to finding a talent to outshine her brother. *Why did it happen dis way,* she wept into her pillow. *How come it work out so bad?* It seemed as if her escapades too often ended in disaster. But her reflections soon swung to her grandmother, who would certainly fret about her soiled school uniform. Neela changed into house clothes and hurried to the backyard.

As she scrubbed the grass-stained patches on the washboard, she heard far-off knocking at the front door. She ignored it at first, anxious to wash away all evidence of the spoiled race, but someone began to call her name.

"Good afternoon," Lenda said, standing on the porch. She held two snow cones, one in each hand, both half liquid and dribbling red and orange syrup over her knuckles. Bringing the red one to her mouth, she licked its sticky overflow and took a long slurp from the top. "I see you does get de orange one after school," she said.

"Lenda, I busy," Neela grumbled, unwilling to let go of the injustice of the day's events. "I doing housework. You can't stay today, Granny gon' get vexed."

"Aw, Neela. You gon' make it go to waste? Don't do dat." Lenda had another mouthful of her cone, purposely wet and tempting; a few icy clumps dripped on the porch's sandy wooden boards.

Neela pouted and observed the lost pieces. "Alright, come then," she sighed.

The two girls sat on a plank that had been laid on blocks to form a wobbly bench. They ate in haste before the snow cones could dissolve in the afternoon sun.

CHAPTER 4

*T*wo *birds depart from their nests, located in trees that are 100 kilometres apart. One bird flies at 24 kilometres per hour, while the other flies at 28 kilometres per hour. At what point will* . . . Navi glanced up when he felt something poke at his shoulder, pretending that he was just observing the clock. Thirty minutes remained. He peeked at the floor between his legs and saw a tiny chunk of eraser, pink and moist as if it had been bitten from a pencil and spat. *Ahem,* he heard appeal in his direction, *a-hem!* The headmaster slumped lopsided on a metal chair at the very front of the classroom, reading a newspaper. It would be safe to curl around, slowly . . .

A boy two desks back in the next row over jiggled his pencil rapidly to catch Navi's attention. *Question seven,* he mouthed, eyes peeled, flitting between Navi and the headmaster. Navi discreetly flipped through the bottom corners of his test papers; he was almost finished his exam, yet he could see that students around him were still wrestling with their second and third pages. When he had found question seven, he brought his hand under his desk, fingers upside down and signalling to the ground—a flash of four and a flash of two. *Cough, cough!* the boy replied, causing the headmaster to snap his head up and inspect the classroom. Navi slapped his suspicious digits against his pants, madly scratching his thigh and staring into the test papers. Yet he was assured that he wouldn't be accused of anything; adults knew that Navi Keetham did not, would not and need not cheat. The headmaster returned to his newspaper and recalled how his mother too used to overstarch his uniform, making it itch like a thousand mosquito bites.

Navi rotated his neck and his schoolmate mouthed, *I can't see!* Navi narrowed his eyes and put his lips in the shape of *Forty-two!* The boy nodded, smiled craftily and jotted his ill-gotten answer in the allotted space. Returning to the last page of the exam, Navi found where he had been interrupted. *Two birds depart from their nests, located in trees that are 100 kilometres apart . . .*

Navi was seventeen and writing his entrance exams to apply to universities overseas. Only a handful of students from Marasaw High School were allowed to take these tests— the ones who the headmaster believed would reflect most favourably upon the state of their country's educational system. Some students had outshone their classmates in science or history or language arts; of course, Navi still excelled in mathematics, but now the town knew him for brilliance in all courses, and as usual, they congratulated themselves for it.

But Navi was too busy studying and crafting personal-interest statements for his applications to notice anymore.

"Hey!" a boy yelped as Navi stepped along the front planks of the high school, arms quivering under his load of textbooks. "How did you do with de exam?" Three other boys hurried forward to hear his answer for themselves.

"Alright, I think."

"Just alright? I see you finish long before all of us!" one said, chewing loudly on a cheese bun.

"You mus'-ee get a perfect mark," another declared.

"A-plus-plus-plus!" yet another chirped.

Navi shrugged. "It was easy."

"What?" objected the one who had begged Navi for help. "Dat was de hardest exam I ever take, man!" The rest nodded in agreement. He put his hand on Navi's shoulder jovially. "So, hear. For tomorrow's calculus test, you can help us out, nah? Since, you know, it's easy for you and all?" All of the boys circled him expectantly.

This always happened. Boys, or sometimes a select collection of girls, would approach Navi with the same friendly small talk and warm hands. They would drift toward him in the school-yard before a test, or after a class during which they had been too preoccupied with spitballs to take notes. But when they had gotten what they needed, these fleeting acquaintances would act as if they had never known him or owed him a thing. Navi understood exactly why they gravitated to him—yet for some reason he still found himself flattered by their on-off attentions, shy at their declarations of his intelligence.

A boy piped in to support the request. "What you say? You smart, man. You gon' share those smarts with us?"

Navi shrugged the shoulder that his classmate's hand was planted on. "Alright, I guess."

They patted his back to say, *Thanks man, you good, you good,* and strolled off together, chatting amongst themselves. Having Navi join their walk home wasn't a serious consideration, either for him or for them.

His grandmother was on the front porch of their house, carefully folding somebody's laundry. "How was it?" she called when he came within earshot. She didn't mind if her neighbours overheard their exchange.

"Easy," he shouted back.

As he approached the steps, Granny forsook a garment on the porch railing and grasped her grandson's cheeks in her hands. "Oh, good, good boy!" She kissed and firmly embraced him, even though he cringed and nudged her away. She was impervious to his dissuasions.

"Granny, come on, stop," he moaned, when he noticed their shirtless neighbour on the next porch over, peeping from behind a bottle of Shawlster beer and grinning without his dentures.

"He did good on de big exam, uncle! Say it easy!" Granny said, when Navi had finally managed to squirm into the house. The man nodded and waved; she was never certain if he could hear her, but she construed his ambiguous replies into whatever she wanted at the time. "Yes uncle, de boy bright indeed."

Navi escaped another disdained okra-and-rice dinner by asserting that he required every last minute to study for his calculus exam. Neela argued that she needed the bedroom to work on her school assignment too, so their grandmother separated them, Navi in the bedroom and Neela at the kitchen table. *But Navi does always get to be in de bedroom! It ain't fair!* It was no use, as Granny's arbitrary decisions were always final.

He shut the bedroom door delicately and propped himself on the bed. He spread his calculus textbook across his knees, although there was no need to study—sine and cosine flowed through him as satisfyingly as water when he was thirsty. Instead, he placed a blank sheet of paper over the formulas and wrote on it with a pencil, trying to prepare for the exam that he was truly concerned about.

He is eating fish-and-chips and drinking a mug of ale at the bistro on the corner of a cobble-stone lane. "What a magical atmosphere," he thinks to himself in contentment. He turns to the bartender. "This night is like nothing I have ever seen when I was living in Marasaw. It is entirely lovely."

The bartender passes him a lit pipe. He is a friendly and cordial bloke.

"Thank you, sir."

Navi squinted over his words sourly. His story always started like this; even if he wished it to start differently, it had to begin this way.

A mysterious man enters the bistro, taking a seat in a dark corner. Norman puts the pipe to his lips and pulls a deep breath. The taste of fine tobacco thrills him. Suddenly, the mysterious man departs his seat and approaches Norman. The bartender exits the dining room and slips to the back, in fear.

*"So you thought you could sneak up on me, stranger?"
Norman's catlike senses allow him to notice things that other
people cannot. He turns around, pipe hanging from the side of
his mouth.*

"We meet again, Norman," the mysterious man says.

*Norman chuckles coldly. "You are mistaken if you believe we
are on a first-name basis."*

*The mysterious man continues. "You and I have not seen each
other for a long time. We have not crossed paths since . . ."* Navi
paused and scanned the bedroom. *Since . . .* This was where he
usually got stuck. He read the story from the top to buy
more time. *Since what?*

He began to scrawl circular doodles in the page margins—
have they not crossed paths since the war ended? Since the
previous top secret assignment ended in tragedy? Since the
marriage of Norman's betrothed to this mysterious man?
He wriggled the pencil between his fingers to make it look like
rubber, relieved by sudden grumblings in his stomach. Hunger
would save him from this impossible story trap.

Granny was out making her last round to return clean
laundry, so he knew it was safe to leave the bedroom. He
stepped downstairs cautiously, not looking too intently at
Neela as she pouted over a piece of paper and shifted on her
chair uncomfortably. She was still moping at being forced to
do her homework in the kitchen, and he knew not to harass
her when she was in this mood. But as he retrieved one of
Granny's black bean cakes from a biscuit tin, he couldn't
help but notice that she was writing a story of her own.

He came beside her and scanned the paper. "What are you writing?" he asked. "What's it about?"

Neela didn't turn to acknowledge him. "Nothing," she sulked.

"For English?"

She nodded passively and stared deeper into her sheets so that he would go away.

"About what?"

She breathed heavily and slapped her pencil to the table. "A creature from outer space, alright?" She tried to keep her answer short and stinging, like a whip on his skin, but she couldn't leave her story so unattractively exposed. "It's trapped in Marasaw," she sniffed, "and, um, de alien's in disguise so people don't know. But it can't hide for very long and when people find it, they gon' want to run it out-a town. Or kill it. I trying to get ahead with it, so leave me alone." She snatched her pencil and wrote frantically.

"Can I see it when you're done?" Navi asked. "You got any others you can show me?"

She raised her eyebrow in distrust. "Yes, I do. Plenty. And they good too. Why you want to see them?"

He examined the bean cake after he had bitten into it. The sight of its filling, a black wad of paste, made him retch. "I just want to see, dat's all."

Losing interest, Neela bent close to her paper to scrutinize the line she had just completed. "No," she muttered, "they mine and I keeping them private." She planted her elbow on the table and used her fist as a shield to block her brother from her line of vision. "I don't care to show them to any old body. But trust me, I know I can do better writing than you!"

Navi kissed his teeth and thundered back to their bedroom, stomping crazily on the stairs. He thumped the door shut this time, noticing Neela's bookbag tossed haphazardly in a corner. *She don't care to show them to "any old body," huh?* He dug through it in a passion and yanked out her *Fine Classic Poetry* textbook, a staple that all high school students studied across the country. *Well, I don't care to* listen *to any old body!* The book was stuffed with loose papers with Neela's handwriting. *She think she's better at writing than me? I don't care what she says, stupid girl . . .*

Navi didn't expect to be so taken aback. Paper after dog-eared paper, short story after short story overflowed from her book—romances, fantasies, intrigues. Each was graced by a colourful block-letter title like "The Golden Steed" and "Nothing but a Lonesome Sinner." He read them one after another, with sluggish disbelief. They might be snippets of writing, with dreadful spelling and reckless grammar, but they brimmed with variety and confidence and imagination— most of all, a mysterious, marvellous talent. He had had no idea that his sister, the bony, petty girl who reflected his antagonism and only waited to undermine him, had a magical ability with words. *How did she do dis to me again? How does she always know to do de things I can't do?* he wondered. *Why does it seem like she takes away what I need right when I need it, just to spite me?* He rested his pounding skull against the bedroom wall.

No one could say he lacked talent. His skill at manipulating numbers grew more impressive by the day, and he soared through every science class—most of Marasaw High School's students studied more for their low grades than Navi would ever need to study for his high ones. And no one would claim he was a failure in the humanities, either. His history and philosophy marks were equally excellent; even his English teacher gave him her highest grades, because she understood that he had claimed the language better than she, and far beyond most adults in Marasaw.

But now he was plagued by doubts. *First-class read,* the English teacher had praised in the top corner of the story assignment he had submitted just a few months before he started to write his university exams. Her comment had been followed by a big A-plus. *Nice phrasing, no spelling errors!* she had celebrated in red pen. But then he had arrived at her last remark, scribbled at the bottom of the last page: *Work on imagination—be unique—use more creative language—do something different than typical literature in class next time.*

Those partial sentences were messy afterthoughts, as if she hadn't intended to write them but at a weak moment had jotted them down. Although she had given him the highest mark in the class yet again, her comments had puzzled him. He had read them a second and third time, soon disbelieving them entirely. *What happened, she didn't like it? Why did she give me an A-plus? She said it's good, so what's dis she's telling me now? It's not fair!* He had never been assaulted by such criticism from an adult—even when he was young, grown-ups had tiptoed around him, hadn't dared doubt that his prowess exceeded that of the other children. He had smuggled his marred assignment home, poring over those inexplicable comments, in the end unable to discover what had provoked this shocking assessment.

Navi had started to write another story, one that would be uniquely and creatively his, one so bloated with expressive words that his teacher would be proven wrong. It opened in a bistro on a cobblestone corner, where a gentleman spy was greeted by a devious dark enemy for some intriguing reason. Yet despite working on it every day for the past few months, he couldn't coax the story beyond that point, even as circumstances, characters and common indulgences—gambling, drinking, beautiful women—were altered. Inspiration had left almost as soon as he had begun. Stubborn, he had persisted with his spy and bistro and cobblestones, refusing to entertain another idea until he finished this one. But after he had spent so many evenings locked in that suffocating bedroom in front of a blank piece of paper, it seemed as if the story was truly foiling him.

Navi's calculus exam was to be followed by the final exam, creative writing and English literature, the morning after. He didn't have concerns about reciting and analyzing poetry passages, or demonstrating what was a simile for what. It was the last portion that troubled him, the one the headmaster had already warned students to ponder in advance: the short-story question, where they would write an original piece of a thousand words. "You must excel in all your exams in order to be considered for an overseas scholarship," the headmaster had reminded them, lest his top students overstudy for math and science and neglect English.

And Navi was excruciatingly set on going overseas. It had started when he was old enough to understand that his mother was there; he was curious to see her surroundings, especially when his grandmother claimed, *It's cold where your mommy lives! She's struggling with de snow and de ice! I told her to wrap herself tight, it don't matter if they laugh at you, or you gon' catch pneumonia and go to de grave without seeing your children again* . . . Granny might have been chastising his mother for leaving her life in Marasaw's warmth behind, but Navi heard those words with great wonderment. When they read of unthinkable things like snow angels and frost and snowmen in elementary school, he pictured his mother skating along glassy streets with other overseas people, white crystals swirling about, ice twinkling and coating the city's surface. In his mind, it always seemed like Christmastime over there.

When Navi entered high school, he considered that his father might also be overseas, doing something important that was probably impossible to do in backward old Marasaw— engineering or doctoring or research, most likely. He knew the man wouldn't be with his mother, since Granny had long made the reality clear; *Your parents are like oil and water,* she would repeat to her grandchildren, ensuring that they built no illusions, adding a customary sharp eye to Neela that said, *and don't you do what your mother did* . . . But Navi still wondered if they could be in the same country, maybe even the same city, and if his father was the one who had blessed him with his smarts. For young Navi, new to the pressure and promise of Marasaw High School, it seemed so plausible that his father was the enigmatic man he envisioned.

"Granny," he asked one day after school, "you think my father might be overseas?"

She was standing hunched at the kitchen table, frowning at a mound of roti dough she worked with whitened fingers. "I don't know." She was hardly paying attention, in light of the frustrating texture of her mix—too gooey, prone to deteriorating into granular bits.

Navi scratched his ear and sat across from her. "Mus'-ee so."

"Give me dat oil by you, Nav." He passed one of the countless soda bottles his grandmother had salvaged to store her cooking ingredients. Its greenish-yellow cola label was slippery and see-through from the overflow of oil. "He must be an engineer or banker or something, eh?"

Granny measured a little pond of oil in the crease of her palm, slapping it against the dough and kneading again.

Four hundred and seven pounds of dough by thirty-two pounds . . . he calculated in reflex. He watched how strands of dough twisted in and around her fingers, oil squirting glossy bubbles between them. "I mus'-ee take after my father then," he said, immersed in the thought.

But his grandmother glared back. "What you mean? You don't take after your father, understand me?"

Navi didn't understand. "I think I get my good grades and thing from him . . ."

"No child in dis house take after dat man," she cut in, massaging the roti dough madly. Hearing irritation in her voice and sensing that it had emerged with reference to her disappeared father, Neela crept to the doorway; she leaned on the rough frame and scratched her left toes against her right calf. "You know where he is? Mus'-ee pass out in some nasty alleyway in de capital, right in dis worthless country! De man ain't overseas and he ain't doing nothing more then fulfilling his calling to be a drunkard." Granny swung her head to Neela and gave a quick stare before returning to her recipe: *You bett'-had listen to me and don't get in de mess your mother get herself in . . .*

If his grandmother was right about his father, that he wasn't achieving important things but lying intoxicated in some littered, stinking alleyway, Navi couldn't see what this country could possibly offer him. The desire to leave was rudely planted in his mind, more urgently than ever before. *I don't take after my father and I don't want to take after him and I gon' leave dis backward place.* He swamped himself in studies and exams; he was going to get out as soon as possible, no matter what.

~~

Navi ripped through the calculus exam the next day, finishing twenty minutes earlier than everyone else and sparing time to signal correct answers to the other boys. He scurried home, barely acknowledging the presence of his family as he rushed upstairs, Neela squabbling that it was her turn to use the bedroom and Granny scolding in response, *Shut your mouth, de boy got to study for his last exam!* He slammed the door and knelt over a piece of paper on the bed.

You and I have not seen each other for a long time. We have not seen each other since . . . He drew a deep breath and pressed his fists against his forehead, dropping his pen. *Not seen each other since . . . come on . . . come on!* Trembling, he glanced at the paper's surface, only to be angered by the loops of his own handwriting. *How come Neela can always do what I can't? How does she have what I need? I don't understand!* He yanked his hands away and pounded the paper a few times; it didn't rip apart with the abuse, but the sight of his own distorted words offered some relief.

He crawled up on the bed, dejected, face throbbing as if it had been punched, and noticed Neela's *Fine Classic Poetry* textbook helpless on the floor. Only a few days ago, he would have never contemplated wasting effort on anything she did; now he hungrily eyed the sheets that spilled out and threatened to burst the book's spine. He snatched the pages and attacked the first story, reading it crazily, whispering words aloud—even now, the enchantment of his sister's writing dazzled him.

The first half of the exam went by fast. Navi quoted soliloquies, provided definitions and corrected the grammar of intentionally ridiculous sentences with ease. But when he landed at the very last page, he paused to survey the other students, their serious brows puckered in exasperation over how hard it was to cheat on a test that required sentences instead of pat numbers. He had an hour left; it didn't seem like nearly enough time when he read the last question. *Story Exercise: write an original short story no longer than 1,000 words. Selected stories will be eligible for entry in the New University Scholars Short Story Awards.* He checked the question again, wondering why they labelled it a mere exercise and wouldn't admit to what it really was—the heart of an examination to determine if he was indeed smart enough to transcend lifeless figures and memorized ideas. This was not his spy story, re-enacted over months with no resolution or movement. This was no exercise.

Navi stared at the headmaster, at how the man drooped in his metal chair in a manner that made him look asleep under his newspaper. *Stupid fool. I hate you.* He rubbed his finger over his forehead, sweeping its dew and realizing how hot, stifled and disgusted he felt in the windowless classroom. He snuffled loudly and returned to his exam paper, doodling spirals in the margins around the so-called exercise. He scratched his scalp until it stung, and watched the clock again—fifty minutes left. He completed the bend of his final spiral and started to write.

~~~

Granny was delighted when the results came back. *I know long-time he would do well in his exams,* she assured her lady

79

friends, *but top-a de class and top-a de country, how I'm filled with joy!* Marasaw fawned over Navi more than ever, neighbours, teachers and fellow students alike. *I know it's a sin to be proud, but how I proud, Lord, I proud!* His headmaster assured him that he would have an enviable choice of prestigious overseas universities, and that he needn't worry about costs—he would easily receive a full scholarship. His performance on the exams switched the order of things; now it was not so much that Navi wanted to attend these schools, but that they wanted Navi, a splendid young jewel in the aged crown of the colonies.

So it was hardly noticeable that Navi's story exercise was being submitted for the New University Scholars Short Story Awards. Any prize he might win would be an insignificant flourish compared to the inevitable trip he would make across the waters. And in morning assembly, after the students had sung the national anthem and before they droned through the school prayer, the thrill was muted when the headmaster broadcast that Navi's little *exercise* had come third out of thousands from the smartest young scholars around the world. Students yawned and passed notes as usual when he boasted that "Alien in a Hostile Town," an inventive piece about a space creature who learned that the harshness of the universe was nowhere harsher than in their own Marasaw hometown, was an amateur masterpiece. "If Mr. Keetham can achieve such heights in de time it takes to write an exam," the headmaster gushed to an oblivious crowd, "we anxiously await what he will achieve over. a lifetime."

Navi made no claim to the bedroom that evening. He stayed downstairs with Granny, choking on a meal of fish stew and rice as they thumbed through a stack of glossy university pamphlets.

"Where's Neela?" his grandmother asked, suddenly struck by the girl's absence.

He dragged the fork through his plate, clearing a narrow path in the grains. "I think she's working on her English assignment . . . ," he answered quietly.

"Neel? Neela!" she called. "Answer me, nah?" But there was no reply. Granny wiped her hands and went upstairs.

After a few minutes of grunts and rudeness and violent moping, Neela abandoned the mess of her homework and cried into the front of her grandmother's dress. It was the washed-out one she always wore to cook food, the one she nicknamed the *old house duster;* it had absorbed varied scents of many dinners over the years.

"What happen, ba-ba? Tell me, nah?" Granny pleaded, and hugged and rocked back and forth, but Neela wouldn't say anything. "Ow, you mus'-ee got too much school work to do, it's bothering you, nah baby?" She stroked Neela's hair away from the line of her brow and the path of her tears. "I know it does be too much for you sometimes."

She didn't confirm or deny her grandmother's theory. She knew that the power of her storytelling had been snatched from her by Navi's theft, that it would never mature into the unique gift that she so longed for. There was no use attempting to reclaim it now, and there was nobody she could complain to about such a mystifying thing. She just closed her eyes and sniffled into Granny's house duster, inhaling the fabric's sugary saltiness as consolation.

PART TWO

Neela was offered a modest bursary at the end of high school. Even she was surprised by the headmaster's typewritten letter, stuffed in the same envelope as her average final exam results: *Dear Miss Neela Keetham, I am writing to inform you of a scholarship that will be provided, should you enrol at Marasaw Training College for Teachers . . .* She registered dutifully at the age of seventeen, with the vague idea that learning how to guide children through multiplication tables and the *Royal English Reader for Students* might finally unveil a true calling.

By the time she had attended college for a whole year, her mornings had settled into a predictable pattern—she got up before the sun began to warm, bathed in dribbles of cold water, and arranged herself in the standard grey-blue uniform. Granny would have already awoken and made her presence known by knocking containers in the kitchen and fussing through mumbles. Neela always rode her bicycle to school; it had been old when she had bought it from a neighbour's son and its paint was littered by rusty splotches, but it rolled smoothly along the side of the road. Its wheels had a tendency to kick up more debris than a typical bike, so she rode faster than she needed to, only to whip a lingering cloud behind her. *Nice vehicle,* the neighbour's son would call if she passed him on his way to school, *I should-a raised de price!* She would speed down to the old lady's shop, the one near the college, with just enough time to buy breakfast.

Auntie Daity's Nice Eats sold a cheese bun and bottle of coconut water for less than a dollar. Neela hoarded change for her mornings, although her grandmother would complain—*You only wasting money we don't got!* But Neela wasn't too concerned because Granny grumbled against most things these days. She simply followed her custom and asked Auntie Daity for the biggest bun on the tray, going outside to eat against the store-front's panels and wait for the *clink-clink* of an approaching bell.

"Hurry up, nah," Lenda said, gliding to a stop and hopping off her bicycle, "we gon' be late." She kept hold of the handles and stood neatly dressed in an identical outfit.

Neela took a loud gulp of coconut water and wiped its dribble from the corner of her mouth with her knuckle. "Don't worry. Bite?" She held the bun out but Lenda shook her head tightly, crinkling her nose. "What's wrong with you?"

"I tell you, I don't trust it." Lenda glanced at the propped shutter that exposed the store's innards, where colourful bottles of pepper sauce lit the shelves with their oily heat. Auntie Daity, a stern old woman, frowned at the two of them through the window as she struggled to twist a soda bottle open. "Dat lady's mad. Always eyeing us," Lenda whispered, quickly repositioning her view when she noticed Auntie Daity's flared, trembling nostrils. "She don't do dat to you. I don't think she likes black people."

Neela shrugged *me nah know* and gobbled her last piece of bun. "Don't take it on. She's mad." She tossed the empty bottle in her bag, tangled by its straps between the bicycle's handlebars. When she leaped to the seat and pedalled with charging force, Lenda clumsily attempted the same.

"Not too fast, girl, why you got to pick up speed so!" she scolded. Neela shooed the complaint with a flick of her hand.

They dropped their bikes into the tall, wispy grass at the side of the building and rushed up the front entrance's planks. Fellow students stood straight, hands to breasts, singing, *Natural wonders from the mighty hand of God, my country, 'tis blessed to thee,* when they made it to the classroom door. Although Lenda was prepared to be counted late, Neela ducked and snaked down the aisle to the back bench—in the haste of the moment, Lenda had little choice but to follow. *Free to serve our fellow man in filial love, my country, we're blessed in thee,* the anthem concluded. The professor turned his gaze from the flag pinned above the chalkboard and scanned the room slowly, suspiciously, probing every student's face. He squinted when he arrived at Neela's poised expression and Lenda's shifting eyes. "Let us begin our lesson," he declared after a thoughtful pause, slipping his spectacles on.

"How you know how to trick de old man so good, Neela?" the young man beside her whispered when the class took their seats. She mashed her lips to bury a naughty snort and shrugged her usual *me nah know*.

"You gon' kill me, true," Lenda breathed from her other side, flicking the pages of her textbook in annoyance. "You gon' take away my life one day, Neela."

Each morning they started with the basic principles of teaching elementary arithmetic, and moved on to classic English literature—Shakespeare and Kipling and Conrad—until lunch. Afternoons would alternate between such subjects as creative writing, science and history. Certainly the course load for Marasaw Training College for Teachers was heavy and its standards were high. The college had been established by a group of missionaries who believed education to be an essential element of redemption; their motto, *Higher Knowledge Leads to Higher Ground,* was in decorative fine script at the head of every classroom, above every overetched chalkboard. After three full years and above-average grades, successful scholars received their First Degree in Instructional Sciences, and were eligible to earn their second and third degrees after yet more years of schooling. Neela planned to stop at the first, knowing that she would be qualified to teach starting grades in her country. It would be just enough to get her out of Marasaw for good.

Neela had never enjoyed school and it hardly improved when she enrolled at the college. Lenda would chatter about books she was to report on and the varied array of possible essay topics—*I'm looking at early childhood development according to Freud and Erikson, but I don't really know, maybe I should do Vygotsky* . . . But Neela would always respond with bored eyes that read, *I ain't care;* she was too preoccupied to put genuine energy into her schoolwork. Her grandmother would caution her to study properly, lest she *get trap-up in housework like your old granny,* but that would urge her into studiousness for only fleeting bursts of time.

She had long ceased wishing for Navi's fortunes—the full scholarship, Granny's boasting to the whole neighbourhood, an excited reception at a foreign university—yet she was indignant nonetheless. She wanted to escape Marasaw and find her passion just as her brother did, released from the same dirt roads and trenches, overly familiar neighbours and her grandmother's unbearable strictness. She sensed it was her fate to leave. The outward drag in her restless spirit was excruciating, but so far, the farthest she had been able to go was the front planks of teachers' college. And the schooling she had left to complete felt like a bland eternity.

At the end of the day, Neela and Lenda rode to an eatery fronted by a generic Marasaw Restaurant sign. Although the building's outside concrete walls were a cheery reflective gold, inside was shadowy, dull and empty, save for some men who played an endless game of dominoes. They were used to the restaurant's claustrophobic cloak and the clacking of black-and-white pieces deep in the back—*Eh-eh, I win 'pon you now, boy!* A light-skinned waitress carried cheap drinks to Lenda and Neela as they lounged, trying to ignore how the woman would examine them mistrustfully before twisting their bottles open.

"You should see de city, it's looking better then ever," Lenda said, placing her glass on a soggy coaster. She turned to the laughing of the domino men, smiling from the infectiousness of their chatter. "Last weekend we went to visit my auntie in de west end. Roads clean, working streetlights and all. I don't know. Maybe dis new government ain't really as bad as people say."

Jaroon Begwan flagged the waitress by pointing at his empty glass. "So how come de people still protesting against them?" In the most infamous protest, people had rushed through the city smashing windows, lighting fabric-and-stick fires, waving signs that read *New Builder Party government: built on lies and corruption!* and *New Builders: profit first, people last!* But real chaos began when government supporters swamped the streets to fight, detonating a chain reaction—the crowd split itself down lines of skin and class, casualties on every side becoming martyrs. The event pulsed through the airwaves and sparked bitterness and accusation, fostered by the party itself, encouraging people to turn against each other as never before.

The waitress refilled Jaroon's glass the same moment a succession of dominoes hit the back table—*brap brap brap*—and concluded with an explosion of joyful cursing. One domino man hobbled over to ask the young people to spare change; *Sorry, uncle,* they apologized with shrugs, forcing him to return to the game empty handed.

Neela pushed her glass around, the lazy motion creating a low dragging sound on the table. "Dat's how dis damn country does stay these days. It ain't no promise land."

Lenda cut a gulp short. "Speaking of dat, Jaroon, you hear de radio dis morning? They talked about de Eden Development."

"It's de town de party's building in de bush, right?"

Neela pouted. "Who gon' want to live in bush?"

"It's a big thing, girl. Everybody's saying they gon' make plenty money. People around de world gon' gladly pay for a visit down there, especially by de waterfall. It might be only bush to you and me, but de place is full-a beauty."

Natural wonders from the mighty hand of God, Neela pictured her classmates singing into the flag's bands, *my country, 'tis blessed to thee.* But she knew that none of them had ever witnessed it for themselves. In the insular world of Marasaw, the rainforest was no more than rumours and myths and ghost tales. *I gon' tell you about de bush spirits, child,* old folks would explain to their grandchildren, *I know a man who see them with his own two eyes . . .*

"They searching for more workers these days," Lenda said. "Looks like it's taking more men to build it than they thought."

"For true? Alright, we gon' see," Jaroon said.

Neela noticed Jaroon's interested face and hastily moved her focus to the obscene banter and hoarse cackling of the domino men.

They left the restaurant when the sun was setting in purple hues. The three strolled down the road, Lenda pushing her bike in front, Neela and Jaroon behind. Jaroon rolled Neela's bicycle between them, one hand steadying the handlebars— when it got dark enough, he switched the responsibility to the other side and brushed Neela's fingers. They clasped hands tightly all the way to her grandmother's house.

Neela abandoned her shoes on the porch and carried her books solidly in front, in case her grandmother was geared up to argue about her coming home so late. *I was studying, Granny, you want me fail my classes?* But ever since she had started cleaning in the new part of town that had sprawled out from where they and their neighbours lived, Granny seemed to work non-stop. Neela plunked her books on their crooked kitchen table and sat in front of one, scanning words without making a real attempt to read. Instead, she waved her hand to deflect fruit flies and worked on summoning every detail of how it had felt when Jaroon had kissed her good night. All she could remember was that it felt good.

"You want to go away?" she had whispered, after they had kissed in the shadowed side of the house, out of sight from where Lenda waited. The flesh of her hand warmed his neck. This close, she could smell his tart musk, and she imagined he had patted it on his chest in expectation of seeing her. She let a fingertip roll across his collarbone, hoping to collect some of his perfume for a lonely moment later on.

"To paradise?" he smiled, equally quiet. "With you, yes."

"No man, you really want to go work there?"

Jaroon looked at the grass. "I getting weary looking for work here, girl. My cousin says dat nobody's really hiring brown people from dis town no more. They say we too mixed up with all kind-a other people. I don't think I got much of a chance to get a proper job in dis area." He squeezed his hand on her hip. "But you can come with me. You say you want to leave Marasaw in any event."

Neela didn't answer. Her eyes fluttered to the same spot where his had been a moment before.

"Your granny gon' be fine. And we wouldn't have to hide from her no more. Don't you want to be with me? For real?"

She looked back at his face and he came closer, tighter.

"Is what y'all doing, pray?" Lenda called mischievously, making them both jump. "Do tell, sir," she said in a singsong accent, "dish de gossip for me, old bloke!"

Jaroon and Lenda giggled back and forth, repeating accented phrases. *Cheerio, kissy-kissy! Tut-tut, keep your knickers on!* Neela had to choke down her amusement. *Neela dahhling, be a lady! Guard your fish-and-chips!*

Jaroon pecked Neela on the cheek and jogged away. "He's daft and peeved, Len, run!" she cried as Jaroon went to play-fight Lenda on the road.

Neela's grandmother arrived to find her nodding at the kitchen table, which was covered in half-open textbooks. "You late bad, Granny," she murmured, eyelids falling.

Granny looked around the room. "What did you eat?"

"Food from yesterday . . ."

"Dat's all?"

"I ain't hungry."

"And you didn't bother to cook nothing? What you gon' eat for lunch tomorrow?"

"Granny, I been studying . . ."

"I see you expect me to do all de cooking, nah?"

"But Granny . . ."

"And de housework too." She snapped her handbag on the table and marched to the cupboard, pulling things onto the counter. "Get de flour. And you bett'-had come and do these dishes."

"I—"

"Pickney."

She didn't have to say more. Neela got up to start kneading flour and oil together, pulling off chunks of dough and flattening them into white discs with a rolling pin. Her grandmother fried fish and okra while Neela cooked roti on the burner beside her. They were both silent.

As the last piece of roti was still ballooning, the kitchen lights clicked off. The roti wheezed and collapsed as if it were giving up its spirit, breathing its last.

"Get de candles," Granny ordered, wondering what had possessed her to spend the money Navi worked so hard to accumulate on the stove. *Buy an electric stove. It will make cooking easier for you,* he had cheerfully written to her. *All of the families over here use them.* It was as if he was eager to forget what living in Marasaw was really like, how disordered and disconcerting the country had become, and she knew that, in blind delight of her grandson's accomplishments, she was too easily sucked in.

Neela fumbled about to find the right container. "Mustn't bust nothing!" her grandmother huffed, encouraging her to clap things together on the counter—rebellion, however petty, came easier under cover of night. Neela finally lit candles around the room and they sat together at that late hour, smelling beeswax and chewing dinner with sullen mouths.

"De market didn't have no good fish today," Granny said, almost to herself. She kissed her teeth delicately. "I tell you, dis country is going down. Before them people stir up all dat trouble, we could-a get any kind of fish our hearts desire."

Neela rolled her eyes and took a big bite of food. "Um-hum," she answered, vacant. She was accustomed to tuning out grumbles about *them people*. It was more common amongst everyone these days, even in their seemingly harmonious town.

"But it tastes okay?"

"Um-hum."

Granny dipped her finger in the sauce and tasted it again to evaluate her stew's culinary merit. "It got nuff salt, right?"

Neela nodded without elevating her head.

"I gon' make beef curry tomorrow. Navi gon' be hungry when he gets in from de airport. It's been a long time since we had beef, nah?"

"It does usually be too late to cook it by time you get home," Neela mumbled.

"You right." Granny observed the roti in her hand. "They come out good. You made them alright dis time."

"Um-hum."

Straining to see the ceiling beams, the older woman wondered if they would have to wait till morning for power to return. She brought her eyes back to her granddaughter, who was gawking at her plate and shovelling the last of her dinner into her mouth. "I hope you and your brother gon' get on good and enjoy each other's company . . ." The wish evaporated with the candle's smoke.

Neela didn't reply or look up; Navi's theft of her high school story, his vexing successes for as long as she could remember, found their way to the front of her mind again.

"We gon' eat beef curry as a family tomorrow," Granny affirmed. It was an ignored promise.

~~~~~

The professor made an unorthodox announcement to open class the next morning. "Our newly elected government has embarked on a new project for de betterment of de nation," he read from an official memo, causing most students to turn blasé and resume conversations amongst themselves. "It is de creation of a new town in de heart of de interior of dis great country."

Lenda elbowed Neela. "He's talking about Eden, you know."

"Alright, shhh!"

"In partnership with Omega Global Ventures, a world-renowned leader in travel-tourism," the professor continued from his script, "the Eden Resort Development will be a state-of-the-art ecotourism destination. It will bring unprecedented growth to our economy."

"De old man's looking *miserable,* boy!" a classmate giggled from the back bench, confirming what Neela had noticed herself—his poised shoulders were shrunken inward and he perspired so heavily that his chest muddied the whiteness of his dress shirt.

The memo explained that Eden was to stretch along the Nasee-Ki River near the landing of the great national waterfall, a fully functional resort town with private residences, schools, hotels, restaurants and its own airport. *The democratically elected New Builders Party is fulfilling our promise of prosperity to all citizens. Your service is necessary to make Eden a reality. We are looking for aspiring young citizens to establish quality child-rearing and educational services.* Anyone who had attended teachers' college for a year was eligible to apply for a position in Eden's new daycare centres and schools—the government even expected that workers would move to the region permanently and populate the new town. The announcement concluded with the popular New Builders Party motto, *Prosperity for citizens built on a prosperous tomorrow.*

But the professor's face betrayed an acidic thought. "Class, I've been instructed to bring de matter to you and register you for dis development if you so choose. If you would like my opinion, I do not believe going to dis place is wise. Especially in de hands of a government dat builds power by promoting disunity amongst citizens." He cleared his throat and hid himself under normalcy once again.

But Neela couldn't heed such warnings, not when she was so energized. There was no need to continue at school, no need to waste more time—she could leave her hometown immediately. The announcement introduced unforeseen possibilities—most of all, an opportunity to be with Jaroon freely. It seemed to be the beginning of a new fate she had sensed for so long.

Neela recognized the smell of roasting beef as soon as she entered the house. Half-opened travel bags cluttered the narrow hallway, transforming it into an obstacle course.

"Where you been, Neela?" Granny called. "We been waiting since afternoon. You brother get in already."

Navi was at the kitchen table, appearing clammy in a long-sleeved collared shirt and dress pants. He looked at her, expressionless. "Hi, Neela."

Although she tried not to look too closely, it was clear that time overseas had washed the depth from his brown skin. "Hello," she answered spiritlessly, books straight and rigid as a shield. "I was studying with Lenda," she told her grandmother, more tentatively than she wanted to; it felt as if her tone had betrayed more stolen moments with Jaroon, more time gliding her hands under his T-shirt to press against his soft bare back.

"With them riots and madness, I does worry when you late. What if a mob catch you? Don't think it can't happen here." Granny kissed her teeth tightly, recalling the radio reports of street brawls that tortured her every morning. "And you still going around with dat Lenda-girl, like it's nothing at all. She and her family ain't like our people, you know, you got to watch out with them or they gon' betray you . . ."

"Don't say dat!" Neela knew what her grandmother, what the whole town thought of her friendship with Lenda nowadays. And even as they avoided speaking about what brewed around them, naively hoping the other couldn't perceive it, both Lenda and Neela felt the blades of eyes boring into them. *Eh-eh, since when a brown and black girl can friend-up each other so? Like they don't know what going on in dis country!*

"Well, don't worry with it now. Go greet you brother. And come help with dis rice."

Neela dropped her books and bent to kiss Navi's cheek unenthusiastically. He didn't kiss back, and was relieved when she popped over to the bubbling rice on the stove. She spooned some to test its softness, trying not to catch the milky water in the ladle. *Granny, de professor tell us about . . . he announce something special dis morning . . . they tell us dat we can all get a teaching job right away, if we want . . .* Every time Neela started this mental conversation, the grandmother in her head would wrinkle her forehead in disparagement. There was no avoiding it, at least not with the granny she imagined, the same figment that became so enraged when Neela revealed, *I like Jaroon Begwan plenty, Granny, I like him bad-bad . . .* Her imaginary grandmother's reactions would stop her from uttering infuriating things to the real one.

"De beef taste alright?" Granny asked as the three of them ate, questioning her skills to make cheap meat palatable. She had attempted to compensate with a pile of starchy potatoes. "Not too thick? Nuff salt?"

"It's good, Granny," Navi answered. "It has de right amount of salt too. You cooked it nicely."

She was relieved by his confidence, as always. "So, must tell Neela how you doing at school. Neel, you know they got more than a hundred buildings at Navi's university? Big fancy halls with oil paintings and stain glass and thing. Tell her."

Navi don't own *the university,* Neela thought. She let her eyes blur over a stray ant making its way up to the tabletop, scaling a wooden leg. *He had to beg their charity to pay for de visit home!*

"They have a lot of buildings," he said hurriedly, cutting his account short with a gulp of juice.

"And nice-nice trees and gardens and courtyards," Granny added. "Just like de children's stories you used to read in school said, right? Grass green and full and mow down clean. It's very pretty over there, girl, well kept. You ain't see nothing like dat here, nah?"

Navi smiled uncomfortably at his plate.

He should go back, then, Neela answered in her head. *Why is he wasting his time here? Just go back to your new home.* She watched her brother and he returned her look with darkened eyes.

"If you want to come and visit me, Granny, I can show you around de university."

"Oh, dat would be nice!" she answered, pleased in a way that Neela never experienced when the two of them were in that house alone. "I never left dis country before, you know dat? Maybe I can save up a little money and visit you, after I finally get to visit where your mommy's been living all dis time. Maybe I can collect her and we can fly over to visit your university together . . ."

Neela tried to remain uninterested in the whole conversation.

After dinner, Navi took over their old bedroom and Neela had to share her grandmother's creaky bed. An inevitable argument arose when the two attempted to get in at the same time—*You using up all my space . . . Well, you gon' only block breeze from de fan!* As Granny snored into the night, happy that both of her grandchildren were with her again, Neela's eyes stayed fixed open. She could never be restful when her brother returned to Marasaw, doted upon by the whole neighbourhood. All she could do was trace the trails of her resentments, rooted solid as an old tree, and wait for the two weeks to pass.

They were like ghosts to each other—Neela and Navi rarely made eye contact and only conversed when their grandmother acted as the portal. While Granny had become preoccupied with Navi's presence, consuming his overseas tales and forcing him to regurgitate them to the neighbours, Neela found every excuse to stay away from home. She spent more defiant time with Jaroon than before, both hesitant and thrilled by its risks. He would slink to back doors of the college and lead her behind the fence, clinging to her in the breaks between her classes, whispering folk melodies into her ear— *How my mother warn me, a man can lose his mind with a brown-skin girl, so lovely as you . . .* She would lean her body against his, wrapped in his heat, hearing the counterpoint of her own grandmother humming the same melody when she was a child. *Stay away, she tell me, a man can lose his mind with a brown-skin girl, a beauty like you.*

"They got a big display set up in de government block downtown, I went to see it dis morning," Jaroon said when they returned to the Marasaw Restaurant, familiar domino sounds peppering the background. He had heard that workers were being paid well to build Eden, promised an even bigger cut if they signed a contract to stay when the town was completed. "It looks like de Builder Party's doing alright, man." Enamoured, he grinned and stroked Neela's arm.

"But how long it gon' take?" Lenda asked.

"They expect to finish it late next year. Can't do these things overnight, you know."

"So you decide to go then?"

Neela stared at Lenda, upset at them both but knowing that she shouldn't be.

Jaroon arched his eyebrows and rubbed the back of his neck. Neela usually loved to watch him perform that gesture, but this time it disquieted her. "I thinking about it, man."

The light-skinned waitress swaggered to their table and plunked another beer in front of Lenda, proudly displaying her irritation; she let her wrist slap against Lenda's arm on her way back to the bar. Flustered and without recourse, Lenda mistakenly caught Neela's eyes and they both bowed away from each other fast, as if they could so easily erase the woman's hostility.

Jaroon confirmed that he had done more than think about Eden when he and Neela were hiding in the restaurant's alleyway. He cupped her face as if he were catching water. "Girl, come with me. You can get one-a them teaching positions. When you gon' get a next chance to leave dis town?"

"But Granny won't let me go." She knew that she sounded like a whining child. "She gon' murder me. And what's Lenda going to say about it?" The alley's pebble pavement poked sharp under her feet and she leaned against the concrete wall.

Jaroon leaned in. "But you old enough to do what you want now. You ain't a baby no more." He moved his fingertips to her shoulders and massaged them slowly. "You my baby now." He smiled. "What, you only staying in town for your granny and your friend? But what about what I want, Neela? You don't care about dat at all?"

"I do care, Jaroon, it's just . . ."

"Listen, de old lady gon' be vexed with you, and yes, I know Lenda gon' miss your company at school. But they gon' be fine. You just got to get up and go, you got to do things for yourself." He kissed her forehead lightly and kept his lips tickling against her skin. "Your granny won't let you go nowhere easy like your brother, yeah? You got to make de decision on your own."

Neela closed her arms around his waist and drew him closer. She could smell that musk again. "I know. I want to go with you. I want get out-a dis town, I know in my heart dat I need to be with you. I just don't know how to do it. It's so hard." She felt her breath reflect from his neck. "But I love you, Jaroon. So much."

He lifted her chin and kissed her for a long time. "I love you. I need you bad. Find a way to come with me, girl, please."

Neela returned to the quiet house and made an attempt to study until her grandmother and Navi got back. But instead of chatter introducing them through the door, there was only silence. Navi hustled to the bedroom and Granny entered the kitchen, clanging things around with a brooding way about her.

"Granny, what happen?" Neela asked, but received no acknowledgment. She realized that the fury in her grandmother's movements had something to do with her. "What's wrong?"

Granny slapped a wooden spoon on the counter, never able to contain her anger for long after being questioned about it. "You going around with dat Begwan boy?" she asked curtly, face creased.

Neela cast her gaze down.

"Answer me!"

Neela's head barely moved side to side, as if to say no and yes at the same time. She had anticipated that it would eventually come to this, but she wasn't ready for it tonight. The whole idea made her hot and tired.

"Don't lie!" Granny shouted. "Don't you dare lie to me!"

"I don't want to lie to you," she muttered to her hands, coiled into fists on her lap.

"So why you tell me you been studying when you really been running around town with dat boy? You know how I hear about dis foolishness? No, not from you." Her index finger shot up and ricocheted back down. "Your brother have to come all dis way to tell me dat he see de two-a-you going round de square dis whole week . . ."

"What?"

" . . . in plain sight for everyone in town. And how long you been hiding dis from me? Months? Years?" Granny reclaimed

THE SUDDEN DISAPPEARANCE OF SEETHA

the spoon and aimed its warped handle at Neela. "You think
it's okay to lie to your grandmother, I see. I know I didn't raise
you like dat, but look how you do me now."

Neela's fury rose and pulled her to her feet. "What did
Navi say?" She couldn't truly be angry at her grandmother
for reacting the long-expected way. But Navi's treachery was
intolerable—against him, she was completely enraged.

"Don't get dat way with me . . ."

"What did he tell you? What did he say to you!"

"You bett'-had make up your mind right now to stop going
around with dat worthless Begwan boy and concentrate on
your school work, Neela! I won't stand for it! Them Begwans
are lawless, always been lawless, they ain't got no education or
ambition, bringing a bad name on we brown people! If you don't
stop with him right now, I gon' make you stop, you gon' see . . ."

Neela flicked her eyes to the kitchen doorway and saw
Navi peering in, serious. "How dare you!" she screamed.

"Don't speak to your brother like dat!" Granny scolded. "It's
you who's doing dis nonsense!" She smacked her spoon into the
sink. "It's dat Lenda girl, eh? She's influencing you! She's
telling you to sneak around with dat boy and lie to me? Them
people don't care about proper behaviour, you know, they . . ."

"Don't talk about Lenda! Don't talk about things you
don't know!"

"Don't you talk to me so! You best stop it with dat boy!"

"You can't tell me what to do! It's my own life! You can't
make me do nothing!"

Navi attempted to cut in. "Neela, don't . . ."

She grabbed one of her big textbooks and slammed it to the ground, glad for the echoing thump it produced. "Shut your mouth, Navi! How dare you come back to dis house . . ."

"Don't talk back to us!" Granny yelled.

Neela stopped abruptly and stared at them with wide, astounded eyes. "Don't talk back to *us?*" she asked, through gritted teeth. "Since when I answering to *us?* Navi, are you my mother? Are you my father? You got any say over me?"

"You disgusting, you know," Granny chided, "you must show Navi some respect! He's your older brother . . ." But Neela thundered off, rushing down the street with her grandmother shouting behind her, "Get back here! Don't you leave dis house when we speaking to you . . ."

It was oppressively dark, save for waves of light from a neighbour's garbage fire. Neela focused on her own fuming breaths, how they blended with the driving beat from nearby speakers that thumped bass over the road—*When de music play, we gon' say "par-ty," oi-oi! Is another day in de car-ni-val, oi-oi!* The soca rhythm caused house rafters to buzz along the road; it thrust the muscles in her legs forward and she welcomed how it quickened her pace.

"Neela!" Navi called, running to catch up. "Neela! Stop!"

She snapped around. "Best not follow me, Navi, you gon' regret it."

"What's dat supposed to mean?" He met Neela with half her face lit by the flickering of the garbage fire.

"How dare you come back to dis town and assume you got de right to tell Granny my personal business!"

"I was only answering her questions. I didn't say anything she wouldn't have found out on her own, in any event. It's your own fault for not being more careful with dat Begwan boy, everybody saw you going around with him . . ."

"Shut up!" she screeched. "Don't you ever talk about him! Don't call his name! No more excuses!"

"Neela, you're really out of line. You're going to make Granny sick with all de trouble you're causing. You want dat?"

"Your whole life you always get your own way, Navi, but you ain't getting your way with me no more, hear? You ain't got dat right no more."

"Oh, alright, dat's what you think?" he said. "And you do whatever you want at everybody else's expense, Neela. You don't think about anyone but . . ." *I hate you,* Navi heard, deep in his belly. He flinched. "What . . . what did you say?" *I can't stand to even look at you.*

Neela didn't answer; she just glared at him, jaw clenched. *I wish you was dead.*

He recoiled, stunned at this painful voice rumbling to his ears from inside. *I hate you so much. You should die.* His body seized as if a jolt of electricity had pinned him where he stood.

"Don't ever come back," she snarled, stepping toward him. "So long as I'm in dis town, don't you dare come in front-a me. I can't even look at you." *Never come back or you gon' be real sorry . . .* She could see her thoughts resonating in him, somehow tearing him from the inside out. It was the first time that she was fully attuned to her power. Instead of being shocked by its emergence, she chose to bask in its darkness, to take pleasure in the vigour that enclosed her bones the more he suffered.

Navi pressed his stomach protectively. "How you . . ."—he trembled, shrunken—"how you do dis, Neela?" He bent his head, entreating himself to consider that this was completely illogical. Yet memories of growing up with Neela, those scattered moments when it appeared as if she could foil him in surreal, profoundly intimate ways, rocketed into his consciousness.

"I wish you never came back." Neela was remembering their childhood too—how her abilities, both creating and thriving upon chaos, had so often brought even her to ruin in their unpredictable, explosive strength. She had limited control over how her powers arrived and ultimately moved. But when they had cast their shade over her, she had never tried to shake them off or refashion them with pure intention; the power felt too good just as it was, raw and spiteful and wilful, a weapon against her brother's triumphs. *Navi, you used to think you was better than me but now you see I can do things you can't. I tell you, it feels right to picture you dying. In pain. Dead. Yes, I wish you was dead.*

Navi cowered lower. "Don't wish dat on me." *You deserve it.*

"What are you scared of, boy? You scared-a me?" she jeered. *Run. Now.*

"I can't do nothing to you. You my big brother."

Run back to your grandmother.

"You are de great Navi Keetham, Marasaw's little god. You can do anything and go anywhere you want. Why you worried about me? I'm nothing to you . . ."

Run. Or you won't live to see her again . . .

Navi stumbled, hardly able to make his legs obey him. He started back toward the house with unsteady footing, feeling as if he would double over and vomit, hoping never to see his sister illuminated by midnight fires again.

Neela didn't return home that night.

CHAPTER 6

Neela signed up for the Eden Development the next morning, so fervently confident from the previous night that she headed directly to the headmaster when she didn't find her professor in class. Although the substitute teacher didn't offer a reason for his absence, the students still gossiped—*I hear de old man get in trouble with de boss for bad-talking! De headmaster and his boys are big New Builder Party men, you know, they won't let nobody disrespect de Party* . . . Neela completed a form and was given sparse information in return: in just a few days, a government bus would pass the edge of town to collect new workers and take them to the Nasee-Ki interior. The headmaster could make no guarantee that they would accept more teachers or child-care workers from Marasaw anytime soon.

"What . . . what you . . . well, when are you leaving?" Lenda stuttered, befuddled, in front of Auntie Daity's Nice Eats. "You nah tell me nothing! I only hearing about dis now!"

Neela hadn't bought a cheese bun or coconut punch, but she had assumed her usual spot leaning against the storefront's panels toward the rising sun. "I decided fast. Len, I got to go. It's my only chance to get out-a dis place."

Lenda raised an angled palm to slow the questions whirling in her head. "So, what now, you leaving school?" Disturbance bathed her face. "What did your granny say?" Her eyes widened. "You didn't tell her! When you gon' tell her?"

No words, more eyes between them.

"What, you ain't telling her?"

Neela shook her head roughly.

"It's Jaroon, then. I see. Jaroon. You running after him and leaving your whole life behind." Lenda touched her fingertips to the middle of her forehead and pressed. "What are you getting yourself into? You gon' abandon your chance for a good career, Neela? How do you know you can trust these Eden people? You hear what everybody says, how de government cheat and steal to win de vote. How can you put yourself at their mercy? And how do you know dat Jaroon gon' really be dedicated to you, Neela? I didn't say nothing before, but I does wonder about him sometimes . . ."

Neela's face stoned up. "Lenda, you know I want to leave Marasaw long-long. I ain't going for Jaroon." She grabbed her bike, propped against the shop's porch. "I'm going for myself and I can care for myself. Just trust me, alright? I'm strong and I gon' be fine."

As always, Auntie Daity glared at them both, lips more wrinkled than usual—those two scamps were causing a scene and they hadn't even purchased anything. Neela lost all patience and cut her eye at the woman.

"But if he wasn't going to Eden, you wouldn't want to leave teacher's college . . ."

"Yes I would . . ."

"No, I know you, you wouldn't."

"Yes! I would!"

Lenda sulked and retrieved her bicycle too, body moving as if she intended to ride alone; she noticed Auntie Daity's disdain and shook her head at her. The old lady finally deserted the window, grumbling to herself about the state of the nation and *them people.*

"I'm leaving in a few days," Neela said quietly, to gloss over their argument.

Lenda walked her bike forward and Neela followed, both without looking at the other directly. "I think you making a mistake," Lenda grunted, after a while of coasting along the road. She wheeled around a tattered baby donkey slumped in the dirt and mewling, and resumed her course to the college.

Neela barely spoke to her brother and grandmother after what had happened. They trod around stiffly, pulling in tight air when they passed one another, as if they wished to say something but held back. Neela and Navi were especially careful to avoid each other—Neela inflated with superiority over her brother, and Navi devastated by the display of his sister's sinister power. But Neela was trailed by a nagging obligation to tell her grandmother that she planned to leave—before words rose to her mouth, the grandmother in her head went insane with rage and bawled in ear-splitting screams, *Oh God, my granddaughter's dead, dead, she gone!* A rush of startled neighbourhood women would scurry into the house to find Granny's rigid body doubled on the kitchen floor, hands blocking her ears, Neela standing over her in frozen astonishment. *What did you do?* the women would accuse. *Your brother don't do dis kind-a evil to your grandmother, you know!* Neela could never stir her mouth to respond; she could only watch as they clutched her grandmother, hugging her head and massaging her hair, flashing scandalized glances at the wretched granddaughter. *Shhh, nah worry, it's alright, ow Sugee, poor girl . . .*

～～⌒

Neela got up early the same day that Navi was to fly back overseas. She cautiously slipped from her grandmother's bed and wriggled into her college uniform. As she dragged her suitcase from its hiding place in the basement, she heard knocking on an outside wall. At first she thought the lizards had roused themselves early and were running across ceiling beams, but this was far more persistent than those typical patters.

Lenda was in the grassy path at the side of the house, pelting a handful of pebbles at its panels one by one. She jumped when Neela's crouching figure turned the corner and gestured for her to approach. The two of them made their way down the road, self-conscious because they had had sparse contact after arguing in front of Auntie Daity and her trays of nice eats.

"You going today," Lenda said with a diminished voice, claiming the suitcase from Neela's hand.

"Um-hum," Neela said.

"You alright?"

Neela shrugged. "Yeah."

"You didn't tell your granny or Navi."

Knowing that they were far enough from the house, they straightened their backs yet continued to speak quietly. "I couldn't . . . you know how she is . . ." Neela hadn't expected tears to bulge at the back of her eyes. "But I just can't live in dat house anymore, Len, you see what it's doing to me, it gon' kill me . . ."

Lenda sighed in response.

"I left a letter for her. And I gon' write her first thing when I arrive. And I gon' send money, too. All de money I can spare."

Lenda shifted the suitcase to her other side and shook the soreness out of the hand that had held it first. "You think she gon' come to terms?"

"I ain't sure," Neela said, weaving her arm into her friend's. "But she would never let me leave, even if I was to finish college, even if I was to get a big overseas job, she would never let me leave dis town. It wouldn't be like how my brother left. And Navi, he really thinks he's better than me, everybody thinks dat. I can't be in a place where people are convinced dat boy's better than me. I sick of it, Len. I just know I got to get out-a dis place. I know it in my heart. Listen, I'm stronger than you think, I can't really explain it to you but I can care for myself, I promise."

Lenda scanned houses around them, decrepit staircases slinking up to side doors, cracking plaster facades in peach and baby blue and lilac. "But things are so different these days.

It don't seem like you can trust nothing or nobody." She brushed the suitcase against Neela's thigh and held its handle out to her. "It's like . . . my kind don't care for your kind in dis place no more. It won't be too easy for me to live here without you."

Neela took her bag back, overwhelmed because she had never packed a piece of luggage so full in the past. It weighed at her side, firm and complete. "Even though you and me ain't supposed to be friends?" she tried to say wittily, only wounding herself by finally admitting it aloud.

Lenda tightened her arm around Neela's.

The sky wasn't the same anymore—morning was softening its blackness, and early-day flies hummed to mark the arrival of their brief span of productivity. When Lenda and Neela arrived at the announced location at the edge of town, a bus half-cloaked in rust was already idling, *Prosperity built on a prosperous tomorrow* scribed across it. People crowded around, many who had journeyed from neighbouring villages much smaller than Marasaw; they balanced bags on the crowns of their heads so they could squeeze a little closer against the folding doors. Everybody hollered to win the attention of the two soldiers who guarded the bus entrance, and would-be passengers chattered to each other nervously.

Neela pecked Lenda on the cheek and immediately shovelled her way through the people, evoking many protests— *What's dis! You pushy bad!* But she was spurred by a smug energy that had remained since her altercation with Navi, and by the practicality that it was too late to go home and shrivel in front of her family, too late to wait for future buses to break her out. When she reached one of the army men, she held her papers to his face. He poked around them just enough so she could see the camouflage beret tilted to the side of his head. He smiled, eyelids low and pulled flirtatiously.

"Eh girl," he muttered. "What are you showing me?"

"My citizenship papers and recruitment form. They in order?"

He didn't look. "They alright, sweetie."

"I can get on de bus then?" She lowered the papers to her side and swung them casually in an attempt to appear bored by it all.

"You support de Builder Party?" Neela shrugged *me nah know* and the soldier looked her up and down once. "You got a boyfriend?" he asked, punctuating *boyfriend* with a flick of his head.

"Yes."

He beamed, revealing the curves where teeth met gums, eyes drifting lower. "What he got dat I don't got? You mean to say I ain't got a chance?" An up-down swept her once again. "Not one chance?"

The people behind Neela murmured to each other, impatient with the delay. *What kind of stupidness happening now, dis girl's causing a big backup!* It was clear that the crowd had already swelled, even in the short time it had taken for her to land at the army man's grins; this one vehicle couldn't accommodate them all. *She's holding all-a-we up and preventing anybody from getting a seat!* Neela could still identify Lenda at the edge of the mass, hand over her forehead as a visor against the intensifying sun. "No, you ain't got a chance," she returned to the soldier, with greater boldness for the task at hand, "but let me on dis bus and maybe your chance might come."

He nodded once and stepped aside, snapping harshly into place after Neela had scampered up the steps. "Don't push me or you gon' get de shock-a your life!" he barked when the crowd attempted to skulk through the doors behind her. Neela peered out of a mud-splattered back seat window, laughing and making rude gestures at her friend.

Mad woman, Lenda mouthed back exaggeratedly, trying not to reveal her true distress at Neela's decision to leave, especially as people glared at their eccentric exchange. She would wait until she found a private place in her busy home, separate from her mother and baby cousins and aunt and uncle; then she would smoulder and cry and contemplate why she had been so loyal all these years, especially when Neela didn't seem to waste a thought on abandoning their friendship. *It's always been like dis,* she would conclude, fumbling through her dresser for a jar of cocoa butter, wishing to smooth its chocolate scent over her skin. By then, she would be fatigued by too many memories, and the depressing sensation of unwiped salt water drying on her cheeks. *All dis time, I been letting de girl use me however she please . . .*

The bus was soon bursting with people, mainly lively young men in search of a real job. It lurched through a solid swarm of disappointed hopefuls and some men scrambled alongside it, banging the metal—*I been waiting long! Lemme on!* The soldier driving steeled his sight, jerking the vehicle forward again and again to scare the runners away.

They travelled many hours, whizzing along paved highways and hesitantly weaving through wild dirt roads. Sunny conversation popped around the seats—*Looks like we lucky, boy! Our prayers been answered!*—and somebody switched on his portable radio, saturating the air with long-playing party songs. *Yes, de Lord mus'-ee bless us dis morning . . .* People hummed with the music and rapped their fingers to the beat.

After a stalled, staggering journey, the bus finally reached a strip where propeller airplanes marked *Omega Global Ventures* had been parked in lines. Although the passengers felt sluggish from the cramped drive, their enthusiasm remained high; they willingly clumped together as soldiers pressed them aboard and approved takeoff with white rags. Neela had never been on an airplane before. She gawked out of the small round window and clutched the sides of her seat as the plane rose. Nonetheless, she was quickly thrilled by the view unravelling below—treetops melted into a seamless layer of green fluff, weighty yet feathered; slithering brown rivers broke through the tree cover like hairline fractures. She was most taken by how the plane soared through clouds, how they seemed so impenetrable but instantly evaporated to steam. Although she had learned about the water cycle in high school, how rivers transformed to vapours and chilled drops, she felt she wasn't meant to know that such heavenly structures as clouds could be morphed into a gasp by a moment's passage.

The plane had been in the air for more than an hour when Neela's stomach sprang from the inside out. "Watch!" the man beside her exclaimed, tapping his knuckles on the window.

They were making an unannounced descent over the edge of a great cliff, following the perilous path of a wide river. Neela knew that she was witnessing the bubbling rush of the great Nasee-Ki; when the plane passed the river's curved ridge, she felt as if the landscape had ripped itself open in a single blink.

The waterfall dropped into a tremendous valley where countless shades of green overlapped and tangled into a web. Neela was used to an imitation of this—a photograph from her old geography textbook, reproduced on plaques and sold to tourists in the city's marketplace. But this was the first time it had been captured by her own eyes, swaying, gushing, glint-ing. She held her breath as the airplane tipped sideways and circled over the valley. As they descended, she could identify a maze of interconnected clearings; soon, frames and foun-dations of buildings, a buglike movement of workers and sol-diers. It wasn't long before they were rolling gracelessly beside the river on a strip of beaten soil.

Eyeballs stinging with new sunlight and legs quivering in the flight's aftermath, she hoisted her suitcase and stumbled down the plane's steps. But someone dipped to block her as she followed her fellow passengers.

"You a manual worker, sweetie? But you too small and cute for dat." It was the soldier who had let her on the bus in Marasaw.

She squinted her eyes almost shut to recognize the particu-lars of his face. "I'm a teacher." Her pluckiness had dissipated in the sheer length of the journey to Eden. She opened and shut her mouth, aware of its staleness.

"Teacher!" He grinned. "So when you gon' instruct me, teach? Eh? When I gon' get dat chance you tell me about?"

She became nervous under the weight of his shadow. "You know where I got to go? Where de other teachers meet?"

"Right here, girl." The soldier closed in and Neela stepped backward, shielding her shins behind her bag. "What? Since when a teacher don't want to teach her student?"

For the first time that day, Neela was conscious that she didn't recognize anybody and that Jaroon wasn't due to arrive for another month. Separated from all she had ever known, standing in the rainforest's mire in front of an expectant soldier, she found her sense of power slithering away. No magic was fortifying her as it had with Navi a week ago, and she didn't know how to tap it on command—she had no special way of caring for herself as she had bragged to Lenda. She was just another vulnerable girl. She wished to dissolve into the crowd, to swathe her fragile body in anonymity until Jaroon arrived to protect her. "Leave me alone," she said, in the hardest tone she could find, "don't bother me."

But he gripped her elbow and pulled her instead, causing her to twist on a clumsy angle. "What's wrong, teach?" he huffed.

"We got to meet over dat way right now," a young woman's voice chimed in urgently. She wrapped her hands around Neela's free arm and tugged. "Come on now, they calling for us."

The soldier's desires were deferred in the unexpected change of pace.

"They shouting for y'all dat way." The woman pointed out to him. "You bett'-had go!"

He released Neela's elbow and turned; by the time he snapped back, both women had been enveloped in the horde.

"You alright?" she asked Neela. "I'm Karha."

"Neela. I'm okay. Thank you."

Karha's mouth was inverted with questions. "You a teacher?"

"Oh, yes, well, not really . . ."

"Which college?"

"Marasaw," she answered, shrinking from the unsettling glances of men pouring along the dirt path in the opposite direction. Deflated, she hunched and thought it safest to set her eyes on the young woman's golden, spotted skin, her brown and weightless hair—features different from those familiar to Neela in her hometown.

But Karha poised herself straight and sliced through the crowd, unintimidated by her surroundings. "I was at de college in de capital city."

"You come recently?"

"I grow up in Nasee-Ki but I went to school in de city. My father lives there."

Neela had scarcely considered the people who were born encircled by bush, inhabiting a world that seemed unthinkably remote to her. They were rarely spoken of in the rest of the country. "So, you a . . . red-skin?"

"Yeah. But not my father. He sent for me to go school when I turned twelve. Dat was when my mommy was alive, so I went back and forth between de capital and Nasee-Ki."

After walking some distance they were alone, freed from the Eden Development's strewn hand tools and disordered stocks of wood and brick. The ground wasn't muddy anymore; it was a soft, barely trodden pad of green. Needles of light poked through between leaves as the sunset began gleaming strong. Neela finally noticed the overlapping clicks and buzzes of millions of insects around them, ebbing and flowing like a tide.

"I gon' show you our school," Karha said, leading her down an impromptu path lined by thick bushes and branches. They arrived at a clearing where a modest rectangular slab of concrete lay on the grass; on it, a wooden frame had been erected, empty, without walls and a roof.

Neela was confused by how precarious and unimposing it was, like a child's glued matchstick project. "Dis? You teach here?"

"I got to. It's my only school and I doing de work I came to do, no matter what they try to tell me . . ."

"But where are de other teachers?"

"It's you and me."

Drifting forward, Neela coiled her fingers around one of the frame's matchstick pieces and pressed; she felt the whole thing wobble. "What do you mean?"

"There ain't no other teachers. When I came back to Nasee-Ki six months ago, I was one of three. But the others gone long. One man joined up with de manual workers. I don't know where de other one gone."

"What about students?"

Karha calculated silently into the sky. "Ah, I got about fifty. It does be different each day."

"You alone teach fifty?"

"Yes. Little children, big children, de children's mothers too. They my own people, on my mommy's side." She lingered for another question, but Neela's mouth was drained. Karha had become well acquainted with that face in Eden, the one that signalled a wave of shock before a full flood of disillusionment, the single question bobbing in Neela's mind: *But what kind-a fate led me here?* "Okay, dat's good, then," Karha declared, matter-of-fact. "It's getting dark. We gon' organize ourselves tomorrow. I gon' show you where I stay."

She brought Neela down to another small clearing in the nearby thicket. A round hut had been constructed, and inside, piles of books had been neatly lined along its walls, accompanied by an assortment of writing implements in open cardboard boxes. Neela's eyes were drawn to the taut weave of waxy brown leaves sloping from the roof's apex.

"I got my people to build dis shack for me, you know," Karha explained, lighting a kerosene lamp and setting it on the hut's unlevelled floorboards. "I wanted to keep watch on my school, to make sure dat them men keep it and respect it good. They would-a made me sleep in dat miserable tent with de women workers if I didn't have dis."

Sitting on a tree-trunk stool, Neela listened to Karha listlessly—the voice remote in her ears as she fought valiantly to make some kind of sense of it all.

Karha observed the ceiling too. "We work with them leaves good, nah?"

Before they fell asleep on a bed made of layers of the same leaves, Karha revealed more to her dumbstruck companion.

She had rushed back to Nasee-Ki when she learned about the government's one-year teachers' college agreement. Just like Neela, she had believed she would find a burgeoning new town, a fresh school ready with the typical components—a headmaster, teachers to serve as colleagues and mentors, student uniforms, textbooks from the Royal Reader line—but the town and its school had been no more complete than they were now. Instead of retreating in disenchantment, she had set out to make her school function as she had originally envisioned it; she had instituted classes to teach her students how to read and write English, complementing their general ability to speak it.

The next morning, Neela refused to wake, in protest against the matchstick school and in demonstration of her new-found melancholy, but Karha wouldn't have it. She nagged until Neela bolted into a sitting position and brooded viciously at the slivers of daylight spilling through the hut's walls.

"I gon' show you how to bathe and go to de bathroom," Karha counselled as they dressed in their teacher's college uniforms, the only clothing Neela felt right wearing in a school environment. "It's not de same as you used to."

Neela didn't ask questions—she couldn't stand to hear what attacking insect, deadly plant or violating eyes she was to guard herself against. She suspected all three, and shuddered.

Children were running over the school's concrete foundation, chasing each other and shrieking happily between the bones of the wooden skeleton, oblivious of its shameful instability.

"Don't worry, they loud but they listen when they want to learn," Karha said, her features cheerful as she approached the spot where the chalkboard should have been. "Alright, class, come now. Quickly! It might rain so we need to start."

Neela sat cross-legged at the back of the concrete slab, struggling with the folds of her kilt. While the children chaotically found their places, a handful of women emerged from the bush path and gathered in a congregation behind them, wearing men's T-shirts that draped over the waists of long, colourful skirts.

Karha frowned. "Where are de older boys?"

The women shrugged apologetically.

"But they said they wouldn't have to work until midday." She shook her head and lifted a book. "Okay. Who would like to read de story today?" she called, children stretching their arms straight and high as they would go before she even finished speaking. "Alright, you." A little girl leaped up and came beside her teacher, beaming when Karha passed the open book. "From de top."

Her expression transformed to concentration. "De . . . Country Fair," she read.

"Coun-ty," Karha corrected over the girl's shoulder. "Please speak so everyone can hear you." Her eyes skipped to Neela at the far edge of the slab.

"De County Fair. In de . . . summer, children are . . . ex-ci-ted because de . . . coun-ty fair will come to their town." She inhaled and licked her lips in preparation. "They love candy apples, cot-ton candy, English . . . tof-fee, and bl- . . ."

"Sound it out." Karha pointed. "Blue-ber-ry."

"Blue-ber-ry pie."

Karha raised her finger at the class. "Say it, 'blue-ber-ry pie,'" she instructed, nodding to accentuate each syllable; both children and mothers answered, mimicking the emphatic head bobs, *Blue-ber-ry-pie!*

"Who would like to read on?" Karha asked, again rousing the children's darting hands and drawn breaths. Although none of the women volunteered, she looked to one of them. "How about you?"

This woman was younger than the others and pregnant. She stepped around the children to the front of the concrete slab-room, raising her skirt from her ankles and smiling bashfully.

Karha put a gentle palm at the top of the woman's back and gave her the book. "Take your time."

"When de day . . . c-comes," she began, "de children s- . . . s- . . ."

"Scam-per. Keep going," Karha said softly.

"De children scam-per to de f-fair in ho- . . . hopes of . . . joy-ous fun." The woman had the same gratified expression as the girl who had begun the story, and Karha patted her on her shoulder.

Karha led her class through more exercises. She would declare words and the class would scribble them down and read answers aloud in the required formula: *De word is vase, V-A-S-E, vase.* Sometimes, Karha fooled them by spelling out letters and asking them to produce the word; it took longer for hands to rise, and when they did surface, they crawled into the air instead of cutting it rapidly.

The day was shortened when overhead clouds became heavy and low; the class scattered from the slab before drops pelted them. Neela sat in the hut's entrance and watched how the rain gushed down wide leaves as if taps had been opened. Everything looked green and full, and when the rain came down hardest, the air turned especially sweet and sandy. It was loud, noisier than the rainfall that visited Marasaw—she thought her hearing would surely melt away in the clapping downpour.

"I gon' got to get a leaf roof on dat school," Karha muttered to herself. She was on the floor, going through the *Royal English Reader for Students*. Every so often, she would narrow her eyes and underline something in pencil. "Or we gon' hardly have class in de rainy season. You should see dat, dis ain't nothing."

Neela twisted to look at her thumbing through the glossary. "But they might finish building de school properly by then."

Karha was surprised by the sound of Neela's voice—she hadn't said much since they had met, and certainly hadn't made an attempt at conversation. "I don't think so, girl." She smiled. "I watch what they do. Dis school ain't what they really care about. It can't really make much money. It ain't a hotel or restaurant or shop." She kissed her teeth. "But it looks like they ain't getting to finish building anything much for Omega, mind you."

Neela observed the ceiling once again. It appeared darker in the rain but its inner surface wasn't moist. "I'm surprised it ain't leaking."

"De leaves are waterproof when you put them together like dat." Karha put one hand up, fingers splayed. "On their own, water can jump through de spaces." She wiggled her fingers. "But when you weave them"—she brought her other hand up with fingers stretched, and interlocked the two—"they form a seal. Rain can't get through. It's like they was meant to fit like dat, growing on de trees just to lock together." She dropped her hands, transforming them back to flesh and bone. "Dat's how we build roofs in Nasee-Ki. In fact, they weave them leaves to make all kind-a thing."

"You teach good."

Karha was silenced by the sudden praise.

"It's true. I can't do dat."

"Well, you gon' learn soon," she answered, and glanced at her pile of schoolbooks.

Rain slapped the earth more rigidly now, provoking beetles; the soil appeared to shiver and break goosebumps as they wriggled out of hiding. "So, they take mail from de workers? I can send a letter home?"

"You gon' got to give de soldiers something." Karha was well versed in Eden's bartering system—she had had to bribe the bossier soldiers to allow her to live beside the matchstick school, even to let the older children attend class a few times a week, despite how jealous the men were of the boys' energetic young muscles. "When they fly out to get supplies, I give them cigarettes so they'll bring back pencils and *Royal Readers* and stuff. You can probably get them to carry mail de same way."

"How y'all get mail sent to you?"

"We don't get mail," Karha answered. For a short moment the raindrops lessened, only to explode again. "Who gon' want to send us mail?"

I arrived in Nasee-Ki safely last week, Neela wrote to her grandmother, *and I already started at the elementary school.* She reflected on how to make it more convincing, more buoyant, adding, *Karha, another teacher here, is showing me everything about teaching the children.* Tension clouded her lungs; she pressed her fist into the middle of her chest and cautiously heaved air, wishing to force the angry faces of Granny and Navi from her head. It was late and Karha had already fallen asleep beside her. Neela envied how she could claim rest in the valley. *I hope you are doing well. Have you seen Lenda? Can you please tell her I said hello?*

She stopped to examine the tip of her pencil, dull and writing in artless strokes. Right then, everything was dull—the pencil, the kerosene lamp's feeble flame, Neela's spirit. She was uncomfortably aware of her inability to survive independently in this place; surely her grandmother would see through her cocky words, even though they were polished in fraudulent optimism. *Please don't worry about me or work yourself too hard. I'm doing well and getting good teaching experience.* She knew it was unwise, but she scribbled it and moved on in a hurry— *I'm making good money and I will send you something as soon as I can, I promise, Granny.*

When she asked about their compensation, Karha revealed that she hadn't been paid for the last three months. She had a nervous, giddy air explaining it. "When I first came, they told us we would get cash each month. But soon de workers start grumbling, saying de government been lying to them. Dat's when de soldiers threaten everyone and said they won't send no cash until de workers build de development up more. De Builder Party ain't meeting de contract on time so Omega's refusing to pay." Her hands would have writhed in each other if she hadn't forced them to cup her knees. "So far, I ain't see nothing more than rations and a little supplies."

"What? We . . . we don't get no money?" Neela exclaimed.

A fluttering laugh escaped Karha's throat. "I don't really think so, girl. Not any time soon, I guess. But when you think about it, what you gon' do with money anyhow? There ain't nothing to buy, really. It might help you work with the soldiers, maybe, but I don't think it makes much sense to have money here. Somebody might just cut your throat for it . . ."

"But my grandmother!" Neela was more tempted than ever to let tears finally creep up. She had been quick to leave Marasaw, but with a firm assumption that she would support her grandmother as Navi and her mother were both trying to do. It had been an important element of running away, both a rationalization for her to flee so sneakily and a means of atoning for it. "I got to send money to her, I got to!"

"How you gon' send it?"

"With de soldiers, de mail!"

Karha had a pitying face. "They would thief it, Neela. Your granny wouldn't see it at all."

"But . . ."

"Even if you give them all de cigarette you got, they gon'

lie and say they send it. You won't really know what happen to it."

"What if I bribe them to let me visit her? They bring me here, they can take me back, yeah?" Her tears were tumbling but Neela managed to stuff back her sobs; the water melted along her cheeks in silence.

"There's no way they gon' let you go," Karha answered, regretful. "They under orders to keep us here. I don't know what happen to de teacher dat disappear but I wonder, did he try to get away? They know you ain't got nowhere to go. And is not dat y'all people gon' try to run into de bush either. Too scared. And how you gon' know where to run?"

Neela wanted to press further, to beg Karha to counsel her on what she should do, but Karha's features made it clear that there was nothing more she could do. Neela felt nothing vibrating inside her belly, no magic abilities to impact or sway the brutal operations of Eden and its inhabitants. "Then why don't you people leave?" she blurted, in a defensive afterthought. "Y'all don't have to work in Eden if you know dis bush so good. De soldiers won't find you in there. Why don't you just go?"

Karha laughed, this time abundantly; the liveliness of her glee worried Neela. "You right, girl!" she exclaimed. "When I was a child, we would play where them big bad men too frighten to go." Her chuckles faded to vague amusement and she ran her fingers along her scalp, down the length of her hair. "But dis is our home, de only home we ever know," she said, now pensive. "De valley's everything. We can't abandon it, like it don't mean nothing to us. Dat wouldn't be right. And we know full well what does happen anyway. We can get away from them now, yes, easy. But you best believe dat we and our children gon' have to pay for it later. They always find a way to make you pay, you know?"

But Neela didn't know and she didn't want to ask.

⁓

Early in the morning before class, valley chilly and misted, they walked down to the camp. Karha had supplied Neela with cigarettes. "You sure you want use them for dis?" she asked as they stepped out of their safe area around the school and hut. "Those cigarettes are all we got to care for ourselves."

But Neela had to try to send her grandmother a letter or she feared she would go insane with concern—Eden's weighty, moist air had caused her to vividly envision the sad lines on Granny's face for the first time, given her the ears to hear her grandmother's infuriated sobs to Navi and their mother over the telephone.

The campground was dirty and smoking, a result of dozens of small fires boiling water and warming rations. Green Omega army tents were stacked close together at the water-logged riverside. Neela walked close behind Karha as they weaved along skinny paths between workers' plots, trying her best not to gawk back at the men in the entrances of their sleeping areas.

Karha stopped in her stride. "I gon' get rations over there," she murmured low, eyes darting about. "But wait to find a soldier by himself, over there at them big tents, alright? Don't let too many people see you." Neela was uneasy about being alone, but she didn't want to reveal her hesitation here. "Don't watch de men and don't answer if they call you. And don't you trust no woman if you see one, just mind your business. I gon' meet you back quick."

Neela nodded and, swift to respond to a soldier emerging from his shelter, she jogged forward as discreetly as she could. He stood in the mud with a lit cigarette between his fingers, staring into the distance, while she approached his side with a crouched back.

"You can do something for me?" she asked, holding two fresh white cigarettes that glowed with halos in the dank surroundings.

He watched her tiredly. "What else you got?" He slid the cigarettes from her fingertips and stuffed them under the rim of his beret.

"Plenty more," she answered, ready to negotiate. "You can bring a letter to a post office for me?"

He let the butt drop from his mouth and swept his steel-toe to cover it with mud, breathing a yawn. "Yeah."

"You sure? You promise?"

"Yes. You gon' give it or no?"

Neela hadn't anticipated that it would be so easy, so she fumbled to pull the letter from her college kilt's tight pocket. "Here." She handed the crumpled envelope to him.

"For your old lady?"

"Yes. And she needs it bad. She gon' die with worry if you don't . . ."

"Alright, alright." He waved the letter to direct her to fly away, and peered around to check that the other soldiers hadn't seen him take it.

Karha and Neela hoisted two potato sacks of rations that would stretch for the entire month and made the half-mile walk back to their hut. "De soldiers' word don't really mean dat much," Karha said on the path. "They lie plenty and I suppose you can't expect nothing more in Eden. I only hope they ain't lying to you dis time."

They started a fire on a rocky, charred spot behind the hut and peeled some sparse rations for the beat-up pot of boiling water—plantains, eddoes, potatoes. Neela gaped hungrily. During her weeks in Nasee-Ki, she had eaten hardly anything more than chewy strips of salted fish and beans. Although she had entertained the idea that she wouldn't be able to eat, that she was too sorrowful to stomach meals alone in this valley, she became ravenous when she saw the stew's hot steam; it flirted in a snaky dance and teased by dampening her cheeks.

"We gon' make a little extra for tomorrow afternoon, okay?" Karha said while they ate their decadent breakfast, even though Neela was too busy slurping the stew to reply.

But by the next afternoon, Neela couldn't think about rations stew. She was so distracted that she dropped a precious piece of plantain in the process of peeling it. "Not so careless, watch out!" Karha cried. Neela had been like this the whole day; when a student stammered over a word, she had to run her finger along the page to identify where the child was reading.

"You want see what's going on now?" Karha asked. "I gon' finish de stew, you go."

Neela was perched on the stool in the hut's doorway, the place she had gotten used to as she and Karha prepared lessons. "You sure?" she asked, elated.

"I can't deny you in de state you in, girl."

Neela was breathless as she stumbled from the hut. She jogged down the path to their school and waited, anxiously scanning the area and shooing flies. Night winds had already begun to build speed and they shook the bushes, making trees creak against themselves. Neela didn't allow her eyes to linger on any spot too long for fear that they might miss something; she tried to filter out the noises of animals and birds screaming and squawking forlornly as if lamenting to each other. *If he don't come, I won't survive in dis place, I won't live another day,* she thought, disturbed memories of Navi and her grandmother threatening to flood her consciousness again. *Please, I don't want them to ever know, but I can't stay in dis place alone, not even for one more day. I don't know how to care for myself.*

Mirroring her upset, the wind gusted unpredictably, whirling tree limbs in its thrust. Branches moved eerily, like trembling arms, and she swallowed against the stiff breeze, the dryness of her mouth. *It's like dis place is cursed,* she thought, *de bush cursed and de people cursed too. Oh, Lord. If he don't come, I'll die, I can't survive dis fate without him . . .* Leaves and grass and vines brushed rhythmically, fanning toward the area where she stood, like the tentacles of an anemone. She wondered what the valley was going to do, what it appeared so determined to propel toward her. She refused to form too strong a hope lest she face the further abuse of disappointment.

She tried to set her mind on her new life—the woven leaves that made the hut's ceiling, children reading merrily as if it were play, the fluid lengths of the women's wrapped skirts. But when Nasee-Ki's wind blasted her skin and raised her hair from its underside, her mind was weighed down with Jaroon Begwan—how it had felt when he kissed her on her grandmother's porch, how she had been willing to leave all she had known and destroy her own brother for him, how he had worn his tart musk just for her at the Marasaw Restaurant, how she had missed him so painfully and yearned for him ever since she had arrived in the interior. *There's nothing I can do. If he don't come tonight, I'll go mad in dis haunted place . . . oh, please come tonight, have mercy on me, bring him to me tonight . . .*

A rustling formed amongst the bushes at the edge of the school skeleton, more coherent than the sounds the wind produced. She turned and glowered as a figure slid and struggled along to follow the footpath. *I gon' cuss him bad,* she thought, anticipating that one of those lecherous soldiers was approaching, *I gon' scream murder . . .*

But then a torrent rushed over her as mighty as the flow of the Nasee-Ki River, rippling up from the bottom of her belly, towing with it the deepest sobs, the warmest flood of tears to streak her face. She latched to the back of Jaroon's neck, locking her arms and cupping his hair in the palm of her hands. *I thought you wouldn't come, I thought you was going to stay in Marasaw and leave me,* she tried to tell him, *Oh I thought dat I would have to be here alone but I can't do it, I can't deal with dis fate, I can't care for myself, I thought I was strong enough but nothing is coming to me here and I can't survive on my own but I can't go back to my family, and I thought I was gon' be without you, Jaroon, oh Lord, I prayed and prayed and I thought I was going to die, I was going to go mad, you wasn't going to come for me . . .* The words melded into a stream of shrill whimpers.

"Neela!" Jaroon said, holding her, alarmed at the whirlwind that had been set free the moment she saw him in the dusk. "What happen with you, girl?"

CHAPTER 7

The tailor made a production of taking measurements. He pulled the tape with taut flourishes, solemn professionalism peppered by hints of artistry. *Waist, 34 inches.* He snapped his wrist and the tape uncoiled even more; it flittered down to brush the floor. *Length, 36 inches.* The man's ease with his craft had thoroughly distracted Navi from choosing one of the countless fabric swatches; he flipped to the start of the *Greys and blacks* section of the binder and began browsing again.

Navi was getting a real suit, the first that would be custom-fitted to his body. He had entered the gentlemen's boutique with the intention of purchasing a proper winter coat, as the parka he had originally bought didn't match the nonchalant winter wear of his peers—they survived in little more than scarves, and toe rubbers over their dress shoes. But when he noticed the store's tower of handkerchiefs and catwalk of well-dressed mannequins, he became convinced that it was time to acquire a business suit like those of his colleagues.

The tailor lifted a jacket and gently slipped it on him. Its lining was cool even through his cotton dress shirt; he shrugged his shoulders and allowed the jacket to adjust itself over the curves of his back. Lifting Navi's arms to the side, the tailor pinched the cloth in varied spots, envisioning each potential cut and seam. Every so often, he scratched something cryptic in a notebook and stuffed it back into his pocket.

Navi hadn't been studying business for long before his talents leaked beyond the confines of the lecture hall, pooling out to the university's government connections. With his reserved manner and head-of-the-class grades he made a fast impression, and was offered a desirable paid internship with the newest governmental branch, the Ministry of Foreign Investment. He understood that the faculty was grooming him to apply for a prestigious position in the rapidly growing field. As he had desired for so long, he now had a chance at staying overseas and forging a prosperous life for himself.

Full shoulder, 21 inches across. The store had a limitless stock of ties, so the tailor brought his personal favourites forward and held them against Navi's jacketed chest. The man's preferences were obvious—he scowled and chucked ties he didn't like on a chair set in the corner, passing serious contenders to his assistant for the next round. Navi, completely discouraged from offering his own input, observed the tailor as he progressively narrowed the options. Soon, a distinct winner was pressed to the suit's fabric, a rich paisley in gold and navy. The man promptly recorded its inventory number, without asking a thing of his customer.

Overseas weather had turned out to be manageable. Navi still found it a novelty to glide over ice patches on the sidewalk and feel snow collect in his hair, but he actually preferred the cold to Marasaw's heat and humidity. It certainly wasn't as bad as the neighbours had warned—*People get chills from dat cold,* they had told him with great alarm, *It can get into your bones so you must make sure you dress properly!* Even his grandmother's prejudice against winter seemed exaggerated when he stepped on the sloped stone walkway in front of the student apartments, catching an early panoramic view of rolling streets on a brisk, dimmed morning. He would enjoy the city's peacefulness as his breath misted warm into the sky, drifting into the path of an occasional grey-blue winter bird. He had only experienced the marvel of cycling seasons a few times by this point, but he didn't loathe cold the way his classmates did—how they complained through half the year, and worried through the other half.

So when he awoke in the middle of the night, beleaguered by a convoluted dream about his old neighbourhood, he couldn't understand what was hassling him so. He couldn't fathom why he would gravitate toward the saturated scent of frying oil from a nearby restaurant or why he would bother to brush the leaves of potted palms in the government building's lobby.

"Maybe you're homesick," a fellow intern, Tarika, suggested. She sipped foam that had spilled over the rim of her steaming drink; a puddle of milky liquid was growing around the bottom of the mug. "Did you ever consider that?"

Navi regretted revealing anything so personal in the first place. "No, no. It's not dat, I suppose I just . . ."

"What's wrong with being homesick, though?" She bent her head low and gestured for him to do the same. "Don't say anything," she whispered, "I wouldn't admit it to just anyone, but I got so homesick when I moved to the city."

"But you said you like going to new places."

She scanned the faces that populated the café, an after-hours gathering place for employees at the Ministry of Foreign Investment, and smirked. "Well, I do now, but it was different for me back then. Something about being around all these old white men made me want to crawl into bed and cry for my mommy. No?"

He couldn't help but chuckle when she spoke so familiarly— they had started their internships only a few months ago, but Tarika treated him as if she had been working alongside him for years. "I really don't think I have dat problem," he answered, scalding dribbles of coffee rippling over his knuckles when he raised his cup. "Ouch!"

Tarika sat herself straight. "You alright there, boy?"

Navi believed that she was kind to him because her family had immigrated from the same country as he had. Although she had been born and raised overseas, experiencing little of her parents' old lives and ways, she had founded an instant, comfortable connection with him. "I'm okay," he answered, slightly embarrassed, working a napkin between his fingers. He was hopelessly awkward around her. Entertaining himself under cover of books and homework

and tests as a child, he had seldom practised how to negotiate polite chatter.

"I think you need to do something to make yourself less
homesick. Why don't we go to the Westside Village? My family used to go at least once a month when I was a kid. We can
buy oxtail or kingfish, whatever you like, and I bet they'd have
all the fruits you used to get in Marasaw." She took a bite of
biscotti and pointed the untouched end at him. "I love it there.
You want some?"

He smiled stiffly and shook his head. Navi hadn't developed a taste for biscotti, and the Westside Village was the last
place he wanted to visit.

⁓

Ever since he had begun making real money to send back
home, Navi had been receiving weekly phone calls from his
grandmother in addition to letters. She was thrilled to relish his
grown-man voice, how it would give her news to brag of with
the neighbours—*Even de government people see how bright de
boy is, and you know them people over there don't play!* As soon as
she hung up the phone from speaking with him, she would
ring his mother to relay the updates. *Mira, you gon' be so pleased
to hear how your son is doing dis week* . . . He didn't mind any of
it, but lately, after a good deal of ranting about his sister's mis-
deeds, Granny would push him into a different topic entirely.

It had started with an innocent statement, posed passive
and delicate—*You mus'-ee meeting plenty people over there, right*

Nav?—that turned to a specific question—*Must tell me more about de other students at your school.* Soon, it slithered into something much slyer and more ominous to his ears. *De young ladies in your class mus'-ee watch you plenty, yeah, they mus'-ee like you bad . . .* He took a laboured gulp of air, anticipating what would happen next.

"No, Granny, I don't . . ."

"I don't mean right now, I'm talking about when you done your schooling . . ."

"But I don't want you to . . ."

"How you can tell me no before you even hear what I telling you?"

"I don't want to!" He stopped himself from blurting that he had no intention of returning home, especially after everything that had happened with Neela. He knew that, deep down, his grandmother understood that he didn't care to come back, that it would be utterly dissatisfying after all he had been promised overseas. Nevertheless, she insisted that he fly down sooner or later to find a girl to marry, perhaps even one of the girls from Marasaw.

"Plenty-plenty nice brown girls all over de place, you know," she said, competing with the crackle of Mr. Jenhard's phone, "especially in de city. But I see some pretty ones around town too, Nav. You know they would really love to meet you . . ."

"I don't want to think about dat kind of thing right now . . ."

"But you must think about your future, you gon' want a family one day, nah? Even your mommy was asking me about it on de phone de other day, she been thinking about it too! At least consider it, Nav."

"I've got too much to do these days, I'm still in school, I'm just starting here . . ."

"And you are such a nice boy! So smart and handsome . . ."

"For goodness' sake, Granny . . ."

As usual, his grandmother had erected elaborate plans for him, long before he had formulated any for himself. He pushed the receiver down after making a narrow escape from the conversation, and drew open the heavy winter curtains insulating his apartment window. Clumped flakes were descending outside, glimmering densely and illuminating the whole street—instead of floating, they plopped to the ground and coated the neighbourhood beyond recognition. Fellow students, cackling raucously, had already pitted the fresh landscape with unsightly footprints even though it was close to midnight, heaving snowballs at each other and collapsing backwards into the frigid padding. Navi followed the drudging grumbles of a single car making belligerent, uneven tracks along the road. He was crestfallen. *I don't want a girl from back home,* he thought, finally turning to slip under his comforter, *I want Tarika.*

Navi hadn't realized that he cared for Tarika right away. In fact, he had hardly formed a reply to her *good morning*s and *good evening*s at the Ministry of Foreign Investment, just as he would rarely encourage anyone attempting a conversation with him. When she invited him to eat with the other interns at lunchtime, he didn't view it as an exceptional display of kindness, especially since she had taken to asking him personal questions so flippantly. *Which town did you live in, is it by the river, I only know about the places around the river.* She didn't seem to notice how he recoiled at her intrusiveness in front of everyone—it was the kind of thing that had turned him off friends in the first place. *Do you still have family back home, are you still in touch with them?* He had decided to avoid her, to remain in his private thoughts and continue reaching for his overseas goals alone.

But something started to change, something so gradual that it hardly made an impression as it happened—he involuntarily began to expect her greetings, even unaware of himself as he answered in kind. On campus, he wasn't put off anymore when she waved enthusiastically across the grand lecture hall, half of her body imprinted by multicoloured shapes from stained-glass windows. She would soon appear at his ministry desk in the middle of the afternoon, reaching into her coat arms; he'd lay his assignments aside to accompany her wandering around the city block. It was no longer so strange when she made him pause to explain what it was like living in the sun, ordering him to speak for himself when he implied that he didn't miss it.

The awareness rushed to his consciousness one day over lunch—the other interns were caught in insular cafeteria prattle, gossiping about another evening at the pub. He wouldn't normally have cared to eavesdrop, particularly since Tarika wasn't at the table; in fact, their storytelling, shaped by counterfeit twists and climaxes, annoyed him greatly. But their giggling started to cling to his ribs as they recounted the resolve of near-drunk men—*Did you see the guy hitting on Tarika? He was so sloshed . . . I would've slapped him, man . . . You know she can't do that, she's always too nice with those idiots.* Navi's interest was strummed. He felt unsettled at the notion that she appeared to befriend everyone, any man, as if by default. He ping-ponged back and forth between the interns over an untouched bowl of onion soup, hoping to catch a contrary analysis of her kindness. *I always tell her, if you're too nice, some of those guys'll get the wrong idea . . .*

Navi was exhausted by the time he returned to his desk, newly disengaged from industry research. *Dat's why she's been so friendly with me?* he worried. *Because she's nice to everyone?* He recommitted his attention to the afternoon department meeting, but the thought still prowled at the back of his mind, nipping incessantly. *What if she's too nice to everybody? Then what does she really think about me?* When he returned home and found it chewing his stomach between textbook chapters, he made a mental leap into his cup of black coffee—*I suppose I like her,* he thought, taking a mouthful. He had to like her, if this trivial issue was concerning him so much.

To Navi's dismay, admitting it didn't win him any measure of control; it simply caused him to smile at her unsteadily and observe her more keenly. Moments that Tarika wasn't in his view, those hours between their classes and ministry internship, became ordeals of endurance. He felt the gnawing weight of her absence yet he was disappointed in himself when relief and shyness heated his cheeks upon her return. He would ready himself for her to come near and ask him something else, rehearsing the plausible replies in his mind—*I know it's typical of me, but I think mango is my favourite fruit . . .* He couldn't remember another instance when he had waited for time to pass this way, and he knew that he could never find a girl like Tarika back home.

She was not like the ones he had grown up with. In Marasaw, he had failed to acknowledge their existence—those girls had occupied the background scenery of his daily routines, usually creating too much of a racket for his liking. *And you know what she told me next, you know what kind-a gall she got? You wouldn't believe it, girl, hear dis . . .* They would snicker and link arms when he walked past them in the schoolyard, sometimes scrambling to adjust their hair, sometimes cutting their eyes at him and skittering away. The drama had made no sense to him. *And watch here, look at dis story, girl, I gon' tell you something real good now . . .* When the other boys swooned over a popular girl, exchanging unrealistic boasts about what they'd do if they were her man, Navi couldn't fathom the depth of their obsession. None ever seemed that beautiful or compelling to him. Marasaw girls were just like the other people in his hometown—inconsequential and rather silly.

But Tarika's smooth brown skin had a novel effect upon Navi; as he took a customary break with her along the hectic street, he admired its glossy sheen in the afternoon light. His fingertips rubbed together inside his pocket, as if they could feel her softness—and he stopped himself abruptly.

"What's wrong?" she asked, halted in the middle of the crosswalk in mid-sentence. The sun skidded behind a cloud and the whole city block dimmed.

His eyes drilled into the cracked pavement, traffic rushing close beside them over a clinking grate in the intersection. He was unable to answer her.

"Was I wrong to ask a question about your mother? I'm sorry."

He was in a shameful panic about this sort of unconscious reaction to her, reflexes that were becoming more common each day. "No, no, it's okay," he said. He pointed a hand out and waited for her to start heading toward the sidewalk's safety, without meeting her eyes or daring to meet anybody else's. He felt as if people were passing him bristled, disdainful, as if they could detect his secret desires for her. "My mother doesn't live in Marasaw, she's in another country doing babysitting work. She was actually overseas when I was a child. My grandmother raised me and my sister."

Navi disclosed more to Tarika than he ever had to anyone, as if he had an obligation to satisfy her curiosity. He knew that he could have kept her at a safe distance if he had truly wanted to, but he enjoyed her attention too much. He was energized that she would inquire about his past, his thoughts, his ambitions. Back in Marasaw, forming explanations for himself had often been a nuisance—*Navi, smartie-boy,* old-lady neighbours would beckon as he attempted to creep home after school, *come by dis way, nah, talk to me, tell me what you been doing . . .* But now idle dialogue was granting him permission to gaze at the form of Tarika's face without reservation.

"So you don't get along? Why?" she asked, taking a slow, casual slurp of an enormous slushy.

He stiffened, just at having to draw his sister to the forefront of his mind. He and Tarika sat on the square base of the campus's landmark statue, a large, scowling army man straddled over a stern horse. It was an exceptionally mild day and soggy patches of yellow-brown grass poked through brittle ice littering the courtyard. "Long story." He braced himself against the horse's veined front leg.

Tarika unzipped her coat and tugged at her scarf, wishing that the breeze would find her neck. "What happened between you two?"

Tiny birds had perched on the horse's head and were making a commotion of cheeps and chirps, of superimposed call-and-answer melodies. "I'm not too sure. But I don't think my sister likes me very much . . ." He let the statement escape and hoped that it would dissipate in the open. He was impatient to forget the bewildering terror he had last experienced with Neela, and had rushed out of Marasaw with the hope of never thinking about her again. With a tentative sense of relief, he noted that his sister's malice didn't appear to be undoing him in this faraway place, yet he couldn't let himself become overly assured. He looked to Tarika with hesitation and found that her expression petitioned for more. "Um . . .

well, last time we talked, she was very angry with me. I don't think she wants to see me again."

He expected her to snap another prickly question, but she remained pensive and observed the bird convention above. Her hair tossed flightily in the breeze and swept back down over her shoulders.

"I . . . I guess I might have contributed to some of de problems," he added hurriedly, wondering what she was making of it, if she perceived his lack of detail as stinginess or worse, if she could sense his disgraceful weakness that night with Neela.

"What did you do?"

"Well, she was going around with dis, dis boy, and she didn't say anything to us, me and my grandmother, and . . ." His voice became self-conscious, fracturing and melting even though her face hadn't changed—to speak of what had happened with his sister sounded distasteful in this new country, amongst the grand statues and structures, trivial even to his own ears. He wished to disown it, to deny its reality and frame it as a ridiculous childhood nightmare. "I was just trying to . . . my grandmother wanted to know what was going on and I was just answering her questions . . ." He compressed his hands together, realizing that they had progressively stiffened; the early spring air didn't seem as warm as before. "I don't know. She got really angry at me."

Tarika placed her cup on the smooth charcoal stone. "Sometimes I think families are too hard on each other, you know?" She put her arm across Navi's shoulders and braced her body in close to his. He couldn't help but be astonished at her sudden gentleness, warm, remarkably rousing. "But I've learned that we really care about each other too. I hope you two can work it out. I don't know, Nav. Maybe your sister just loved the guy a lot."

Navi hadn't thought about it in those terms, but by the time she slid her arm off, he knew that he loved her.

Ever disciplined, Navi maintained his goal, that voracious desire to exceed his superiors' expectations of what an intern could accomplish. He would arrive at the Ministry early and leave late. He tried to construct a rapport with his supervisors, just as the other interns had automatically done—for the first time, he was concerned about presenting himself as charming, as personable. He was soon informed that he had been chosen as one of three students to participate in interviews for a coveted managerial position at the Ministry.

But he wasn't driven solely by motivation to impress the government. Navi would glance at Tarika from his desk, her expression blank when she was writing a weekly report, instantly livened by conversations with the other interns, the soft fall of her black hair and float of her hands as she returned to the keyboard. And something in his chest would squeeze and twist when she grinned at a passing intern; she'd make a sound, *pssst* or *ahem,* and cause the young man to double back on his path. Before he could properly interpret the outline of words on her lips—*Did you see what happened at that meeting, it was absolutely hilarious*—Navi would crumple into the spiral centre of his book. He would yield to distraction for a single moment, chasing one looped thought: *I wish it was me.*

Nights were restless. He would break free from another prying telephone episode with his grandmother, yearning for sleep yet alert and staring at a square of moonlight plastered on his apartment ceiling. If Tarika wanted to marry, Navi would certainly marry; if she wanted to have him without those tangles of commitment, he'd gladly accept that. Slamming doors and heavy feet along the building's creaking hallway would frame his future plans—she had often told him how much she longed to leave her common city life and experience the world. *My family says I'm going through a phase, but I know it's more than that, Nav. I just really want to live . . .* Now that he was in this adopted country, he could hardly imagine being apart from it, but he would prepare himself to travel any place she desired, anytime she wanted.

He would kick the covers off, sweaty and unsure with almost bottomless longing, and apprehensive about his new-found weakness for a woman. He worried that Neela was somehow the source of these feelings, that she had discovered a mechanism through which to sap his strength. This was when he was most incapable of pushing Marasaw and its inhabitants out of his thoughts; the humidity and teasing spices of back home would stalk around the room, crawl up the bed's legs and seep into his skin. *Is Neela haunting me, making me feel dis way? Why can't I stop thinking like dis?* But he would consider how it felt to be close to Tarika, closing his eyes to recall the stirring at those few instances she had touched him, and he would doubt that Neela could be behind something so intrinsically marvellous.

Shivering, he would feel around for his covers. The square of light would have deformed into a crooked rectangle. He would be unable to find a diversion from whatever had happened earlier that day, another one of Tarika's unaware brushes against his leg or touches of his arm. If only he could remain in such a luxurious state of awe. Yet it wouldn't be long before his mind curdled into reservations, the dread that she might not even want to be his.

"Nav, do you have a second?" Tarika mumbled from the doorway of a meeting room as he stepped by. It was another early morning and the office hadn't yet begun to reek of coffee. "Can you close the door?"

He was again coy at the prospect of being alone with her, but it was clear that she didn't intend to romance him. "What's wrong?"

"Nothing, really." Tarika's hands were tight fists, her face soured. "Well, yes. Something is wrong." It took her conscious effort to unclench her fingers. "Listen, I overheard the other two guys last night at the pub. They think they're so damn good just because you haven't been here that long. They think they're better than you."

Navi wanted to claim her tense hands but he kept his locked to his sides. "But I don't care what they think about me . . ."

"You should've heard them talking their heads off, saying that you have no chance of getting that job, and why would you? You're fresh off the boat, right?" She squeezed his forearm. "But I know you deserve it more than either of them. I'm not just saying it because you're my friend. You've worked hardest and you're the smartest one here. I've seen what you've done, you're brilliant."

Legs never so unsteady, he sagged into a chair. "Dat's very . . . thank you," he breathed.

She was unaware of his debilitation at her confident touch. "Well, you don't have to take their arrogance. I spoke to the director's assistant this morning and she wasn't able to tell me very much, but she did type up the interview notes and she remembered seeing some things on the page . . ."

"Tarika, I don't care about those two," Navi said, staggering back to his thinking self. "I know I've done well. I don't need to do anything else."

"No, you do need to do something more. Everyone knows you're smarter than the others, but it's not just about smarts." She saw confusion swipe over his expression and tried to redraw her words more tactfully. "She said that what they want is someone who can . . . well, relate."

"I'm not that different from any of the other interns, am I?"

"I don't think they mean that. I think the directors want you to be able to relate to people you'll be dealing with when you do foreign work. Why do you think they brought you here in the first place? They want someone who can set up deals, win people's confidence, make investing easy for them down there.

From what the director's assistant said, they don't seem to see that in you very much." She faltered. "I think they think you're too uptight."

Navi looked through a window that opened toward a neighbouring building's shadowy brick, puzzled. He had done everything to make the right impression on them, to slot into the environment around him—he had spent most of his life preparing to fit in with what he imagined they would want. Suddenly, he felt as he had when he was back in Marasaw, like a boy who didn't belong. "I can't . . . I can't see how I can change," he grappled. "Did they really say that? I mean, I'm not sure what they want anymore, I'm not sure what I could do to please them, then . . ."

"You have to give them what they want. You just have to." She tapped the table restlessly and flicked her hair behind her shoulder in a way that he found striking. "You have one inter-view left. I think you need to show them what you know about back home. Tell them what it was like, give them the facts, the politics, everything you saw. Show them that it makes more sense to have you at this Ministry than the others, that you can fit in wherever you go. You have the experience, you lived there! I think they need more people like you."

"I . . . alright, okay. I'll try," he answered, rubbing his hands along his thighs to become assured of himself again, "I'll try what you said." He touched his fingers to his heart lightly, almost unable to force out more words. "Thank you, thank you for helping me. I don't know how to thank you properly . . ."

"I know you think I'm not really like you because I grew up here," she cut in, scratching her head agitatedly and surveying the room. "But by now I've seen it all, okay? I know how things work here. People like you and me have to help each other out." She tried to disguise the welling in her eyes by blinking, by staring at the points of her dress shoes. "Sometimes I can't stand this place."

He desired to inch over, imagining how breathtaking it would be to cautiously wrap around her in a slow embrace, even for the short time before the others arrived at the office. Yet all he could do was pull out of his chair and hold the door open for her.

He wore his custom-made suit on the night of the cocktail party, sombre as he slipped into each piece, silent during the taxi ride downtown. The ministry interns stood in a loose ring that constantly broke and reconnected at the edge of the marbled great hall, drinking as happily and carelessly as they would in a nightclub. Wives of the government men crammed the room in cocktail wear, greeting each other and perching over displays of food and wine.

Navi weaved into the hall to establish a place to stand close to Tarika; *You look very pretty tonight,* he tried to tell her, gazing at delicate purple beads strung across her collarbone. But her friends arrived as his lips parted, giggling some silly anecdote about one of their supervisors into her ear, and he was glad to busy himself with trays of caviar and brie that were drifting about.

The house lights rose and the music faded away. "Can I have your attention, please?" The Minister of Foreign Investment stood at a weighty podium under a collection of massive paintings of unnameable grey-skinned dignitaries and wrinkled statesmen. "We're very pleased to be here. Tonight we celebrate another milestone for our ever-growing Ministry with the establishment of three groundbreaking ventures. As all of you are aware, these opportunities will not only benefit our nation, but also bring needed infrastructure to the developing world, infrastructure that *we* will supply. In partnership with visionary corporations and industry leaders, we can build our economy, our nation and our world. *To progress.*"

A multitude of half-full glasses were raised to the ceiling in concert. *To progress,* they repeated, sacrificing an offering of applause. Navi noticed Tarika's polite face from the corner of his eye; while she peeked regretfully into her empty glass, he flagged a waiter to pour more red wine for her.

"Before we return to the revelry, I believe some congratulations are in order," the Minister continued, gesturing to the musicians to delay starting into their next set. "Over the past year, the Ministry of Foreign Investment has been fortunate enough to have the energetic presence of some very gifted and driven young people. Every one of them contributed to the success of this department. But after much difficult deliberation and discussion, one intern, brilliant as they all are, stood above the rest."

Pausing for emphasis, the Minister lifted his spectacles and leisurely scanned writing on a card in front of him.

"I am pleased to call Mr. Navi Keetham to the podium."

The interns broke out in hooting applause, slapping Navi on the back and urging him forward; *Congratulations, well done, good work*, the government men and their wives mouthed as he zigzagged through the crowd toward the front of the room. The Minister gave Navi a vigorous hand-shake and stepped to the microphone again. "We are pleased to announce that Mr. Keetham will be our newest manager, surely the beginning of an esteemed career with this govern-ment. His migration story is certainly an inspiration—such great success in a short time. It demonstrates what deter-mined immigrants can accomplish in this great country of ours. Let's make a toast to Mr. Keetham and to all of our dedicated interns."

Navi rested his eyes on Tarika's delighted countenance, how she raised her glass highest and drank a grinning red gulp. As much as he had done this for himself, he had done it for her too. His thoughts had overflowed with her when he had gone into the office early and caused a jam in the photo-copier at the other end of the floor, requesting urgent help from the director's assistant to repair it. Tarika had burned inside him as he dug around the assistant's desk drawer, deli-cately uncovering a key to the director's office. And he had found those confidential interview notes she had mentioned, barely masked inside an envelope the colour of butterscotch, and had secretly made a copy to study for his final interview.

Navi was more than ready to provide the Ministry of Foreign Investment with what it wanted to hear from a promising young intern, in point-by-point harmony with the director's notes, convinced that seizing the job by any means would not only ground his career, but also enable him to create a life Tarika would want. She would discover that he was worthy of more than friendship, and his prosperity and achievements would launch their future together—he would be a grown man, finally matured from an ignoble childhood amongst the mosquitoes and brown water and dirt.

But as Navi strode back down to merge with the cocktail guests, the Minister presented a final toast. "And we cannot forget to bid farewell to those interns who are assuming our new international positions. They will serve as fine representatives of our country for the next four years, truly ambassadors for progress overseas. I would like to give our very best wishes to Michael Linnard, Janice Wiley and Tarika Lapandoon on their exciting journey." *Hear, hear!* the congregation answered.

Oh no, no, no . . . Navi's stomach dropped and his body went cold. He was back in Marasaw, back in that terrible night—the night his sister had taken control from him, the night he had feared he would lose his life. *No, not dis. I can't lose her now. Is Neela doing dis to me? Please, not again, not Tarika . . .* As the Minister promised not to bother his audience again and the music and thunderous chatter resumed, he gaped, stunned at how people were casually crowding around her, patting her shoulders and tugging at her arms for hugs. *Excellent work,* men and their wives praised Navi, claiming him with their torrent of handshakes; he wanted to give them the eager, fresh visage they expected but he could hardly keep his floundering head up.

People were still congratulating him as he reached for her. "Nav, oh gosh, I'm so proud of you!" Tarika beamed, throwing her arms around him. "I knew you could do it! You did it!"

His mouth trembled and he was without strength to hug her back. "I . . . didn't know you were leaving."

Other interns swirled about, speaking laudatory things to them both. "I made my decision only a week ago," she answered remorsefully, breaking off to respond to an accolade. "I didn't tell anyone. I didn't even say anything to my family at first. I was afraid that I'd change my mind." With a concerned smile, she took his limp hand. "It's a hard decision, but I think it's the right thing, Nav. I know myself. I need to get out of this place and experience life. If I don't go now, I'll never go and I'll always regret it. Aren't you happy for me?"

Navi had to set his eyes away from her. *Neela, please, if it's you. Not dis. I don't want to lose her. Please, hear me, not dis.*

She wiped water from the corners of her eyes and embraced him again. "Oh, I'm going to miss you too. So much." She stroked the back of his suit jacket, tracing the line of its middle seam. "I hope you'll keep in touch with me."

This time, he managed to lift his dead-weight arms around her body and hold on tight.

The interns celebrated at their favourite pub later that evening, completely out of place in their dresses and suits and yet most appropriate with their tipsy banter. But Navi left early, whispering a subdued good-night to Tarika alone and ducking out into the breezy evening. He boarded an empty train and resigned himself to a lengthy ride, all the way down to the Westside Village. Even though it was late at night, many of the scruffy, stacked-close restaurants were informally open and old people relaxed in their doorways, smoking and weaving joint commentary together—*Eh-eh, watch dis boy here now, he's looking dapper tonight, whaaat* . . . The streets were fully active, animated with the *ping-ping-ping* of calypso and unparalleled midnight energy. It was the same buzz that Navi had grown so familiar with during his time in Marasaw.

He nodded at the old folks, finally acknowledged to himself that he could never forget his old home and old life, nor was it likely that he would ever escape them for good. And he accepted that he would always ponder what Neela was doing to him, how she might be ruining his accomplishments and drive and ideals from afar. Even as he drowned in such looming realizations, he tried to salvage a sense of relief in surrendering to them.

He found the first place that served rice and oxtail and claimed a seat in a dark corner. When a steaming plate was set in front of him, he didn't bother to wipe away the dhal that splashed onto his suit sleeve.

CHAPTER 8

Neela turned nineteen in Eden, still longing to unearth teaching talents alongside Karha in their matchstick school. Soon after he arrived to drown in Neela's torrent of tears, Jaroon also became acquainted with the common disenchantment of Eden's dwellers. At first he spent difficult days sweating in the bushes and enduring stinging bites, labouring with the other men to build what amounted to nothing. They toiled aimlessly as soldiers stood in groups and smoked, sometimes pausing to bark threats—*If you don't work properly for de Builder Party you ain't getting no rations next month, yeah!*

But no matter how hard they worked or didn't work, there was no escape from the Nasee-Ki Valley. Wood ants bored into freshly cut planks and split them along their grain, rain pelted ugly pits into concrete before it could dry, overnight winds shattered recently erected building frames. *Dis place is cursed*, workers whispered, relaying rumours they had long overheard from the people who had been born and raised in Nasee-Ki, *De waterfall is rebelling against us.* But Jaroon didn't respond to such claims; he simply watched the sky and returned to grating a handsaw across logs to the point of exhaustion. Whether or not Nasee-Ki was haunted wouldn't affect him.

What did change things were the prolonged evenings that he spent with workers like himself, his own kind, assembling to commiserate and grouse about the other men in the development, *them people.* His untailored charisma made a fresh impression each night. Jaroon would wrap two fingers around a smuggled cigarette, gulping contraband Shawlster beer and manoeuvring domino pieces with the tips of his remaining fingers. His free arm found rest across Neela's shoulders—her unusual presence at the crooked game table only sharpened his magnetism. Although she slouched beside him bored and pouting, she was certainly no *loose woman* from the camp. She was a real girl, a good, devoted girl who did what the others couldn't imagine convincing a woman from back home to do—she followed her man into the depths of the Nasee-Ki. They admired and envied Jaroon for it, even as they wished for Neela themselves.

Brap! "What you mean, boy, here!" A worker slapped his double-one domino down, causing the table to quake over everyone's knees. The other players cursed leftover pieces that were caved in their hands, and reluctantly chucked clean cigarettes to the winning team.

"They robbing us, girl," Jaroon commented merrily, but Neela only curled her lip and shrugged, *I ain't care.* He leaned close to her cheek and rounded his arm around her waist. "What happen? Eh?"

"I tired," she huffed, "and I want to go." She turned her face to the exact angle where she could look away from him but still feel his breath gliding over her neck.

"Alright, we gon' go just now, one more game." Jaroon nodded to the man across from him. Neela puffed an irritated sigh. "Let's go, deal quick."

The man clacked the pieces together, white and clean as pretty teeth, shuffling them in and out of each other on the table-top. "I going, man, I going." He caught Neela's sulk and winked. "You gon' get to be alone with your honey just now, girl," he quipped. The other workers smirked, *eh-ehhh, whaaaat . . .*

Instead of cutting her eye at the dealer, Neela pressed against Jaroon's side, brushing the knuckles of his loose hand as it dangled over her collarbone. "Don't you worry yourself," she answered, mocking his tone, "I can wait."

"And good things come to those who wait!" someone's drunk mouth tumbled, and all the men laughed. *Eh-heh, you right, boy, you right!* Jaroon grinned and squeezed Neela's hand as he raked in his share of dominoes.

"Who's got de double six?"

Jaroon was the one to answer the call this time. He theatri-cally readied himself to smash the piece on the table, only to jerk back and offer it dot-side up and flat on his hand to the girl beside him. She scanned the jealous, captivated eyes of the men and bent close to the domino piece, unhurriedly blowing good luck over its etchings. *Brap!*

"I mus'-ee cut a million pieces-a wood already. True," Jaroon mumbled, caressing the soft cluster of Neela's hair, swept into a ponytail. "I getting too good at it these days. Who would think?"

"So y'all should be moving forward with de work then, right?"

He frowned at Karha and Neela's hut. The surrounding shrubbery was populated with invisible insects that seemed to screech at him in spitefulness. He had walked Neela along the gloomy path, and they stood facing each other as they had done almost a year earlier, in the hidden area near her grandmother's house. "They always talk about how dis place won't let us finish nothing."

"Karha says it's cursed." She laid her hands on the middle of his chest as if blessing him, eyelids shut in concentration on his fingers in her hair. "Cursed from long time. She say de government does always come to do things on de land but they does always fall apart. De valley don't let people do what they intend to do ... ."

"I don't believe them people when they talk so."

"What you mean?"

"They talk pure jumbie-story, spirits in de bush and all dat. They only trying to scare us, you know."

"Well, Karha said . . ."

"But it scares you, right?"

Neela shrugged *me nah know* and peered into the bush herself; it had turned into cavernous shadows at this hour.

"It certainly scares de men, especially our own kind, girl. Trust brown-man to take on dis stupidness de most. These Nasee-Ki people believe pure nonsense, man, pure superstition. I can't understand why they got to put it on us too." *Them people!* his withering expression read.

"Then why y'all can't get de building done?" she asked, trying to find his eyes, to compel an answer, but he only surveyed the night sky as if predicting rainfall.

It did rain that night and Neela couldn't stay asleep in the midst of the downpour, the sharp-odoured riot. *It sound like de rain is washing away some good buildings tonight,* she thought, observing her friend's shape in the darkness. Karha had grown up in the middle of nighttime deluges and was sleeping soundly, unmoving except for a gentle up-and-down of her chest. Neela took comfort from her soft snoring—it was the same as Jaroon's as he slept.

But her awareness switched to what was underneath the snoring. *It's like someone breathing heavy*, she thought, yet she didn't hear rhythmic respiration of lungs. Instead, her surroundings hummed a connected breath, a long exhale; the more she attended to it, the more real it became. She felt her way out of bed and tottered to the doorway in bare feet, cranking the elastic of her shorts up over her stomach. She squinted to perceive silhouettes of foliage, eerie images undressing in cloud-covered moonlight, holding a movement she hadn't detected in daytime hours.

In the shades of the night, Neela sensed that the Nasee-Ki had its own breath, that it was indeed alive, and she was awed.

Her rational mind told her that her own heartbeat was projecting life outside herself. Yet ever since she had first landed, she had felt something strange about the river, the valley, the waterfall . . . *dis whole bush is haunted, fed up with dis lying government and dis damn development and these reckless people . . .* She felt the bush's intensifying anger rubbing her spine, its desire to promote human chaos and, at the same moment, to be relieved of it. When the bush had propelled her reunion with Jaroon, Neela had experienced a connection. Her acute awareness of its life made her the custodian of another gift, another unsolicited secret in this far-off place to swell her up. *I know things other people don't know, things my brother will never know,* she boasted in her mind. Returning to bed, she burrowed close to Karha and wondered about the place where they lay, the true nature of those Nasee-Ki leaves they spread themselves out upon each night. *What Karha says is true, de bush can't be tamed, it gon' always fight back . . .*

Neela had developed the habit of crouching in the hut's doorway when she couldn't fall asleep, and staring at the bush. She knew that she should be terrified by the possibility that the Nasee-Ki was sentient and lurking, but the bush's life made sense in the same way that her curious ability to experience it now felt so ordinary. *People don't get what they want in life,* she thought, *but at least de bush know how to get its own way . . .*

If living in Eden was disheartening—Neela was still trapped, unpaid and irreparably disowned by her family—working with Karha wasn't. Karha was an unyielding teacher, determined that a proper school should exist in Nasee-Ki.

Her passions easily transferred to Neela; although she had spent her time inventing daydreams at Marasaw's teachers' college, she had now become peculiarly desperate for her students to stumble on words and claim them as their own, to shout them aloud in victory—*Trol-ley-car! Bung-a-low! Trou-sers!*

"Why you teach, Kar? Why here?" Neela asked, one dazzlingly bright afternoon; it was a rare day when a flash shower hadn't interrupted class. College had held a singular promise for Neela to leave Marasaw, but Karha seemed to have had so many other options—a father in the city who would have let her learn what she wanted as long as she tolerated him, and beyond that, she was a young woman so clever and brave and full of energy. Neela had come to believe that Karha could accomplish anything.

"I feel blessed." She gathered textbooks from a neat grouping on floor, exercising special care over copies the soldiers had delivered last week. She brushed the valley's earthy debris from their covers, already building a film in the course of a single school day. "I had de chance to learn. Mind you, I didn't want to go with my father. He forced me to leave my mother and my home. But I fully learn dis language in de city, and my people don't really get to do dat."

They followed their dirt path, arms strained by books, moving in tactless strides that startled tiny frogs into breaking their camouflage.

"I suppose children who got to wait to learn know what a good thing it is," Karha said, "especially English. When you know it, no one can do you bad and get away with it."

"People do y'all bad, nah."

"You bett'-had believe it. Do you know what de Builder Party did during de elections? They came out in dis bush to force de village people into marking ballots for them." Karha laughed the noisy, almost hysterical laugh that Neela supposed she did when she was angry. "Lord knows what else de people was pushed into signing."

"Man, how they can do dat?"

"I don't know. But dat's why I teach and why I don't want to let dis damn government forget to build a school here. We gon' learn to use they own ways to defend ourselves."

They approached the hut and Karha bent her head away, spitting into the long grass that curled out over the edge of the path. Neela thought of her saliva soaking deep into the earth, nourishment to be reabsorbed into the valley's vast cycling life.

"But Neela, de question I got for you is, do you *really* feel to eat rations for dinner again?"

Beyond the pleasures that Karha's infectious teaching had stirred, Neela now had Jaroon to herself. She was already used to freedom as if she had owned it for a lifetime, the worry and anguish over prying neighbourhood eyes and her family's disapproval already a blurred memory. And she would never again face criticism for her mother's previous indiscretions. "Don't let me see you do as your mommy did, you hear?" Granny had threatened as they had scrubbed soiled cloth pads in the backyard. It was only a few days after Neela had gotten her period, at eleven years old—she could remember those bizarre buried muscles bursting sore for the first time, expanding deep within her body. "If you run around with boys, you gon' get yourself in trouble, yeah?"

But she didn't comprehend this *trouble* her grandmother spoke of until they visited Marasaw's modest outdoor market another afternoon. As they traced cramped spaces between stands, Granny and Neela approached a group of teenagers who had gathered near the ripening fruits. Neela immediately noticed that the girls had removed their high school sweater vests, outlines of severe white brassieres contrasting brownness underneath their blouses. Even in the brief moment it took to walk by, she observed so much more—how the girls conversed boisterously with the boys; how one had propped herself barefaced on a boy's lap, arm laced around his neck; how the boys talked to the girls so differently than boys in Neela's class, eyes communicating captivated messages to each other. She was spellbound and let herself loiter with them, her vision still affixed when they were behind her. She couldn't prevent the birth of a smile.

And Granny knew it. She snatched Neela's hand and tugged, forcing her past crates of mackerel and okra and off-colour eggs. "See how them girls loose themselves just so?" she complained, half to herself, half to her granddaughter. "See how they does let boys touch them and watch them up?"

Instantly, Neela's delicious curiosity morphed to humiliation and Granny's pulling turned aggressive. They left the market without buying anything they were supposed to.

Neela was directed toward home, although she wasn't resisting. "I see you watching them good-good," Granny charged, "eyeing them proper with your little eyes, like you want follow them." *Slap*. Neela was struck on the back of her arm; it stung and she frowned, out of confusion more than physical pain. "Mustn't follow them, hear me?"

She didn't dare answer back to her grandmother, yet she was delivered another blow.

"Don't do what they do, or you gon' get yourself in *trouble* like your mother, hear? You bett'-had behave yourself or I gon' cut your tail. Mustn't make them touch you there. Or anywhere. You think you can ignore me, right? I gon' cut your tail!" She carried on in the presence of neighbours on their front porches, all assuming that Neela was reaping the consequences of some sort of rudeness.

But I'm free now, freer than my family could-a dream, growing and doing what I please, like de Nasee-Ki itself . . . She savoured her liberty in this valley as Jaroon gladly carried the easy power of having his own girl. The men's initial surprise at this sociable young man grew into a respect that he nurtured. Chucking his handsaw to the grass, he chatted up the soldiers to get extra beer and cigarettes smuggled into his side of the camp, eventually ensuring that his closest friends were given more than their share. Soon, men came to him for whatever they needed—*You can get de soldiers to bring me something from de city, 'Roon?*—and he always delivered. Eden's dwellers came to know him by face and name, lifting their hands and shouting greetings at him through the valley's never-ending dew. It wasn't long before Neela realized the benefits too; the matchstick school amassed more crisp books and crayons and lined paper than Karha had ever imagined possible in Nasee-Ki.

But it didn't happen without an early miscalculation on Jaroon's part, when he limped into the hut bloodied and sullen, refusing to account for his monstrously swollen face. He squeezed his cut lips and brushed Karha away when she approached with a damp cloth. Planting himself on Neela's doorway stool, he glared at an empty spot on the ground. It was only after she poured him a bowl of rations soup, its boiled plantains and potatoes possessing the capacity to soften misery, that he revealed to her how he had put himself in the middle of a fight in the campgrounds.

Some of *them people* had been arguing with his people; they broke out punching and dragging each other to the ground. Jaroon threw himself in and began to brawl wildly, unaware of the transgression that had triggered the fight but eager to demonstrate his loyalties. Yet he was still inexperienced in Eden's intricate, shifting maze of power; he had chosen the wrong man to lash out on, and soldiers from the opposite side of camp—*them people* soldiers from *over dat side*—formed a confining circle around him. They kicked with the heels of their boots and thrust their rifle butts, all in the sight of the workers. Some cursed in Jaroon's defence and some only observed.

"You lucky you alive, jackass," a soldier spat as they sauntered off and left him crumpled in the mud. "Next time you won't be so lucky, eh?"

After his mate had dribbled liquor pungent as gasoline into his mouth, Jaroon was revived; he wobbled to his feet, every inhalation jagged inside his lungs. Pain had schooled him in Eden's law of friends and enemies—whom he had to become, whom he had to ally himself with and, most important, whom he would have to settle scores with. His opportunity came swiftly, one critical night.

Neela marched off with echoes of coarse laughter and belches shrinking behind. *Damn drunkard,* she thought, stiff-lipped and gripping an empty rum bottle at her side, *he says I humbugging* him! Jaroon had been wrapped in a booming game of craps that had lasted well beyond midnight. Fed up with the lateness but mostly exasperated by his inability to pay her any mind when he was drunk, she had snatched the rum from his hand and christened the dirt with what remained. *Ohhh rooks!* everyone had exclaimed, and flicked their finger bones together, but Jaroon had only laughed vibrantly in response. "Girl, stop dat now," he had mock-reprimanded, with the countenance of a crotchety auntie, "you *humbugging* me!"

Neela had run off when the men burst out in amusement at his antics. She wondered why she even attempted to compete with him in these situations—despite the attraction she inspired, he had won their true admiration. She left the glowing reach of the camp's fluorescent tent lights, stepping suspiciously along the narrow mud path toward the hut. *It's pitch black tonight,* she noticed, *like de leaves are crowding out de moon and advancing on us.* It was difficult to cleave to anger in the shapeless isolation of the night.

There was a rustling. "What's going on, teach?" somebody asked from close behind, making her start and stop. She knew that Karha's bribery to prevent soldiers from wandering around the hut and school didn't apply to this area. "You don't want to answer?"

"Go away." Neela hadn't forgotten the voice of the soldier who had guarded the New Builders Party bus in Marasaw. She was unable to face him, her stomach frozen solid in a lurched state.

"Well, I come for my lesson, girl . . ."

Another noise was layered underneath his voice, a sniffle or perhaps a snicker from someone else. "What, she got a nice body indeed, yeah . . ."

"Get away from me!" she roared, and whipped around when a malicious hand swept her arm. The soldiers' faces were veiled by the night but she could perceive the outline of two berets, two sloppily arranged uniforms. She tightened her squeeze around the bottle's neck.

"What you mean? I staying right here and you gon' teach me like you promise," the one soldier said, jabbing her in the shoulder. "Don't you break your promise now."

"Don't touch me!"

"Alright, we better go . . . ," the other soldier muttered, trying to conceal the sudden apprehension in his voice.

"Come on, girl . . ."

"Take your hand off me!" Neela's words barely puttered

through her breathlessness, expiring the moment they left her mouth.

" . . . man, leave it now, they gon' find out . . ."

"Come on!" He shoved Neela and she staggered back many paces, narrowly recovering her balance.

"Let's go," the other pressed, "Jaroon-them gon' hear!"

"You lady-man! What they gon' do?" He forced Neela close to him, cupping the base of her neck; her forehead skinned the fabric of his chest before she could stiffen in reflex. "Dat's right, teach," he snarled. "Don't leave your student waiting . . ."

Fierce nausea overcame her. She wanted to double over and protect herself in her own embrace, but the soldier's grasp strained her upright and he struck her in the stomach. She rippled and coughed liquid, suddenly windless from the shock of his body over her.

He didn't anticipate the swing of Neela's arm—she smacked the empty bottle across his scalp. Its hollow impact woke her legs and as the man winced, she squirmed from his cover and set off.

But her knees stung against the thick clay-mud when she was jerked to the ground by the other soldier. "Let me go!" she yelled, blinking and disoriented in the darkness. "Get off me!"

"You think you can get away just so?"

He yanked her arm at a bad angle and she fell flat, shocked by a blow to her lung as he stamped on her side. "Ah!" She twisted under his weight. "Stop, stop!" She thrashed her fists and tried to hit out, to block the wrenching, rushing, angry hands, unable to see the soldier's face but terrorized by it still.

Then she sensed a resistance that was not her own and the soldier's body swung away; a beam of light pierced her eyes and flailed madly as someone joined in a nearby fight.

"You alright?"

When she heard the question from Jaroon's mate overtop the growling curses and slaps, she understood that some of his men had rushed to defend her. *Did de bush send them to find me?* she asked herself, astounded and stumbling to her feet. She pressed her palm against her wounded ribs and commenced the painful limp to Jaroon's tent.

The bodies of those two soldiers were uncovered a few days later. When the other soldiers had determined that they were truly missing and not truant, it took only a half-hearted search to uncover them; they had been discarded not far inside the Nasee-Ki bush. And it wasn't difficult to see what had killed them, either—they had been beaten to death with nailed planks. No care had been wasted on disposing of them, because the murders were meant to be discovered.

Jaroon's abilities and means were fully accepted amongst camp dwellers now. If they had considered crossing him, their desires crumbled when the soldiers' bodies were laid on dry leaves and reduced to ashes. If they wanted retribution, it had to be measured against the reality that he would amass a force of men—both workers and soldiers, if conditions were right— to reply in violent haste.

And Neela was fully Jaroon's girl. She couldn't be touched anymore. She and Karha no longer had to bother with bribery to hold classes and live in their hut and get supplies. They had only to ask. As Jaroon's influence deepened amongst the workers and expanded beyond the boundaries of Eden, transformations began in the little matchstick school as well—it sprouted four walls and a shingled roof, a green chalkboard, even the beginnings of a modest library. Although they might wonder when the waterfall would wash it away, students were dazzled by their fortune, their authentic schoolhouse, completed long before the appearance of recognizable hotels or shops, and classes that could persist through downpours.

But Karha had concerns, though she kept them to herself. She thought of what she, Neela and their students would have to give in exchange for these improvements. She had observed how Jaroon's more amateur predecessors had operated in Eden before him; their benevolence was always connected to dubious requirements, and they were quick to proclaim debts that could never be repaid. She preferred the blank swap of cigarettes and liquor for books and protection. It was hardly comparable to the extravagant exchanges Jaroon organized throughout the region, but at least Neela hadn't been caught in the middle of the old bribery.

They had been waiting in the school a few mornings after it was blessed with walls and a roof—Jaroon and two oversized, nameless men who seemed to escort him everywhere. Karha and Neela entered with towers of *Royal Readers*, carrying them from the hut to the new safety of the classroom. The escorts, ever busy and always too willing, scuffled forward to help, but only Neela gave them her books. Karha shook her head guardedly and piled hers in the corner by herself.

"So, how does it look?" Jaroon asked Neela, adjusting the collars of her college uniform. "See what I do for you, baby?"

She took hold of his wrists. "It's perfect, 'Roon! De children gon' be so happy." She turned to Karha. "How you like it?"

Karha glanced around, mouth set in a mild smile, watching how fresh plaster reflected emergent sunlight invading the window. A single spiderweb string drew an exaggerated shadow across the wall. "You shouldn't have worried with all dis, Jaroon. We don't need a fancy place to teach simple things."

"Well, now your students can say they go to a real school."

She kept an eye on his two men, who were lackadaisically thumbing through the textbooks in silence. "But still, you didn't have to . . ."

"Karha, de children never had dis before, it's good for them, right?" Neela said. "And it happen, a school in Nasee-Ki, just like you always wanted." She offered her hopeful eyes; they demonstrated how much she had come to depend on Karha's approval. "What you say, girl?"

Neela was too keen to notice Jaroon's stance, how he turned his head on an angle and looked intently at Karha's face with narrowed brows—*Tell her, what do you say for true?*

"Well, we gon' do some good teaching here. They can't stop us now," she answered. "We got to get ready, de children gon' arrive soon . . ." Karha took her place at the front of the room, slapping open a book cover to indicate her expectation of privacy.

Jaroon gestured to his men and they obediently left. He kissed Neela's forehead and followed them at a relaxed, haughty pace, turning back for a parting comment: "You got a good thing here, Karha. Best be grateful and not spoil it."

Eager to avoid the staining taste of rations soup and Neela's usual visit to the campgrounds that evening, Karha brought her to the village where her students lived, the place she had grown up. They followed untraceable paths in the bush, weaving amongst the covering trees and spacious plants and creeping insects. Neela was mindful that they were travelling through the dense bush that soldiers and workers fearfully avoided; even Jaroon stayed out of it.

"It ain't too bad, right?" Karha asked, voicing Neela's unspoken assessment. "I grow up in all dis." She pointed to the top peaks of some trees, where a handful of outrageously yellow birds had perched themselves. "You see them? Watch quick."

Displeased, the birds fluttered briskly and burrowed into the sunless heart of the branches. Neela had almost missed them.

"Those were my favourite birds when I was young, you know, with their pretty-pretty soft wings. We used to find feathers on de ground and collect them. I would brush de feathers all up and down my arms and legs. But they say dat most-a de birds fly far into de interior these days, they don't stay around de waterfall too much. I don't think they like people crowding them out." She sighed. "Dis place ain't so bad, Neel. Not as I remember it. Truth is, I miss de old days bad."

After exploring for close to an hour, they arrived at a clearing where a cluster of huts stood, exact copies of the one they lived in. The village had been built beside a stream that extended into the flow of the great Nasee-Ki. Excited young students ran out to greet them—women shooed them away and led Karha and Neela to a blackening cooking fire, insisting they rest on a fallen log that had petrified long ago.

"We're used to being on our own here," Karha said, watching a delegation of women in wrapped skirts around the fire, pondering the stew. "Even when I was young, de men were back and forth from dis work to dat, going all over de place. Mining and digging and all kind-a thing. They would go away and bring back rations and supplies."

Neela plucked a blade of grass with delicate buds along its tip, round and iridescent like pearls. She twirled it between her fingers. "What did they do before all dis mess?"

"Live from what de Nasee-Ki gave them, I guess." Karha held out her hand to request Neela's blade, squinting at its buds for inspection. "Dat's done now, though. We don't get to live like dat no more. You know, some-a de women does even leave de valley to work in de city from time to time. Cleaning house, selling crafts in de market and thing. They collect what they need and come back when they done." She returned the piece of grass, now limp from handling.

"How do they reach de city?"

"Walk. It takes them many weeks to arrive."

"Really?"

Karha nodded solemnly. "They go in a big curve"—she demonstrated by sketching an arch in the air with two fingers—"walk right around de valley till they catch de road. I tell you, they know what they doing in dis bush."

Neela heard the women conversing in a language that she hadn't heard them speak at school. They giggled and fanned themselves as the stew steamed more aggressively. "You ever go with them?"

"No. I went to live with my father before they could bring me." Karha bent over Neela's lap to select her own blade of grass, deciding upon the one with the biggest, whitest buds. "But you know, I would really love to know how they do it."

They ate exceptionally well that evening—one woman, rounded by pregnancy, kept stubbornly refilling Neela's chipped plastic bowl. Despite her objections, the woman would seize it and bring the stew to the top, silent and beaming. The others disintegrated into laughter every time, poking Neela and sweeping their fingers through her hair with easy affection. *Eat, teacher-girl, look at you, you need your strength, eat!* At first, she returned their gestures with an unsure smile; by the end of the night, she laughed enthusiastically along with them, her mouth wide and cheeks sore even when she couldn't understand what they were saying.

"They like you bad!" Karha said when they were both in their bed. She had propped her head on an elbow to skim a book while Neela attempted to start another letter for her grandmother. The kerosene lamp burned solid yellow, sketching sharp-edged shadows over the hut's walls. "See how they carry on with you? Love you off."

Neela grinned. "See how they fed me, too? More than you, I notice. Mus'-ee like me more than you . . ."

Karha rolled her eyes. "They don't love you *dat* much." She heaved a sigh and it evolved into a great yawn; she shifted to lie on her back and stretched out her arm. "Let me see something."

"What?"

She laid a warm hand on Neela's belly, pensive.

"What you doing?"

She felt around, pressing flesh lightly through Neela's shirt. "I seeing if I can understand what they was talking about . . ." She paused at the bottom of Neela's belly, curved over its curve, her mouth in a reflective frown. "Hum." She kept her hand in place and put the other across Neela's forehead.

"What's wrong?"

"Maybe de women right. They say you look pregnant."

"What?"

"That's why they were pushing food on you. I hear them talk about it in my language."

"How they know . . . how you know they right?"

Karha crossed her arms tight over her chest, suddenly upset by the prospect of Neela's long-term connection to Jaroon. "They usually right about these things, girl."

And when Neela didn't see her blood for a few months on end, she too understood that they were right about these things. "What he gon' say when he finds out?" she begged for an answer in the privacy of their hut, her tears matching the valley's rain. "You think he gon' be vexed with me, Kar? He gon' even worry with me?"

The only reply Karha could form was a pitying shrug.

As her grandmother had so feared, Neela was *in trouble.*

All-night showers had made the rainy season's air heavy and hazy, and Neela knew she wouldn't be able to hide her rising belly from Jaroon much longer. These days, school was held under a sheet of fog amidst the rich stench of roots and earthworms. But one morning, a tale of *gentle ladies dancing in lovely dress* was interrupted by the flustered entrance of women from the village. While Neela coaxed a student through the terrain of a long sentence, they whispered to Karha that two of the older boys were missing—they had prayed for them to be here in class. "But what we gon' do now, Teacher Karha?" one boy's mother pleaded, a threadbare T-shirt of his wrung in her creased hands. "Where you think they can be?"

Class was cut short and younger children were sent home with warnings about playing along the way. As the sky hung low, the women, older children, Karha and Neela began a search in the bush surrounding Eden. They snaked between trees in a wiry line, proceeding instinctively faster when night readied itself to spread over the valley. *Where are de boys?* Neela inwardly asked the rainforest and awaited the bush's exhale, but she couldn't detect it. She was disappointed by the silence and took hold of Karha's wrist, requiring the help of a guide— the noiselessness around her made the valley unrecognizable.

When the boys were finally discovered, close to the campgrounds, the women needed only a glance to know that they had been dead for more than a day. Their faces were flat against the soil, limbs recklessly cast, trapped in crawling escape from a racket of bullets. As was clear with so many incidents in Eden, this was meant to be seen. Karha, Neela and the women encircled the bodies as the children left to fetch woven-leaf stretchers.

It was almost midnight when they reached the village again. Karha sat by the stream with wrappings dangling across her arms as the older women rubbed oils and bound the boys up tight, and Neela accompanied the younger women boiling stew. When the bodies had been embalmed and hidden in a hut's dim calm, they all ate in moonlight, mourning by the cooking fire—even the little ones were awoken to partake in the sorrow feast with half-sleeping eyes. But Neela could hardly stomach more than a mouthful, and when the old women started to sing in sobs, she watched Karha dash her food into the flames and sprint toward the stream.

"Karha! Kar! Where you going?" Neela shouted, straining to match her steps. "What are you doing?"

Karha ran to meet the water's shimmering edge, setting her face toward its choppy journey to the Nasee-Ki. Grey and low, the moon glared at them both.

"Karha, what happen?" Neela breathed hard behind her. "Answer me, nah?"

"I don't want look at you and I don't want talk to you," she said, and wiped her nose with a rough fist. "Go away."

"What happen?"

She barked her sudden laugh. It dissolved as soon as it had arrived. "I can't believe you don't know!"

"No. Tell me what I don't know."

"You won't take me on!"

"Tell me!" Neela exclaimed. "Don't do me dis, girl. Look at me. What did I do?"

Before drops could sear along her face, Karha pressed her eyes with the heels of her hands. "I can't understand you, Neela," she answered sourly, glowering at the water as if it were her adversary. "You didn't know what Jaroon had them boys doing for him?"

"No."

"He was getting them to steal from the soldiers, telling them to sneak behind de cargo planes to thief liquor and thing. He use de boys to do his business 'cause they quick and young and know how to hide. And he think de soldiers won't aim gun and shoot mad at them in de bush . . ." Her voice scattered like ants in the rainy season escaping a flooded hole.

Neela looked to the ground.

"You carrying his baby. How can you not know? How can you know so much about everything and not know dis?"

"I don't know," she whispered.

Karha sniffled and sucked in an aggravated breath, returning her attention to the stream once again. "It seems like you don't want to know."

Neela was tempted to argue—*And how I gon' know about all de nonsense them boys do, tell me, pray?* She wanted to defend Jaroon against the dark red circles burned in those boys' backs, against the accusation that he had caused the soldiers to shoot. *You don't got no proof,* she wanted to yell,

You always talking like a big woman, like you better than me,
you like my brother, just like him, but you wrong, you ain't bet-
ter than me . . . Yet those words wouldn't come to her lips.
She could only keep her head down and listen to Nasee-Ki as
her breathing, shaky with sudden tears, stammered over the
bush's steady, undaunted breath.

They spent the next few days in the village, around bonfires
of cooking and cremation, beside the women and children.
Neela tried to devise a strategy to get Karha to speak to her
again, quietly considering how she had managed to keep herself ignorant of what Jaroon was doing, how he had amassed
the immense power that he had. He was involved in things
she didn't care to know about, yes, but convincing the boys
to steal for him on the promise of a stray cigarette? Leftover
Shawlster? Minutes alone in the tent set apart, that dwelling of
Eden's handful of women labourers? Neela had been so quick
to enjoy the spoils of being untouchable, so intoxicated by the
respect that came from being in a place like Eden with a man
like Jaroon, that its hazards had rarely troubled her at all.

When Neela finally revealed to Jaroon that she was pregnant, he conceived the idea of moving overseas with his
woman and baby and starting some sort of business—surely
they wouldn't dare raise his children in Eden or Marasaw or
anywhere else in the country, the whole place was useless.
Overseas guaranteed fine houses in place of tents, imposing
schools in place of makeshift classrooms, order and civility in
place of brutality and contraband. Jaroon's plans became more
detailed, more lavish, through their retelling. "We gon' get a

nice house made-a red brick," he declared to Neela in his tent, "and it gon' be surrounded by proper flower bushes. Red roses to match de house, how about dat? And I gon' get a big car to drive around and do my business. And I gon' have plenty more children, yeah? Strong boys and pretty little girls."

Neela wanted to believe it, to swallow his dreams and become drunk on Jaroon as she had been when they were back home in Marasaw, despite the malice she had come to discern in his dealings in Eden. Perhaps she would have let herself keep faith in their future if she hadn't seen what happened in the campground, when he and his mates had suspended their game of dominoes. She spied through a break in the tent's vinyl and saw one of her students dragging wooden crates in front of them, a skinny, lively nine-year-old boy who wore a blue T-shirt with a chipping cola decal—he would gawk absorbedly as Neela read stories, eyes tinged with displeasure when they finished. One of the men cracked the top of a crate to survey its contents and, his expression set in approval, handed the boy a carton of cigarettes. It was Jaroon's response that ignited her; as the child cradled his carton, Jaroon tousled his hair and patted his shoulder to send him away.

"How can you do dat?" she whispered when the men returned to their game, nonchalant. She pushed her hands taut against her stomach. "Dat child is my student!"

"Why are you hassling me now?" he complained, and took a sloppy mouthful of beer, mouth curled in irritation.

"De boys! You getting them to do your badness! You mixing them up in your mess, Jaroon? How can you do dat? And you continuing to do it even after those two little children got shot up!"

Jaroon studied his dominoes, pulling leisurely drags from his cigarette. The other men didn't look at her either.

"Answer me!"

He crashed a piece down. "You hear me," he replied quietly. "Those boys ain't *children* and they ain't *students*. You wasting your time with them dirty red-skins. It's just like you used to friend-up dat black girl in front-a everyone back home without a shred-a shame. You don't know a damn thing 'bout loyalty, Neela."

She fumed at him as he paused to examine his remaining dominoes, running a thumb over their indentations.

"And don't you ever ask me how I can do what I doing. For all your big-woman talk, it's you who's benefiting from it, yeah?" he said. "Remember dis. It's *my* business and it don't got nothing to do with you. Not one thing."

She cracked a large cynical laugh, just like Karha's. "How dare you disrespect me and disrespect Lenda like she wasn't good to you! You get sweep up in all dis nonsense now too? You want to talk about loyalty? I want to know where *your* loyalty's gone . . ."

But in a flash Jaroon turned and slapped her hard across her cheek. "Don't ever talk back to me again!" he screamed, pointing into her face and returning to his stance at the table as if he had done nothing.

Neela was startled, spine inflexible, cheek and ears aflame with dazed embarrassment. She had been thrust into the same old state she had once known battling her brother and grandmother, that clumsy, in-between condition of part-child, part-woman, foolish and slighted and put in her place. Jaroon's mates were now observing her silently; she couldn't help but return their looks in the reflexive confusion of the moment, *What was dat, what just happened, did he really do dat to me?*

But she knew not to rely on any of them to answer such questions. She stood up, arm guarding her belly; without a word, she left the tent at her own measured pace and did not return. Jaroon didn't bother to watch her go.

When Karha did finally forgive Neela, she boiled their rations soup for dinner and they sat in the hut eating reservedly, as if they hardly knew each other. The door was left open and they both shivered when an uncharacteristically brisk wind whirled in, causing the hut to shake and groan. "Well," Karha said, smiling gently. She rested her empty bowl near her bare feet, licking the wooden spoon and then fiddling with it in her fingers. "We got to start dis friendship up again sometime. It can't stay bust-up."

Bashful, Neela smiled in return. "You're right." She was relieved, especially since Karha was the only one who had endless courage to bolster her own resolve—she had to reject a battery of supplies and peace offerings that Jaroon's men were delivering from the campgrounds. Karha didn't even allow the gifts to touch the school's dusted concrete floor, no matter how the men whined and begged, *'Roon gon' kill me, please take de thing or he gon' be vexed with you and me both!* Even if they did need a box of pencils or coloured chalk, they both tried to break their obligations to Jaroon. Karha returned to her favoured method of bribing soldiers for essentials—a sack of rations every month, small bunches of books, sometimes letters for Granny in Marasaw. More dependent than ever, Neela relied on her friendship with the Nasee-Ki women to help her through her progressing pregnancy. They quieted her when she was sick to her stomach and told her what she should do to prevent the nausea's return, they gave Karha ointment to soothe Neela's skin so it wouldn't crack, they even collected fabric so Neela would have something to wrap her newborn in.

"Don't worry with him," Karha admonished as she massaged ointment over Neela. It had been extracted from stalks that grew in clusters at the most fertile edges of the stream by the village. The women had squeezed some into a sack woven from flexible bark strips. "Me and de women gon' be with you now. I really don't know how dat man thinks he can get away with anything and just buy you back. You ain't like dat, hear? He should know you ain't going to take it."

Neela raised her arm and exposed her side to Karha. She was well into her eighth month now, riddled with previously unimaginable sensations—her muscles throbbed and the baby ranted inside her, eager to be born. "But how long will he keep his peace? De men are already saying dat he's getting fed up with us. With me."

"Lift your shirt," Karha instructed. Neela borrowed clothes

from the women nowadays—those T-shirts and wrap skirts that amiably accommodated her new body. "Don't you lose your determination. You frightened of him and his fools? What they can do to us, really?"

Neela glared at Karha, and Karha realized that it would be prudent to cool her baseless brashness. "Well, maybe he gon' forget and give up soon . . ."

"You know Jaroon don't give up on nothing and he don't forget getting crossed. He ain't like he used to be."

Handling the woven package tenderly, Karha poured some ointment on the top of her fingers and warmed it with the tip of her thumb. "I see being in Eden does do dat to people. I learn it from them camp women." She kneaded Neela's side with both hands, slowly sliding from her ribs down to her hip. "Long time ago I thought they might want get away from dat place, maybe come and help at school. But when I went over they cuss me and run me out of de camp."

"What?"

"They alright with getting their liquor and rations by freely sleeping with de men, don't want to entertain nothing else." Karha put a greasy hand up to emphasize. "But it make me think. What else women gon' do really in dis place? Is either do dat and get what you need, or break your back building dis damn development and get force to sleep with them at night." She bent forward and started massaging vigorously.

"But don't you think they could try to do something else? Make things better for themselves?" Neela asked. "Dat's what you and I do."

ANDREA GUNRAJ

"Don't know, girl. I wonder if they being there is what's saving us."

They lingered in a pool of disturbed silence. Neela shut her eyes to ponder the women—what man in Eden wouldn't demand them, what man would expect otherwise? "But I would-a never been able to do what they does do. My granny teach me better. Dat kind-a behaviour could-a never come out me."

Karha used the bottom of her palm to push Neela's skin in the opposite direction, producing a grunt in the effort. "But dat's what I mean, de women mus'-ee think de same thing before they come to Eden. They might-a say, oh, I wouldn't prostitute myself for nothing, I couldn't behave so. But I tell you, being here does change people, man."

Neela puckered her lips and, making laborious, incremental shifts, managed to rotate her body toward the radiance of the lamp. Her movements created enough tremors to scare an insect from its dwelling underneath their leaf-bed. "You mus'-ee right. You think it's a curse de Nasee-Ki does put on people?" she asked, with Jaroon's face strong in her mind, its content, tranquil look when they used to spend hours in conversation with Lenda at the Marasaw Restaurant.

"Not really, dis curse ain't de land's fault." With a hovering foot, Karha tracked the creature's skitter for cover in the bare hut; instead of stamping, she nudged it into a fissure between the floorboards. "It comes from people alone."

Neela was bedridden for the last weeks of her pregnancy. Karha would bring some students to the hut, providing a

venue for them to show off sentences they had learned—
Thanksgiving is a marvellous holiday for de whole family—
these were cheerful moments. But during her plentiful
hours of solitude, crushing disenchantment bore down on
her, the defeat of Jaroon and their love and future, the un-
amendable estrangement from her own family, the faltering
of her spirit when she considered raising a baby by herself in
an unkind place.

She thought of her mother, for the first time pondering
how it must have been when Mira was pregnant with her and
Navi, exiled and afraid. As a child, Neela would never have
believed that such a thing would happen to her—she had been
convinced that one of her magical talents would save her, grow
her into someone influential and adored, prevent a tragic
repetition of her mother's failings. But now she couldn't even
conjure one single little story to distract her as she lay in the
dimmed hut, as she had done so easily in high school, before
her brother's interference.

She began to dream of home, the same hectic scene repeating again and again. *Oh God!* her grandmother would wail
when she discovered that Neela had given birth to Jaroon
Begwan's baby out of wedlock. *I dead!* Neighbourhood women
would rush out in a panic as they always did, *Sugee! Sugee-girl!
What happen?* Navi would be there too, fully suited in jacket
and tie, observing the whole mess in revulsion; it would
quicken Neela's heart although she wasn't in that imaginary
house. *My granddaughter's dead! Dead and gone! Oh God, why
you punish me so? What I do to deserve dis? All I got is my one*

*grandson, he's all I really got left, no daughter, no granddaughter, no
more! It gon' kill me, oh God!*

⁓

Karha brought Neela to the village when the contractions
came, pausing for her to rest on rocks and rotting stumps
along the way, her tears welling in alarm when the pain
caused Neela to grimace and cry out. Neela gave birth with
the composed instruction of two village women—*You just cry
and shout if you need to, teacher-girl, and when we tell you, push
like you more constipated than you been in your whole life,
alright?* When the baby emerged transparent red and purple,
making hoarse, high-pitched newborn sounds, Neela saw the
room liquefy into blinding beams of sunshine. She fainted into
a deep, overwhelmed and comforted sleep, dreaming of the
valley's greenness more alive and breath-filled than ever.

The women called the baby *pretty-girl* and brought her outside as a wrapped package; the child stared in blurry admiration
of the rainforest as the afterbirth burned in a sweet-and-sour
fire. Neela remained in the village for the next few weeks, permission for her to rise from the leaf-bed adamantly denied. She
was fed bitter herb soup and her skin was cleansed with grainy
balm slathered on wet cloths; the women refused to let anyone
see her, lest a careless negative thought be cast to hinder her
recovery and undermine the baby's good health. Even Karha
had been banned. Finally Neela insisted on returning to their
hut and preparing to work again. She clutched the baby to her

chest, overtaken by the wealth, the brimming abundance of the girl's presence inside her, and named her Seetha.

Jaroon's men carried a different kind of offering to the schoolhouse now—expensive jumbo packages of disposable diapers, canisters of infant formula labelled with grinning white infants, stuffed animals in pastel colours—but Neela refused them all. She knew that the men delivering these presents had been ordered to spy on Jaroon's new baby, slung across Neela's breasts in a traditional Nasee-Ki contraption. "It's my child," he told his mates in the campground as they listened timidly and drank rum, "what does she think, I gon' have patience forever? Dat she can keep me from my own child? I ain't gon' let dat happen, mark my words, yeah?"

The submission of scorned gifts tapered away, but Jaroon's surveillance intensified as the baby grew. *She gon' learn dat she can't disrespect me, watch, I gon' teach her and dat red-skin to conspire against me. After all I do for her! If she don't know her place, I gon' got to teach her . . .* Neela and Karha could smell cigarettes from Jaroon's men, a constant cloud outside the schoolhouse window. And as Karha cooked stew and Neela nursed Seetha, they sensed shifting figures around the hut, barely hidden by darkening sunlight between the bushes. *I gon' give her what she deserves if she thinks she can cross me and keep me from my child, I gon' teach them both to never cross me again . . .*

By the time Seetha turned one, Jaroon's tolerance had dissolved and sabotage had begun—Neela and Karha couldn't gather enough contraband to get the soldiers to bring supplies or send letters to Marasaw, and they had to barter belligerently to get the monthly rations they had once received without headache. Karha tried bribing soldiers to allow the older boys to attend class, but mysterious counter-bribes would send them straight to the development at five o'clock in the morning, to shingle plaza roofs and nail planks on rustic resort cottages.

Jaroon even had his men play pranks—thumps on the hut's walls late at night, obscene threats shouted into the classroom, shards of glass to litter the field around the school. But Neela and Karha persisted the way they had always done, refusing to do things any differently, refusing to abandon their work and run to the village for cover. They were too stubborn to show Jaroon that they were demoralized and intimidated, that they understood his menacing arrogance wouldn't allow this to end well. *After all I do, she want to reject what I give her? Then I gon' take away everything she got . . .*

"Your father's a real jackass, baby," Neela told Seetha with an animated voice one afternoon. She said it loudly so the men stalking the school window would hear clearly.

Karha laughed heartily, causing the baby to crawl toward her with an unaware, toothless grin, her knees whitened nubs on the concrete. "What does dat mean, Mommy, eh ba-ba? Must ask her what dat makes you if your father's a jackass," she said, eyes open big and clapping to dot her words.

Neela crept to the baby with her hands clawed out. "It makes you . . ."—Seetha giggled and squirmed when her mother dove to tickle her bare belly—" . . . a donkey-baby! Baby-donkey!"

Karha crouched behind Seetha and did the same on her rounded back, causing her to shriek in amusement. "Little donkey! Pretty little donkey-donkey!"

But they couldn't have imagined how Jaroon would react to their insolence.

Seetha had fallen asleep between Neela and Karha as they thought up new spelling exercises. It drizzled outside, a fine but deceivingly heavy mist.

Neela sat up sharply. "What's dat?"

"You hear something?"

She froze at sounds of popping and crackling outside. "You hear it too?"

"Yes."

Bowing her head, Neela listened some more before she peeked outside. "Oh God!" she yelled, swinging the door open.

Their schoolhouse was on fire, half-swallowed by dazzling flames and releasing a swirling tunnel of fumes into the air. Karha was shocked to her feet and almost out of the hut when Neela grabbed her arm.

"You mad?" she cried. "It ain't de school he wants to burn!"

They gaped at each other, but when Seetha let out a cry their attention snapped from their melting school to the true danger they were in. Neela hurried to the bed and calmed Seetha in her arms, turning to see that their hut was also ablaze. Karha frantically slapped the wall with an empty rations sack.

"We got to go! Go, go!" Neela screamed. Anguished, Karha watched the fire flash toward the woven leaf roof, and darted out behind Neela and Seetha. But when they noticed frightened young faces haloed by the burning school, they were shaken to a halt; Jaroon's men were restraining the same boys who ran their errands and lifted supplies from soldiers. The children wailed in a shivering clump, made to watch their schoolhouse engulfed by flames—*Them teacher-whores think they can mistreat Jaroon? It's them who cause dis! Watch what gon' happen to them now!*

"No, no, dis way!" Neela cried when she saw Karha's dismay transform into resolve to protect the boys. "It's too dangerous! We can't help them!" Neela pulled at her and they swung around, only to be startled by two new figures in their way, Jaroon's closest companions and guards.

Karha bolted between the men and Neela, face planted firm in front of her. "Let de boys go! They didn't do nothing to you!" she snapped. "They just children!"

"Dis don't concern you, red-skin!" one answered.

Neela stood behind Karha, body curled stiffly around screaming Seetha. "Go along your way, leave us!"

The other came up. "Shut up, whore!"

"Don't talk like dat to her!"

"Shut your mouth!" He shoved Karha clumsily on her chest but she didn't allow her feet to be lifted from their place.

"Keep your hands off her!" Neela said, grabbing hold of Karha's shoulder. "Lawless fool! Go back to de camp!"

"You got dis bitch defending you, eh Neela! After all

Jaroon do for you, dis is how you behaving! You really an ungrateful whore!" He tried to clap the sides of Karha's head but she swiped her arms out hard, flinging his arms away.

Karha put her hand behind her and clutched Neela's waist, backing close against her, and Neela dug her fingers into Karha's shoulder. "Move back!" she barked. "Don't you dare come one step closer . . ."

Swiftly, unexpectedly, one of them lunged around the side, the force of his move shoving the women into each other and onto the dirt.

Neela didn't understand what was happening until she hauled her head up and felt emptiness. "No!" she shrieked, and leaped on the leg of the man who was grasping Seetha to his chest. "Let her go! Let my baby go!"

Karha rushed to her feet and scratched at his arms, fighting to pry them open.

"Don't hurt my baby!" Neela tugged at him with all her might, kicking wildly when she felt the other man attempting to tow her off.

"Step back! It's Jaroon's child!" he bellowed, and squeezed Seetha harder, turning the child's crying into sputtering breaths.

Neela was flat on her stomach and hanging from his feet, still struggling with the man behind her. "Give me my child!"

"Let go! She's Jaroon's, not yours!" he screeched, kicking his heels at her head.

But Karha yanked his arms apart just enough for Seetha to tumble out onto the grass; Neela scooped her and jumped up, swinging out of the other man's grip.

And they were all struck by the hot blast of an explosion—the fire had swallowed a gasoline barrel that Jaroon's men had used to fuel it in the first place. Sounds of shrieking brought Neela back to consciousness and she tried to refocus, a fuzzy image of one of Jaroon's trusted aides blanketed in flames and thrashing in front of her. Stunned, she tightened herself around Seetha and cringed, straining to see if the boys had been harmed.

"Neela, I'm on fire!"

"Oh God!" Neela scrambled, slapping the flames that were consuming Karha's clothes and steadying Seetha with her other hand. Karha's exposed skin glinted in the firelight, patches of her arms and neck already blood-red and raw. "We got to go!" She could see a group of men charging toward them in the distance, and she made an effort to heave Karha up, even as she hollered in agony.

"Watch out!" Karha cried.

It was too late. Neela resisted the instinct to release Seetha to the grass, to clutch the fresh wound in her shoulder blade. Jaroon's other mate had crawled over and stabbed her with a utility knife with his last bit of energy, loyal to his superior, determined to get her although he had been injured by the explosion too. He dropped to his face, knife still in hand.

"Karha . . . ," Neela exhaled, shocked and stooped, squeezing her baby to her body.

Now it was Karha who had to force Neela to run, propping her up with one arm, grappling to support Seetha as well. They scuffled into the shadows of the bush, unresponsive to the messages beating them from behind—*You gon' get your tail cut . . . Jaroon gon' teach you good . . . He gon' get his child back, wait and see . . . You gon' be sorry!*

As they stumbled into the dark mass of foliage, the sensation of tiny droplets prickled their skin. Seetha howled dryly; her tears had been spent. *It's alright ba-ba, don't cry, we got you now,* Neela wished to pant into her baby's ear, too stung with pain to form the words aloud. Karha continued to drag her as they both groaned, Neela from a throbbing shoulder, Karha from skin that still felt aflame. Neela feared that Jaroon's men were directly behind them, ducking low to scrape Seetha from under her.

She twisted weakly and saw the leaves curling in behind them, cradling their escape and sweeping them deeper into the interior. *Oh, thank you,* she thought, *even though you vexed, you hearing me, you choosing to help us. Only you can keep us safe now . . .* She held to the reality that few knew how to navigate through this bush—only the villagers who were attentive to it. Certainly not Jaroon or his men, they wouldn't dare follow them into it this moonless night, especially if they could hear what Neela heard along the sightless stagger, clumsily weaving between tree trunks and stepping around mossy bushes. Through it all there was the breath that didn't inhale, the life of Nasee-Ki making its presence known once more beneath the falling dew. *Don't worry ba-ba, don't be frightened by de bush, people can't get what they want but leave de bush be, it knows how to fight for itself . . .*

PART THREE

CHAPTER 9

N avi rooted through his closet, hair still damp from showering, hangers squeaking over the pole as he shuffled clothes aside. He extended his arm to reach for a dress shirt tucked at the very end; when he lifted it for inspection, its whiteness glowed, made heavenly by the bedroom light. He brought the shirt against his face, unable to determine whether the smell of curry that had infiltrated his new off-campus apartment now permeated his work attire. Endlessly wafting spices had compromised his nostrils and he was no longer a reliable judge of such things.

Ever since his grandmother and mother had arrived at his place, they had cooked non-stop—currying every meat available in the supermarket, baking yellow tarts, frying up tangy stews. *Look how skinny you get over here*, Granny had exclaimed when she threw her arms around him for the first time in two years, Mira watching behind them, *You gon' get sickly if you don't eat proper food!* He hadn't anticipated the culinary flurry when he purchased their plane tickets for the visit, nor had he expected to witness his mother and grandmother's synchronized, word-less manoeuvres in his kitchen. It was unusual how his grand-mother, while attending to something on the stove, could sense that Mira had eased away from her roti dough. The two of them would seamlessly switch tasks without even lifting their heads to avoid a collision.

It seemed that they had re-established an old rhythm living together again—after Neela had left home and Granny had spent a fruitless year waiting for letters and messages that never arrived, Granny had decided that it was time. She had retrieved the immigration papers that Mira had long ago filed for her, and cashed Navi's money order. By then, the stream of neighbourhood rumours concerning Neela and Jaroon's scandalous affair and getaway to Nasee-Ki had dried up. Granny had flown to her daughter's country and settled in Mira's concrete high-rise, ready to assist in the babysitting work. She could hardly bear to reflect on how those things that had once held her in Marasaw were now entirely dispersed—Mira overseas in one country and Navi in another, Neela fugitive in unknown bush.

A tentative knock tapped the bedroom door. "Come in," Navi called, buttoning his shirt.

"I ironed dis tie for you, if you want to use it today," Mira said, entering with eyes scanning the floor. She carried the aroma of breakfast in with her. "I ironed and folded de rest of your laundry and piled them on de couch."

Navi observed Mira stroke his tie on the unmade mattress. Her bare feet were bony; she seemed childish in her pink fleece pyjamas. Her hair was layered in a lackadaisical braid, longer and more youthful than Navi had expected it would be, even after the many hours he had spent as a boy examining the photographs she used to mail to Marasaw. "Thanks."

"Your grandmother's calling for you. She made a little something for you to take to work."

Granny stood in the kitchen wearing a pair of velour slippers, fitting an assortment of containers into a plastic grocery bag. "You leaving already, Nav? I putting your lunch together." Although she had come so far, travelling across three countries in a short span when she had been hardly anywhere beyond Marasaw before, she insisted upon wearing her ancient house duster to cook. Its edges were more tattered than ever, its flowers an indistinguishable collection of colours. "I cook-up some stew beef and rice and put some dessert in there too. But sit down and eat breakfast before you go."

Automatically, Mira responded by organizing plates and mugs on the little dining-room table. Navi noticed a tray of steaming scrambled eggs and bacon, guarded by jars of chutney and guava jelly that his grandmother had flown over with as gifts. "You shouldn't have worried with all dat food, I have a lunch meeting today."

Granny wasn't deterred; she spun the ends of the bag and secured them with a twist-tie. "Bring it for snack. I know they don't like to give people a good amount-a food at them fancy restaurants." She handed him the package and Navi obediently trailed her into the sun-washed living room. Curtains had been thrown open and the air conditioning was turned off, making it seem as if they were in Marasaw again. "Now don't dis boy look nice in his business clothes, child?" she asked, pleased.

Mira smiled and nodded, hurriedly glancing at Navi's suit and pouring him coffee as he took a place at the table. He kept his eyes on their breakfast.

That evening, after returning from his managerial work at the Ministry of Foreign Investment, Navi brought his mother and grandmother downtown to the annual Culture Share Festival. Rows of temporary booths and food stands lined a barricaded street like malformed teeth, selling souvenirs and art and meals to the slow-moving crowd. Performers in outlandish costumes danced down the sidewalks; more modest performers claimed territory on the curb and strummed folk songs to earn their change. Granny strolled ahead of Navi and Mira, completely enthralled by the festival's colourful excitement. She lingered to scrutinize unfamiliar candies and treats, to run her hands over silks and shawls and textured beads.

"Look there, they even got things from back home!" she exclaimed, weaving her arm into Navi's and dragging him into a booth crammed with souvenirs. "Mira, you see all these?"

Mira lifted a long-necked bird cut out of glued pieces of dark and light woods. Tiny black beads served as a pair of eyeballs and its lacquer finish reflected the orange street lamps.

She had been searching for something to discuss with Navi. "They used to sell these in de market. You remember them?" she asked timorously, pointing the statue at him.

Navi's belly churned dully when he saw the bird's graceful lines and arched wings. It was almost identical to the little figurine Tarika had kept on her desk at the Ministry. That one had been fashioned into a slender woman with exaggerated breasts—a bowl of fruit was balanced on the top of her head, steadied by one curved arm. He moved his eyes from the bird and forced the comparison out of his mind, just as he tried to do when anything reminded him of Tarika. "Yes, they used to have ones just like it."

Granny pored over the table and selected a crouching monkey statue playfully carved to convey its trickster personality. She stroked the figurine gingerly. "How about dis one, Nav, you like it?"

"I do."

"Then let me buy it for you, nah?" She turned to locate somebody she could pay, enthusiastic.

"Oh, don't worry, Granny," he answered, having to speak over a travelling troupe's blaring speakers; dancers flipped and leaped and cartwheeled along the road to frenetic dancehall, evoking cheers from the crowd. "I don't have many places to put stuff like dat."

"But you don't got nothing pretty to decorate your apartment. It's too bare! How you can live like dat?"

"I'm not going to stay there for very long. When I buy my house, I'll get all those nice pieces to put around."

Disappointed, Granny looked at the monkey and shook her head before finding its original home on the crowded table. "At least it would give you a little joy when you walk into de room."

Mira moved around other browsing shoppers to reach a table at the very corner of the booth, where wide-brimmed hats and purses for little girls were piled in wobbling stacks. The handicrafts were earthy greens and browns, made of intricately woven leaves and adorned by fabric flowers. "Mommy, look over here," she called brightly, "they even got things de bush people who live by de waterfall does make out-a leaves. All de girls used to carry these handbags when I was in junior school."

But Granny's face dropped when she saw them, and Mira realized that she had drawn attention to a forbidden subject. Granny hadn't uttered Neela's name in Navi's presence, and even when Mira wanted to bring it up with her mother, she knew that it was wisest to avoid the subject.

"Let's go," Granny mumbled with darkened eyes as the dance troupe's beating bass passed, making ordinary festival noises oddly mute in contrast. She seized Navi and made her way back out to the road, pulling him along. Mira let them both go ahead of her.

Granny was glum and untalkative for the rest of the night and it dampened the mood for all of them—Navi and Mira strained to make conversation. After all those years of being apart, no communication other than letters and phone calls that tapered away as he grew into an adult, Navi had little understanding of what he and his mother had in common. It wasn't long before he stopped hassling himself to draw her attention to festival sights, since she barely responded anyway, too shy to offer him much of substance on her own.

When they returned to the apartment, Navi was eager to excuse himself and crawl into bed. He was exhausted with battling the recollections that had been trying to bulldoze into his consciousness all evening. *I'm having a wonderful time,* Tarika had written him in an email that morning. *There are so many beautiful places in this city. There's a three-thousand-year-old temple right beside the embassy! It's like living on another planet. I'm even learning the local languages and my friends say I'm getting pretty good . . .*

Despite his attempt to maintain lowered expectations, the email had wounded him as soon as it popped open—one casual paragraph made of trivial, patched-together observations of her new international life. *Please say hi to everyone at the Ministry for me.* The sentence triggered fierce irritation in him, not simply because she had typed him into the same category as all of the others. It was clear that she was too far removed from him and even if she did return one day, he would have nothing to offer a woman like her. He was convinced that whatever chance he might have had was ruined, sabotaged beyond repair by his sister's mysterious intrusion.

He was tugged out of dejection by sounds of urgent whispers from the living room. "But why we can't at least try, Mommy?" he heard his mother ask, as he cracked the bedroom door's seal. "You got to give me an answer."

"Why you insist on bringing dis thing up now, Mira? I tell you already," Granny answered. "I ain't doing it. De girl want her own way so bad, let her get her own way, alright? I don't even know where de child's gone!"

"You know she's in de Nasee-Ki. Yes, she was wrong for running after dat boy, I know she done you wrong. But you got to remember she's only young and foolish."

"Young and foolish!" Granny scoffed. "Dat's it? Everything explain away so easy? It can excuse how she been so cruel to me? It can excuse how she break my heart?"

"I don't mean it dat way. It's been two years. Maybe she gon' listen to some sense now. Please, think about it," Mira pleaded, "she might respond to you now. We can at least ask around de old neighbours and find some way to get a message to her . . ."

"You don't understand, Mira. She don't want me. She don't want none-a-we. I ain't going where I'm not wanted. If she were to come to me herself, dat would be one thing. I ain't a hard-hard woman, you know, I don't hold spite like dat! But why I gon' kill myself finding her when she done show me such . . . such hatred?"

"But Mommy, you know she don't really hate you. She made a bad mistake. What if she think different now? You can't let your stubbornness get in de way . . ."

Navi pushed the door in again. He sat on the mess of covers on his bed, tired and irritated, rubbing his eyes until rainbow splotches appeared. *Damn Neela*, he thought bitterly, *stealing every chance of happiness!*

Navi took his grandmother and mother to a new place each day after work, trendy diners and tourist destinations and water-front attractions. Although Granny had suggested that they tour his office, he formed weak excuses to get out of it—*We aren't allowed to bring visitors, government security has become very strict lately* . . . He felt a twang of guilt for lying, but he was too averse to the uncomfortable impact of worlds if his family were to enter that building and be introduced to his colleagues. *What a plain box of a room they give you,* he envisioned his grandmother complaining too loudly when she stepped into his office, Mira creeping like a timid shadow behind her, *Dis is how dis government rewards its most valuable employee?* If he allowed it to happen, he feared he would never recover.

Instead, he brought them to the most prestigious mall in the city. He tried not to show his exasperation at accompanying them in the labyrinth of exorbitant designer stores, how they insisted upon going through every almost identical shop, purchasing little but pondering the price of everything—*What? How dis belt can be three hundred dollars, it's made of gold?* He averted his gaze each time they neared a supermodel splayed over one of the mall's enormous advertisements. But he was socked with embarrassment when he noticed the recognition in Mira's eyes, her detection of his discomfort with such images in the presence of family.

"Y'all go on without me," Granny said, her skin looking suddenly pale. She put her fingertips to her temple and bent forward to slump on a bench that was framed by indoor trees. "I gon' catch up with you later. I need to rest a little right here." Her elbow released slackly and the purse and shopping bags anchored around it slid to the ground.

Mira cupped her mother's arm. "What happen? You alright?"

"I ain't feeling too well . . . I don't know why all de sudden dis bad feeling come upon me . . ." She only vaguely realized that shoppers were dawdling by the chlorine-blue water fountain to observe her pallid features. She tried to set her expression normally but found it difficult to smooth its contortions.

"What's wrong, Granny?" Navi questioned, crouching and leaning his head close to hers. He had rarely heard her complain of pain or seen her face so feeble. "Do you think you might've picked up de flu? Let me see if you have a fever." He laid his hand on her forehead and discovered that it was peculiarly sticky and cool. Mira sat down on the bench beside her, frowning.

The sounds of the mall swelled and condensed into a high-pitched squeal in Granny's ear; tiny white dots materialized and exploded at the edges of her vision. "I don't know, boy," she panted, surprised by her failing voice. She pinched her eyelids shut. "Something ain't right . . ." She felt her hand tingling as she rested an arm over Navi's shoulders.

"Do you want to go to de doctor?" he asked. "Or maybe we should take you to de emergency room . . ." But Granny couldn't answer him anymore—her head drooped and pressed dead weight against her grandson's.

Right before she came to and attempted to reply to her name, Granny felt triggered by the intertwined odours of strong chemicals and food. She opened her eyes and gradually realized she was lying in a hospital bed; the yellowness of the room's walls jarred her head. Mira and Navi were frozen on her right and left, gripping the bed's plastic rails and urging her to recognize them. They twisted their heads to talk to somebody beyond her vision. She tried to respond again, to shape some sort of noise so her daughter and grandson would know that she was still with them, but she was seized by overwhelming tiredness. The heaviness in her lips and tongue were too powerful.

It was only after several more hours of semi-consciousness that the intravenous liquid cleared her mind and mouth. *It's fortunate that she arrived when she did*, the doctor told them all, after listing a set of regulations she would have to obey to manage her dangerously high blood pressure, *or it could've turned into a full-blown stroke*. Granny was surprised by how disappointed in her the young man seemed as he explained his diagnosis.

Mira wouldn't stray far from her mother's hand, even though it had been marred by a needle and tape and tubes; her body was stiff in a plastic orange chair pushed up against the hospital bed. "De nurse said you must learn to control your stress or your blood pressure could get bad again. I tell you, if something is stressing you so much, you got to deal with it . . ."

"It ain't what you think, Mira, so get dat out-a your mind. You hear de doctor say dis blood pressure problem is caused by many things. And he say de medication gon' fix it, alright?"

Navi sat on the edge of the bed, using a disposable spoon to stab pits in a cup of green Jell-O that his grandmother wouldn't eat but refused to discard. "But stress is usually part of de problem, Granny. You have to take de medicine and work on everything at de same time, your stress level, diet, exercise . . ."

"Nothing's stressing me," Granny declared. "I come through plenty troubles in my life, you know, but you never see me allowing them to make me sick. And I eat properly, I work hard and get plenty exercise, boy."

Navi shook his head. "You shouldn't dismiss what de doctor's telling you so quickly, Granny. He said you can be unhealthy and stressed out without really knowing it."

She kissed her teeth and flattened the blanket over her torso, annoyed. "You getting into dis with me too?" She snatched her hand away from Mira and tugged the sheets tight around her chin. "It's all y'all who gon' make my blood pressure rise now."

Mira's lips parted in rebuttal but she glanced at Navi just as he finally slurped a shuddering chunk of Jell-O; she caught his attention and tried to smile, but his eyes flicked away too quickly. She decided not to harp on the issue in front of him.

Mother and son trundled home together on the subway that evening, after insisting upon staying at the hospital beyond visiting hours. Although they hadn't eaten dinner, neither of them ventured to ask the other about it—they just quietly hobbled around each other to make their preparations for sleep. Yet, as Navi closed his eyes, his stomach began to buckle and groan for food; he tried to ignore it, to leave it until morning, but it wouldn't let him rest, no matter how weary he was. He started out of his bedroom toward the fridge but became distracted by soft talking in the guest room. He skulked to the other side of the hall and carefully placed his ear on the room's hollow plywood door.

"I don't know what happen, she never had blood pressure problems before," he heard Mira speak into the phone with a lowered tone. "It cropped up so fast. I know de doctor says she has to watch her health, but I really think it's dis thing with Neela dat's causing de problem. I see it going on since she came up to live with me, but she would-a never admit it to me. She does hardly want to talk about it with me. I don't know what I can do . . ."

Navi almost resumed his course to the kitchen, exasperated by the invocation of Neela. *I don't need to hear dis, let my mother worry about dat girl from now on,* he thought, *I'm finished with it.*

"No, he don't know about you. I'll tell him I had to make a call to de people I babysit for. At least he won't get surprised when he sees de phone bill. He said Mommy and I could make long-distance calls if we needed to, in any event . . ." Navi's interest was instantly revived; he was bewildered that his mother was concealing the conversation, that she felt apprehensive enough to hide it from him. He pressed closer, frowning and unwittingly holding his breath.

"I want to talk to de boy, but things don't really seem right between us. I get de feeling dat Navi don't want to talk to me too much so I stay back. It's hard for me, you know? He's been so quiet dis whole trip. It's been so long since I left them in Marasaw, maybe it's been too long. Maybe things can't be fixed. I don't know. Sometimes I wonder if it would be better for me to go home." She signed gently. "Oh, I shouldn't start into dis now. I might wake him up. Anyway, it won't be much longer. We gon' get to see each other soon. I think about you every day." Her voice stalled. "Well, it's funny to hear you say dat 'cause I think you more beautiful than me." Navi could perceive an adolescent undercurrent in her voice, bashful pleasure in receiving a lover's compliment. "I know. I love you too."

He almost punched the door in, almost blazed through with a surge of profanities. *Get out of my house,* he inwardly said, fingers tensed into fists and breath accelerating. *You think it's hard for you? It's your own fault things are like dis!* He juddered backward, thinking that he might scream, anger so intense that he didn't care that the neighbours would overhear. He pictured the sweep of Mira's mild grin as she offered affection to a total stranger, her one hand gripping the receiver and the other caressing the twirls of the telephone cord. His teeth locked down hard and hot tears welled. *You liar! How dare you come into my house and pretend dat you actually want to be here! After you abandoned us with not even a second thought, you actually expect me to jump back into everything like nothing happened? Go home to your boyfriend and don't ever think about coming back!*

His own vitriol stunned him, and he managed to shake himself from the runaway thoughts. His brain tilted to a halt and he felt abruptly empty, gaping at the guest-room doorknob, unsure of himself. He hadn't realized that he felt this way about what had happened, and he hadn't thought that he felt anything much for Mira at all. She had become such a remote aspect of his childhood—he had thought she had shrunk to an abstraction in his consciousness as he had grown up. He had assumed that he was content with it, confident that it would stir no buried sorrow or rancour to be faced by her as a real flesh-and-blood woman once again. He couldn't fathom such a fevered reaction to the fact that after leaving them all those years ago, and knowing what she had done, she wished for more from him.

His eyes fixed on the fibres of the pressed carpet and he filled his chest with air, gradually releasing it back into the hallway. Hunger long forgotten, he decided that he wouldn't blast in or curse madly or strike the phone away. He would return to his bedroom and regain his former peace, since peace was really all he believed he could have with Mira.

A couple of days later, after Granny had been released from the hospital with a battery of pills, Navi was awoken by the clangs and fragrance of baking. "You should rest some more, Granny. Mom and I can make breakfast," he said, tying his robe and entering the kitchen. "You have to prepare for your flight dis afternoon."

The room sweltered with oven heat and Granny cracked an egg over a hill of flour in a big silver bowl. "I don't got plenty things to pack. It's your day off from work and you must enjoy it." She pouted at the stained fabric of her house duster. "I just splash-up a whole cup of oil on myself like a fool and now it gon' be trouble to get it off."

Navi braced himself on the counter and poked a set of freshly baked cheese buns that had been left out to cool. Their crusts appeared hard but they were spongy to the touch. "Don't worry about it, I'll take care of it for you."

Her face soured. "Go to de hospital for two days and everybody treat you like an invalid, man," she murmured. "Nav, don't puncture them! Nobody gon' want to eat mash-up buns!" She tried to be stern but relented to an immature grin. "You still a little boy."

Navi smiled back and jabbed his finger into another bun. "But they're too perfect, I can't help it. Dis one's mine."

"Put yourself to use and prepare de cheese for me on de table."

He washed his hands and walked to the living-room table, where a half-block of cheddar lay in a heap of its own grated bits. His grandmother followed, bowl tucked underneath her arm; she glided the curtains open before sitting next to him. Sun blanketed the table and checkered Navi's neck.

"Remember how we used to make buns on de weekend back home, long time ago when you was a little boy?" Granny asked, abandoning her dough to reminisce. "You always wanted to measure de milk and oil and flour but you would never bother to stir nothing together."

"I preferred de technical side of culinary arts." After sweeping aside the tiny spirals of cheese, he planted the grater in the middle of the plate and scraped the cheddar block as hard as he could.

"You don't have to press de thing with such a heavy hand, Nav," she instructed, grazing his arm. She folded her fingers together and rested her chin on them. "Neela would help me with de rest of it, though. I don't think she liked baking too much, but she would always try. It was good dat she tried."

Navi stopped grating to observe his grandmother, surprised that she spoke of his sister. Her eyes were serene toward the bare white wall and her mouth was set in a dim smile. She seemed hazily pleased, escaping in that memory.

"Neela loved cheese buns. I knew you weren't so crazy for them, but dat girl loved them from young. She was de one who made them disappear so fast, you know, sneaking them from de container all day long and filling her belly before dinner!" She laughed to herself. "I didn't prevent her, though. I said, let de child enjoy her buns. We got to enjoy weself however we can, right?" She dragged the bowl of dough close to her chest, poised to recommence mixing. "Nav, you must think your granny's speaking like an old crow, nah? Them days long over and I bothering your young mind with old things."

Navi found that he couldn't look at his grandmother any-more, unexpectedly struck by her evocation of the past. It was unusual for him to be taken in by nostalgia. "It's okay with me," he answered, aiming his vision at the cheese, "it wasn't really dat long ago." A foreign lump lodged in his throat and he swallowed, hoping that it would soon disappear.

They quietly resumed their work, untroubled by the sensation of sun magnifying on their skin through the large living-room window. Neither of them noticed that Mira stepped out of the guest room in her pyjamas, slinking into Navi's bedroom. She'd been waiting to hide a wooden monkey, the one she had secretly bought for him at the street festival, in his nightstand drawer.

CHAPTER 10

As Seetha slept on her shoulder, Neela stepped out of a rattling taxi onto Marasaw ground, only to be taken aback by boarded windows and bolted doors. Porch unswept, littered with dry leaves and ash from cane-harvest fires, Granny's house looked more aged and morose than ever. Slumped against the back door, child still in her arms, she listened to distorted sounds of a neighbour's radio until the sun turned orange.

"We didn't know what to think," Lenda said, when they had finished a rich oxtail dinner at her house and were sitting outside. Seetha's giggling could be heard from inside; the girl was stunned and delighted by Lenda's little cousins—one with a green shirt and no pants, one adorned with dark gold earrings and bracelets, one who enjoyed the rubbery flesh of a ginip and grinned with it plastered over his front teeth. "We didn't know if you was dead or alive."

Neela tugged the corner of her T-shirt down, hard-healing knife wound on her shoulder blade still sensitive. "I wanted to leave but they wouldn't let none of us go. And I sent letters to Granny, I put all kind-a message in there for you, but . . ." She looked to the street, where children shrieked and tossed a scrap of aluminum, running forward and back, forward and back. She had been avoiding the question and knew that Lenda wasn't going to say anything on her own. "So, she's gone to live with my mother, nah?"

Lenda nodded. "She been gone for a while now. From de look of de house, I don't think she's planning to return anytime soon." She brushed condensation from her plastic cup, pressing it against her cheek to battle the humid evening. "But how you manage to get away from Eden then?"

"De village women brought me and my teacher-friend down a path out-a de interior. It took almost fifteen days of walking in pure bush. I don't know how them women knew where they was going, but they did. We finally found de road and followed it to de nearest dock to get back to de capital." Neela's stomach dropped when she remembered how Karha had wept when she and Seetha were about to board the ferry to Marasaw—it was as if Karha hadn't appreciated how far Nasee-Ki and her dream of founding a school were behind her until that moment. She would remain with the women in the city, and return to her father's home when they finally left.

"So," Lenda said tightly, "now you back in town."

"I miss you in the bush, Len, you know. So bad."

She snorted. "Oh, yeah?"

"What you mean?"

"Nothing." She was serious, gazing at the children on the road.

"But what's wrong?"

Lenda made Neela's hand slip from her arm by taking a sip of soda. "You don't care about me," she said quietly, "you never did. You do what you want. It don't got nothing to do with me. And you come back when you need my help." She twisted the cup in her fingers. "Listen, I know it's my fault too, alright? I didn't say anything. I let you get on dis way with me, treat me like I hardly here. Like I don't matter. I was always running after you, Neela."

"But it ain't true, I do care . . ."

"You only saying it to save face."

"No, you my best friend in de world . . ."

"Stop. Please." Lenda moved to take another mouthful but halted as if something unappetizing were floating in the cup. She passed it to Neela and leaned forward, resting her chin on her knuckles. "Don't bother with saying nothing. I know I been de fool all along. You can't deny it. And you can't say nothing to change it."

Neela noticed the braids on the back of Lenda's head, taut and perfect, smelling sweet like coconut oil. She had always thought of Lenda's faithfulness as automatic, claiming that selfless, steadfast friendship as if it were naturally due. She wished to press her fingertips over those braids, anything to convey thankfulness, to demonstrate her mounting regret. For all of the astonishing abilities that had come to her, and for all she had thought she could achieve, Neela had done little for her best friend, and longed to plead for forgiveness. But she only brought the drink to her lips, choked with embarrassment; she blinked to prevent tears, convinced that she didn't deserve to produce them.

After Neela had left for Eden, Lenda would ride to teachers' college in the early morning fog and study until her classes began. She sought to suffocate her loneliness by filling her head with educational techniques and theories, ruminations on combatting the inherent fickleness of childhood with book knowledge. But solitary library time offered surprising joy— Lenda began to bask in her textbooks and scribble cryptic notes up and down their margins. She was drawn all the way up to the highest shelves, plucking the most neglected books, ones with curdled pages snacked upon by paper-eating ticks. For the first time since she had started college, she was truly free to delight in learning, amazed by the pleasure it gave her. She had hardly been able to nurture that desire for knowledge when Neela was in town, set on deterrence, ensnaring her in tragicomic episodes, an endless string of exhausting and time-wasting pursuits.

Lenda discovered companionship amongst her classmates. Instead of visiting the Marasaw Restaurant after class, some of them dragged benches into a broken triangle and assessed what they had learned that day, contesting the professors' viewpoints and, more rarely, reaffirming them. *Yes, I agree you can use child's play to enhance comprehension but wouldn't de teacher then have to learn to play as well?* As she squeezed into the mob of opinions, she realized how simple it was to be witty and confident—she would gesticulate for emphasis and scan face to face, longing to rouse the most satisfying reaction, the nodding heads of her peers. *But I believe adults already know how to play, it just looks different with age, like de game of romance, for example* . . . And when she smiled generously at a supporting comment from the student beside her, she saw that he had been compelled to smile back in admiration and flirty camaraderie. These things hadn't seemed noteworthy when Neela was nearby, arms crossed and foot twitching until the two of them finally left school.

But Lenda felt as if her gains were crumbling, gashes growing over their surfaces. "Well, what can you do?" she said drably, disappointed that her confidence could be so easily threatened, that it was so impossible to find reprieve from the patterns of lifelong friendship. She rested her back on the house to ground herself on something more solid than herself. "What are you planning?"

"Not too sure."

"What you gon' do about Jaroon?"

Neela's body stiffened at the mention of his name. "I don't know. But as long as I don't have to see him or his hooligans again, it don't matter."

"But he gon' stay away? What if he comes back?"

"He got it real good in Eden, he built a kingdom for himself and has everybody answering to him. I don't think he gon' want to come back here, but I ain't convinced he gon' stay away from Marasaw forever. All I know is dat I got to be on my guard and I can't let Seetha out-a my sight."

Lenda patted the corner of her shirt against her neck to sop up sweat. "I suppose you got plenty other things to worry about in any event," she mumbled, limp. "Let's go. Your granny mus'-ee leave a house key with your next-door neighbour."

Not long after returning to Marasaw, Neela started to seek the sort of household work that her grandmother used to do. She collected laundry from her immediate neighbours—*I surprised to see you again, girl . . . Ow Sugee, your poor granny, I miss her bad . . . but eh-eh! Who is dis pickney with you now? . . . Alright, I gon' try find a little wash for you.* She soon ventured farther, circling the streets to babysit children, cook meals and watch old folks. When she had collected enough money to afford electric current in her grandmother's house, she purchased her own plug-in iron and began laundering in the new part of Marasaw where more impressive colonial houses had sprung up while she was in Eden. These clients might be apt to refuse payment if their sheets were not folded perfectly square or their pants were not creased crisply enough, but they were better equipped to pay for amenities.

During every job she did, Neela carried Seetha propped across her hip. It would bother her old neighbours and incite whispered strife between mothers and daughters, aunties and nieces, grandmothers and granddaughters. *Look story. Run off reckless, get mixed-up with de Begwan boy, back by her lone self with his baby!* Neela could hear the women cautioning their girls over the sizzle of frying fish and yelp of babies. *Mustn't follow what dat girl do or you gon' get in de same predicament . . .* Their reactions were just as Granny had envisaged.

And she got the same response from women living in the new side of Marasaw too, townsfolk who wouldn't know her grandmother or her family's last name. They stood in their doorways in front of her brave young face, avoiding a direct gaze on that grinning child straddled over her, tangled in a web of concerns about surrendering their garments. *What do these girls from* dat side *of town get themselves in*, the women wondered, *again and again! How could their mothers let it happen?* Others avoided the confrontation altogether—their cleaning ladies would fetch dirty clothes as Neela waited on the other side of the gate, inhaling odours from the trench and stretching her arms between the bars. *Fold them up nice,* the cleaning ladies would instruct, *and de missus might give you an extra tip for your little baby . . .* Neela resented the reactions of new Marasaw as much as those of her close neighbours.

"See dis?" she said, lifting a dripping piece of cloth from the scrubbing board. She was washing a load from a family in the well-off part of town. "Watch me."

Seetha stumbled around the concrete in her diaper, exploring the backyard and swatting at a pale swarm of fruit flies. She looked to the crisp white briefs, turned see-through by sparkling soap bubbles.

"Dis is a panty," Neela instructed. "Not just any panty . . . a *fancy-lady* panty. You know them ladies. Their panties are better than our panties, you know."

Seetha pointed at it and yelled.

"Yes! You can say it? Pan-ty?" she mouthed. "Fan-cy-pan-ty?"

But Seetha was determined to name it in her own language; she sulked when her mother tried to declare it otherwise.

"Alright, I'm sorry. You can call it what you want, hard-ears donkey ba-ba."

In fact, Neela tried to transform every chore she did in Marasaw into a lesson for her daughter—*You can say 'broom'? How about 'washcloth'? What's dis, you can tell me? Dat's right! Rolling pin! You use it to roll roti. Want to put your hand on it and I roll for you?*

"You teaching de child good!" Lenda exclaimed when she visited Neela one evening after her classes. Her pitying mother had sent her with a spare bottle of Mellow Cola and cuts of fresh fish. "At least you was practising something of use in de bush."

"She been learning quick too! Watch." Neela pointed at the soda that had been placed on the table, fizzing invitingly. "Seetha. Look what I got. What is dis?"

Seetha observed, frowning. "Dool!"

"Yes! Bottle!" Neela clapped her hands and made the child smile proudly.

"Dat didn't sound like 'bottle' to me . . . ," Lenda said.

"Well, her baby teeth are preventing her from saying it properly."

Lenda raised an eyebrow.

"I telling de truth! Listen, you try with her then, Miss Big-Woman-Teacher."

Lenda bent a fork close to Seetha. Its tips were pitted by bites. "Baby, here. What's dis?" She rocked it between her thumb and index finger. "You got to help me show your mommy dat she's mad in de head . . ."

Seetha gaped, captivated by how the utensil flashed in the light; she lengthened herself in its direction.

"No, you got to tell me what it is first."

"You confusing her!" Neela nagged. "Come, Seetha, show dis girl what you know."

Seetha finally shouted a reply: "Poke!"

Neela laughed gaily and rested her palms on the flesh of Seetha's cheeks. "My little donkey! Look how bright she is! Eh, Len?"

Lenda brushed her fingers across Seetha's forehead to sweep her hair away from her eyes, astounded by how the child so resembled Neela when they had been in elementary school, tickling and play-mocking each other until they got in trouble with the teacher. "You de brightest little donkey I know, child."

Neela taught Seetha something new every day, spelling words, telling stories, singing songs as they traced market aisles and scurried about town to finish their work. *Sing along, girl: "There was a happy bird that flew from tree to tree"* . . . Bubbly and enthusiastic, Seetha squealed and gurgled, only to be egged on by her mother, *I can't hear you, speak up!* But their overexcited exchanges were nothing less than impudence in their illegitimate situation, according to old neighbourhood women, as if the disgrace of it meant nothing at all. *I would-a hang my head in pure shame! See how girls carry on nowadays? I tell you dis country is going to de devil,* they nipped, in the thick of hushed conversations about *poor Sugee.*

You did the right thing, Granny, Neela wrote in a glossy New Year's card. She had found a return address for *Miss Mira Keetham* while rummaging through Granny's crate of browning letters forgotten under the stairwell. *When your papers came through, you were right to take the opportunity. Don't worry with me, the baby and I are doing good. Her mouth is full of teeth and she talks and walks plenty now. I wish you could meet her. Seetha is a smart child. She's learning so fast that I think she could be a teacher herself, probably a headmaster! I'm even showing her how to count and spell.*

She started writing many letters to her grandmother, now strangely willing to relay things she would have never disclosed when they were in the same country—the unabridged story of Seetha, Nasee-Ki and Jaroon. More than that, she was ready to reveal how she felt, what she longed for, for herself and her daughter. *I want my baby to do well and I want her to learn. Even Lenda comes by and teaches Seetha while I do the wash outside. I know the child will grow up bright, because Lenda is a very good teacher. She has the highest marks at teacher's college and everybody's talking about it.*

Neela brushed her hair into a messy mass with the tips of her fingers and redid the elastic band. It was late and she had just finished getting Seetha to fall asleep in the cot alone. *You know, I see Jaroon's grandmother in the market sometimes. She's the only Begwan left in town. She watches me and Seetha but I stay away. I don't want to have anything to do with anybody in that family, not even that crazy old lady. But Granny, I think I feel him following us. I can't explain it, but I can feel his spite. Deep down, it seems that he'll come back. I just try to tell myself that I'm too busy with Seetha to worry myself sick with that man. I just have to keep her close and keep my eyes open.*

Seetha loves to talk to everyone. When we go to the market, she touches all the fish and chicken and when people tell her no, you know what she says? She says "Excuse me" loud and proud and goes right back again. The ladies quarrel and say I'm not raising her properly, but Seetha has her own way. They don't know that. But she's a good girl, friendly with everyone. If only you could see what a smart girl she is. Neela stopped herself from writing that her daughter's brightness reminded her of Navi when they were children—she didn't want to let herself start thinking about him too.

I'm so sorry that I made everybody worry when I went to Nasee-Ki. Every day I think about how much I hurt you and Lenda. I wasted plenty energy on those soldiers to get letters to you. Maybe you're still angry with me. Maybe you're still mad that I went away and had a baby. I'm so sorry I did all of this to you. I thought I was strong enough to be on my own. I thought I was special and I thought I had the ability to care for myself in the bush. I was wrong.

Please don't be mad at me. Please don't be ashamed of me. I don't want you to feel that way anymore . . .

~

When a woman from the new side of Marasaw accepted Neela's offer to stay and assist with cleaning when she returned her laundry, Neela woke up early and put on nice clothes borrowed from Lenda, a dark blue skirt and a blouse with an embroidered collar. She had rigged her rusty old bicycle to carry laundry back and forth, strapping a tattered canvas like a hammock between the handlebars and tying a metal basket behind the seat. Even though the whole setup would buck and shudder as if it were going to collapse, it allowed Neela to transport more wash. She left her drowsy daughter with Lenda's mother and cautiously wheeled around town at daybreak, careful to avoid wobbling along the way.

She knocked on the door, hastily planting loose strands of hair into her bun and shrugging to massage the twinge in her shoulder blade. A young girl answered without a word and led her to the kitchen, where an old woman stood by the stove.

"You de girl helping de missus today, nah?" the woman asked, not moving her head from its watch point over the open pot. Her fine white hair had been pulled into a tense ponytail, but where hairline met skin, broken strands had curled from the cooking steam.

"Yes," Neela answered, "I brought de family's clean laundry too."

"Give it to de child."

The young girl silently hauled the bundle from under Neela's arm and scurried off. "You gon' start in de living room," the old lady directed, pointing Neela out of the kitchen with her attention still captured by the stew.

After polishing mahogany furniture, towering massive and self-assured, Neela scrubbed the floors by hand. It was difficult to scour the wood grain with a single worn brush, but the old lady appeared impressed by the results; she supervised Neela's progress. "You know, de other girls don't really know how to do dis kind-a thing," she revealed under her breath. "I don't say nothing to de missus but I notice most-a them got something wrong with their heads. But dis work does come natural to you." Neela knew she had gotten the job when the old woman asked her to stay for the rest of the day.

"De missus sends us here every day," she said, walking with difficulty and cradling a bucket of cleaning supplies. She and Neela were entering the house's expansive back lot, down a path that cut through a wall of lush palms and fruit trees. They reached the far edge of the property, thick with the sort of disordered foliage that Neela knew from Nasee-Ki. A diminutive shack had been built out of sight, lifted on stilts and completely hidden by murky leaves. The structure was dilapidated, as if it had passed through a fire and escaped in charred remains. "Make sure you don't say nothing, you just mind your business and do de cleaning," the old woman instructed as they ascended the deformed plank stairs.

The shack was dingy and crowded by mismatched scrap furniture. Strung-up fluorescent bulbs cast a thin, harsh light on the kitchenette and front room. Neela swept while the old woman replaced linens in the back room—as she toiled with the uneven floor, she was astounded out of her task by strained noises of a baby and a disheartened, meagre voice attempting to console it. *Oh rooks,* she wondered, broom in hand and scanning the sad, vacant front room, *what kind-a mother and baby would stay in here?* She wanted to learn more about the mysterious occupants, but there was no conversation to overhear.

The woman returned in haste and rushed Neela to complete their work, and the two of them bustled out. "I heard noise," Neela panted, hustling to keep up with the old woman's suddenly fast steps. "Somebody lives in dat shack?"

"Don't you worry, it ain't your business," she answered briskly.

"But I think I heard a baby or something . . ."

The old lady curved around. "De missus told us to clean de place and bring little food, dat's all. She didn't tell us to interfere with nothing, you understand?" She gave a biting look and resumed her course along the sloped trail. "If you want to keep dis job, you gon' mark my words right now, yeah?"

Neela cleaned the missus' house for a few hours each morning. She was given a starchy shirt and skirt as a uniform and was instructed to take directions from that old lady who cooked and cleaned, Miss Leema. "She has been working loyally with dis family for more than forty years," the missus explained, for the first and only time treating Neela to a cup of tea. "Miss Leema is like family and we expect you and all de girls to view her as such."

But Miss Leema proved to be a demanding overseer with domineering standards of perfection that the others could rarely live up to—*How you do de folding so mashy-mashy!* she would rage when Neela returned clean laundry to the house. *What nonsense are you doing with dis waxing! I ain't gon' let none-a you roll roti no more! Like you don't see how lucky you are to work here, heaven knows what evil nastiness y'all would-a do to make money without it! How all these girls can be so foolish, not one-a them got sense!* Neela and the other girls were miserable with Miss Leema, but they forced their tongues into obedience with the allotted replies: *Yes Miss Leema, No Miss Leema, I sorry Miss Leema . . .*

I managed to get a little job, Neela wrote her grandmother. *They pay me good money and give me steady work. I can't bring Seetha with me, but I can pay Lenda's mother to babysit her every day. I don't like leaving Seetha but if I have to, I want her to stay with good people like Lenda and her family. I don't really feel safe with anybody else. Every noise makes me weary, you know, even at home. That man and his hooligans are still watching us, somehow. I don't know how, but I still feel it. At least now Seetha and I might be able to save up and come to be with you and Mommy.*

One morning when Miss Leema was engrossed in a particularly complex goat dish, she sent Neela and another cleaning girl to take care of the shack. They received a firm cautioning out of the back door: "Don't let me hear y'all doing any stupidness in there, or I gon' tell de missus and both-a you gon' be gone by afternoon. Hear?" *We hear you Miss Leema.*

"But what can she do to us, really?" the other girl considered as Neela washed dishes in the kitchenette. "If she tells de missus anything, de missus gon' ask, why you *allowing* de girls carry on stupidly then? Isn't it?"

Neela giggled. "Maybe you right." She tried scrubbing the kitchen countertop with bleach but it was so caked in dirt and covered by scratches that it refused to come clean.

"Yes man, yes, I tell you! Anything we do gon' go back to lick dat crazy old devil-woman herself!" she passionately said, giving her mop even less attention.

"Don't go testing dat now. It's like Miss Leema's part of de family. You can't play with dat."

The girl kissed her teeth. "Please. What kind *crap* is dat? De lady scrubs what drop out-a they behind in de toilet. She ain't part-a no *family* and she ain't no better than us."

Neela gave up on the counter and retrieved the linens. "I gon' take care-a dis," she said on her way, answered by the girl's *I-ain't-care* expression. She clutched the sheets to her chest, adjusted her skirt out of habit and tapped on the door to the back room; when she heard no response, she turned the knob and poked her head inside. "Hello? You in there?"

"You want to change de sheets?" asked a small voice.

She squeezed around the doorway. A young-faced girl sat in the corner with a dozing baby near her tiny, deflated bare breast. She wore a droopy printed dress, collarbone jutting angularly, hair loosened in a frizzy tent; she shut a book resting on her knee and swiftly concealed it between the small of her back and the chair. "I . . . yes, I got de sheets here," Neela answered uneasily, "sorry to disturb you."

The girl looked up and, connecting with Neela's eyes by mistake, twitched her head downward in embarrassment. "It's alright," she said timidly, mouth hardly forming an exit for the words to escape.

Neela moved about awkwardly around the wire-frame bed, sweating in the utterly motionless bedroom air. She yanked the sheets off and replaced them with the fresh set, laying the linens as evenly as possible in the confining space. She made every effort to keep from staring at this strange girl and her strange baby.

"I think I'm done here," she said. The girl was now cradling the child over her shoulder and patting its back. It was agitated yet lifeless, griping and gurgling in melancholy. "How old?"

"Oh . . . five months," the girl replied.

"What's his name?"

"I call her Sally."

Neela stepped closer and laid her hand on the back of the baby's head, combing its sweaty jet-black hair. "Oh, I see, Sally's a girl." She smiled. "Pretty." She noticed that the girl flinched and froze, stunned by her touch on the baby. She recoiled and folded her hands into each other. "You trying to burp her?"

The girl nodded.

"If you support de child's neck little more, she gon' be able to pass gas easier."

The girl shifted her hand a little.

"Go more, dat's good," Neela affirmed when the girl's hand was rounded over the base of Sally's head. "Now rub her back with your other hand and move up, push de gas up, gently, yes, just so . . ." She surveyed the girl's efforts until the baby finally burped. "See then? Now de child gon' feel much better. You know, when my daughter was small like Sally, she could belch bad like a grown man."

The girl smiled but compressed her lips before they could stretch too wide.

"If you do dat whenever you feed her, she gon' give you less fretting and her milk gon' stay down good." Neela gathered the pile of dirty sheets and opened the door, a rush of sticky air flowing in as if it had crouched in wait for the opportunity to pounce. "What's your name?"

"Baby," the girl answered to the floor.

"Alright, I gon' come back next time, Baby," Neela assured her.

"I heard you talking in there!" the other cleaning girl exclaimed as she dragged her mop down the shack steps, uncaring that it collected mud.

"What's wrong with dat?"

"You know we ain't allowed to talk to her!"

Neela scowled when the bottle of bleach almost slipped from her grip. "Hold dis, nah," she said, handing it over. "I know we ain't suppose to talk to her," she whispered heavily, "but what I gon' do, ignore de child?"

"Yes!" The girl shivered and drew her mouth into an unsteady line. "She and dat baby make my skin crawl. They ain't normal."

"How you can say dat?"

"They keep them in dat shack, don't they?"

But Neela was intrigued. She returned as often as she could find a reason, volunteering to clean the shack and bring food to Baby and Sally. *Yes Miss Leema, I gon' come right back when I done.* She enjoyed visiting them; between the mopping and scrubbing and sheet changes, she taught Baby to handle her infant, demonstrating how to hold Sally firmly, how to breastfeed confidently, how to play with her energetically. Soon, the pitying lessons turned into genuine conversations.

"What happen to you!" Miss Leema barked when Neela entered the kitchen. "Why you been back there so long?"

"Sorry Miss Leema . . ."

"Don't *sorry* me!" The old lady was even more severe with her girls as the missus and the family prepared to entertain guests for a religious ceremony that evening. "You know we got plenty work to do and yet you dilly-dallying in de yard!"

"Sorry Miss Leema," Neela repeated, replacing the cleaning fluid under the sink. "There was plenty things to do."

"De girls tell me you spend your time gaffing with her. Hmm? Is true?"

Neela casually began to pass a mop over the floor. "Who you mean, Miss Leema?"

"You know full well who I talking about!" she yelled, and abandoned a pot spoon in the boiling rice. Hearing the old lady's accusations, another cleaning girl who was entering the kitchen promptly backed off.

"De little girl who live back there?"

"Do you know what kind-a *little girl* dat is?"

"I only ask permission to change de sheets. I don't talk for no other reason."

Miss Leema wagged her finger, as she normally did to rebuke her girls. "You think you really know about dat girl and her baby?"

Neela concentrated on the mop's soapy yarn strings. "She's just a girl . . ."

"She's slow in her head 'cause she fornicated with her own flesh and blood!" The rice sizzled, erupting with a flow of grains and bubbles; Miss Leema dashed to draw it from the burner. "See what you do? You girls gon' kill me and ruin dis whole house!" She thrust the spoon against the stovetop. "You bett'-had stop dat! Next time, you gone!"

This wasn't the first time that Neela had heard such things about Baby. The girls had their own alarming accounts—*She's retarded, you know, and de baby slow too . . . they call it "inbreed."* But Neela didn't see those distressing things in Baby herself; the buzz about *fornicating with flesh and blood* seemed so distant from her experience with the girl and her infant. *I don't listen to what the others say about them,* Neela wrote her grandmother, *People like to talk but they don't know what other people are passing through. You can't pay attention to it.*

But Baby did pay attention to it. When the cleaning girls entered the shack, she listened through the wall, flushed with humiliation when they fell into their hushed arguments. *You change de sheets . . . No, you go, I had to last time! . . . I don't want go in there or touch nothing! . . . Well I don't want to neither! . . . I can't be in de same room with dat girl . . . But I frightened too! . . .* When one of them was eventually wrestled into the bedroom, Baby silent with Sally in the corner, the cleaning girl's expression always spelled the same message in dawdling, devastating letters: *You nasty and retarded.*

It was when she was alone once again that Baby would crouch under her bed and retrieve her hidden stack of books—assorted holy texts and spiritual musings that she had collected back home, before she had given birth to Sally. Those books made her feel there were ancient secrets in a vast world that even she, scrawny and anxious, might be able to uncover; riddles within riddles that promised to organize life's random difficulties, simply through vigilant reading. Baby found that she needed to look at them each day, back broken and bottom numb, hunched over her books for hours as she fumbled to care for her daughter in the old shack.

CHAPTER 11

I like Baby so much because she sees things differently than most people, Neela wrote to her grandmother at the kitchen table one evening. *Today I told her that I worry Seetha and I may not be safe, that Jaroon is somehow watching us and planning to do us evil. I told her that I don't really know what to do about it right now. Then she pulled out a book and read, "I am safe in their wings, angels are watching me." Baby said that maybe Seetha and I are being watched in a good way, by angels. I had to laugh. I told her yes, she might be right . . .*

"Last week she was barely walking but watch now!" Neela exclaimed in delight. Sally waddled about the bedroom with her mouth open, drooling in concentration for each chubby step. "Look how she grow plenty in one week!"

"Yesterday, I think I hear her say something like *Mommy,*" Baby said.

Neela clapped her hands and opened wide eyes to win some attention, but the child was too mesmerized by her abrupt mobility to acknowledge her.

"Seetha . . . she did all dis kind-a thing when she was Sally's age, right?"

"Dat child walked before she crawled, girl. She's so clever, I tell you. She was a big woman as soon as she was born, almost ready to walk after one week in de world."

Baby listened wholeheartedly when Neela boasted about her smart Seetha, how she had grand plans to teach the girl to read and sew and do math before the other children. "I wasn't sure Sally was going to walk at all."

"Of course she would! Most children do."

"But . . . Sally was born . . . she was born different than other children . . ."

"So what?" Neela bent and began collecting the dirty linens strewn over the floor. "You can't do nothing about dat now. It passed and it ain't her fault. All you can do is bring up de child like any other and see what gon' happen, right?"

Baby knelt by the bed and drew a book from underneath it; she swiped the cover across her belly, leaving a grey streak on her duster. "I been reading my books. My Uncle Byeo said he got dis one from a lady who used to go door to door telling people about her religion." She raised its heavenly pastel scene, airbrushed and calm and dreamy.

"What does it say?"

"Plenty. I read a piece about how things feel bad to you, but they turn out good in ways you don't know about. So you can't really suppose nothing. I guess I can't suppose nothing about Sally either."

Neela came near to pass her palm over Baby's frizzy head.

"You right." She turned to Sally again. "I got to go, you hear me, Sally? I gon' bring you something next time I come." The child twisted her head shakily for a short, indifferent moment. "I'll see you, Baby. I got to get out-a here and fetch Seetha before it gets too dark."

"When you coming back?"

"As soon as I can. Leema getting fed up with me so I can't push her too much. Don't worry. I gon' come back soon. It don't matter what de old woman say."

"Oh, okay. Maybe . . . maybe next time you can bring Seetha and she can play with Sally . . ."

"Girl, it would be nice, but I don't think they gon' let me in de house with her. And I don't like to take her around town too much no more, you know. I frighten someone gon' watch us and try . . ." Neela let the thought trail into the bedroom's palpable air—the fan only stirred waves of droplets to wash over their skin. "I don't really think it's safe."

Baby wrung her hands together, bashful as when they had first met. "Oh, alright."

"Maybe things gon' change soon, yeah?" she proposed, recognizing the slump in Baby's disheartened face. "In fact, I think it might very well change before we know. I might be able to bring her for a little bit sometime, it shouldn't cause too much problems. We gon' find a way to work it out, okay?"

But she was incapable of living up to such a promise, with the growing terror that vibrated inside her belly these days, especially when she was alone with her baby in her grandmother's tumbledown house. She stayed up late that night to boil laundry and finish her ironing, but the truth remained that uneasiness wouldn't often allow her to fall asleep; she did one of the few things she could when she felt that way. *I hear noises still,* she scrawled on the page, *every night they come on me now.* The electricity had already been cut so she squinted to follow her thoughts in the unsteady glow of a melted candle. *I don't sleep well anymore. You must think I'm going mad. But the noises sound so close sometimes, as if someone's in the yard or even inside of the house. I thank goodness that Seetha's asleep upstairs. I don't want her to hear all that and get frightened . . .*

She pressed her hand at the top of her chest and took a weighty breath—it felt as if it were trapped in her lungs, pressing to burst from the inside out, shoulder-blade wound stinging as if air might rupture right through. *You know what it feels like when you're scared and you can't breathe? It's how you feel when you know someone hates you and you can't do anything about it.* She forced a full inhalation and her chest was uncomfortably packed with clammy air. *I feel his hatred. It's like a stone crushing me and I can't escape from under it. It's inside of me no matter where I am or what I do.* She tried to scan the kitchen but it was covered by gaping darkness, the kind that seemed too black to be natural. She wondered if something was lurking about, circling her mockingly, closing in the more she wrote. *Nothing looks or feels right anymore, Granny. I don't know how to explain it to you. What if something bad is happening to me and Seetha?* She considered abandoning the letter on the table and retreating to bed, but somehow she was too intimidated even to leave. Nothing would move but the pen she clutched.

I spoke to Karha. She wanted to argue with her father to let me stay in the city with her, telling me that I shouldn't take any chances. But the truth is that even if her father would let me go, I don't want to lose this job, Granny. I don't want to leave Baby and Sally. I don't want to leave Lenda behind and I don't want to leave this house again. It's all I have left of you. She shuddered as the candle faded low and warned of smoking itself out. *Maybe I might find another way to stay safe from Jaroon. Maybe there's something I can do and it will come to me, come upon me soon. I'll just have to wait for it to come. Please, just pray for us and tell my mother to pray for us too.*

Neela gasped when she heard a clipped shout from the bedroom. *Oh no, no* . . . Seetha's cry had vanished; she fumbled from her chair, the chaotic movement snuffing the last of the candlelight. She stumbled upstairs and groped along the house's rough walls with quivering hands, listening for something—a call, a whimper, a gripe—but there were no such familiar sounds. *Please, please, please Lord* . . . When she finally identified it, Neela slapped the bedroom door open. "Seetha?" she breathed, shoulder pulsing. "Please, Seetha?"

She lurched inside when the child began whining. "Oh my baby, oh ba-ba . . ." She cradled Seetha tightly in the middle of the cot and dragged the sheet over their heads, curling her body around her baby's like big spoon and little spoon.

～

But when Neela woke the next morning, her eyes snapping to light, there was no Seetha beside her. She jerked over the edge of the cot with a jagged fear that the child had fallen during the night; she kicked at the tangle of bedsheets that shackled her legs, and dropped her head to see underneath the cot. *Oh God . . .* She slapped her feet to the floor and wound around the room.

"Seetha," she called, "Seetha!" *Oh Lord, no, it happened . . .* "Where are you? Answer me!"

Neela bolted through the house, coiling around the meagre furniture, shoving creaky chairs aside, livid, terrified. *Damn bastard, I didn't even hear, he took her from my own bed! I should-a left, I should-a left!* "Seetha!" she cried. *Oh God, he take her!* She dashed into the backyard. "Answer your mommy! Seetha!" she screamed, assaulted by the emptiness, the vivid presence of her daughter now wrenched away. "Oh God, answer me!"

She went to find the only person she could trust in Marasaw—Lenda rushed down the road in her sleep dress as Neela jogged ahead. They stirred a whirl of interest from porch-dwelling onlookers, neighbours who strained to hear Neela's gasping explanations for the early-morning ruckus. "Oh Lenda, I thought she mus'-ee gone outside, you know how she's got her own way, but I calling and can't find her, and I come to you thinking you mus'-ee bring her over in de night, I don't know, Lenda, I don't know what to do, I don't feel nothing!"

House to house, neighbour to neighbour, they asked the same thing—*Neela's child disappeared last night, you see her anywhere?* It wasn't long before others had enlisted in the search and scurried about too, half-excited and half-alarmed, temporarily setting aside the suspicions they held against each other—*You see de girl's baby anywhere? Sugee-granddaughter-child, man, you know which one, you see her?*

"We got to get de men searching further," Lenda decided on the road in front of Granny's house, with a spray of new resolve. Groups of neighbours were digging around bushy patches and examining the trench's brown water, not quite as motivated as before.

Neela squinted into the sky. "How long we been here, Len?" she asked groggily, wiping fluid from her nose.

"A couple of hours."

They both turned when a neighbour shouted animatedly, but he was only greeting a cousin-neighbour across the road.

Lenda scowled at the false expectations. "We got to start moving to de fields. We got to organize ourselves."

"Jaroon take her," Neela whimpered, her fighting presence sifting away, even at the moment she needed it most. "Right from my own bed . . ."

"None-a dat now. Uncle!" Lenda lifted her hand and a man still in his sleep clothes rushed over, flip-flops hardly sticking to the bottom of his feet.

Neela tugged at her arm. "No, Len, you don't understand, she ain't in Marasaw, I can't feel her near me no more!"

But Lenda was facing the other direction. "We got go out further," she said, and waved a finger like a tornado above her head.

"Please, hear me . . ."

"Where you think we should go?" The man brushed sweat from his forehead; his features were tattered, skin pitted by many years and many drinks, but in searching for Seetha he had taken on bright young eyes.

"We can split in two and some-a we can go there"—Lenda pointed to one edge of town—"and de others should go through de fields."

But Neela shook her head manically. "He's already gone from town with her, I tell you . . ."

He jogged backward. "Alright, I gon' round de men up. Y'all ladies keep looking in town, yeah?"

"Thanks, uncle."

"Seetha's gone!" Neela shouted, jerking Lenda's arm. "I should-a left dis town, I knew it would happen!"

Lenda ripped out of Neela's squeeze and glared angrily. "So what you want me to do?" she snapped. "Stop looking for de child, dat's what you want?"

"But she ain't here!"

"Just stop looking, eh?"

"Seetha is gone, I can't feel her no more!"

"I ain't listening to you, understand, Neela?" Lenda yelled. "I'm not going to stop just because you carrying on like dis now."

"But you can't see? I can't do nothing, I can't feel her . . ." She was desperate for Lenda to know the dearth, the dreadful loneliness, her daughter's defining presence disappeared.

Lenda started toward three older women who were sombrely discussing the tragedy on the street, Neela still dragging from her. "You does do whatever you feel to do, don't worry with no one! But *I* nah worrying wit you dis time! I don't know why I been worrying with you all dis time, how you stay, it's impossible to deal with you! Always got your own way! Left me in dis damn town to run off with Jaroon! All dis mess happen and you still want your own way? You can't do me dis no more! I ain't going to take it, so stop it!" She tried to wiggle free but Neela had a grip like steel. "Let go! Get off me right now!"

"No, Len, please!"

"Auntie!" she shouted. "Come take dis girl from me before I get her off myself!" Confused, the women watched as Lenda tried to keep a steady stride while Neela hung off her, almost stumbling back to the ground. "Neela!" she barked. "You mad? Get off me!"

"My child," she bawled, "he took all I got left!"

"Shut up! Stop! Auntie! Auntie!"

They circled Neela—*Come on, come with us, stop all dat now, you gon' make yourself sick* . . .

"Jaroon take my baby from my own bed and I didn't even know and I can't feel her no more! And there ain't nothing I can do, I thought I could stay here but I'm a fool, there ain't nothing I can do! Ow God!"

Lenda tussled away, panting. "Take her away, she's mad!"

Alright girl, come, stop dat now . . . Neela was weeping and shrieking at Lenda and the neighbours, and at the same time crying to no one at all. The women formed a wall and pushed, rough and gentle at the same time. "But none-a you understand! Jaroon take my baby just like he said he would . . ." She was aghast—her silent thoughts had carried such influence at times, yet her screams appeared to hold little weight this day. *Alright, dis way, you got to rest yourself, girl, come with us, come, shhh, stop dat, shhh . . .*

Lenda and the neighbours searched all day long, arranging groups to scour Marasaw's roads and surrounding fields. Some walked out far, to where rows of sugar cane began to stretch into the distance, waiting until night arrived. *Ow Lenda,* they moaned upon return, *I too sorry girl, we ain't seen nothing, what I can tell you?* She soon made up her mind to go to the Begwan house, bitterly mindful that she hadn't seen the boys, Jaroon's plentiful gang of cousins, for some time in Marasaw. She had made every effort to evade townspeople speaking of them, believing the avoidance to be an obligation of friendship. But as the day progressed, her lack of information had soured into resentment. *These Begwans, where are they?* she growled to herself. *De child is their own flesh and blood!*

"Hey! Hey! You home?" She pounded on the wood door dampened by mould. Light appeared in the front window; sluggish steps shuffled closer, irritated.

"I coming, man!" The door cracked open and a short old woman peeped out, truly alarmed by demands upon her at such an hour. "What's dis noise?"

"I looking for Neela Keetham's child," Lenda yapped. "You see de little girl?"

The woman's eyes became large grey discs. "They already come plenty-plenty asking me de same thing, but I tell them I don't know where de child is!"

Lenda pushed her hand against the spongy door when the woman attempted to shove it in. "Where de other Begwans, then?"

"I don't know where them boys gone, they don't tell me nothing . . ."

"When did they leave?"

"Can't remember! I say must come visit me, yeah? But I ain't seen them long time and I didn't ask nothing to let them say I too nosy and want to talk they business . . ." She tried again to shut her door.

"Stop it!" Lenda nipped, set against the old lady's attempt to regain privacy. "So what, you ain't seen them long time and dat's it?"

"Yes dat's it!" she answered, in amazement at the great injustice. "I don't know where they are, them boys don't visit me in dis backwater! They done gone to the city! I don't keep track, not after my husband die and de boys all pick up and leave me, running all over de place . . ."

"So you seen Jaroon? Huh?"

She dug the corner of her eye with her thumb. "Girl, I ain't see dat grandson-a mine from long time. I tell he mustn't trust de government to care for him in dat bush, but he didn't come back. I tell him dat he can't go to live with all *them* people and expect to come out in one piece . . ."

Lenda kissed her teeth furiously. "You best not be lying to me," she said, pointing her finger.

"What, now look! I talking to her and she push her thick finger in my eye . . ."

"Because if you lying I gon' come back to you and cut some good Begwan tail and if I ever see Jaroon, *ever*, I gon' kill him, you hear me, old goat?"

"Look story! Bullying me! These people ain't got no shame! I might get de police on you but I ain't got no money to pay them today, I got get my grocery and thing to do . . ."

Lenda smacked the door, producing only a mushy thud, and stormed down the porch steps, old lady Begwan ranting in the backdrop.

"Watch how she's knocking my house up! I can't repair nothing, I got to go to de market tomorrow . . ."

Lenda returned to the neighbour's house, where the women had holed Neela up since morning. *She needs to stay quiet,* they stressed, threatening that Neela would succumb to illness if she got more agitated, but Lenda pushed past them nonetheless. She knelt on the rough floor beside the bed, resting her elbows on the pillows. Neela was tucked under a psychedelic-patterned comforter that had been forced upon her so she'd sweat it out; her eyes were glazed open, filled with dew and blank. Lenda drew aside strings of hair stuck to Neela's forehead.

"What happen?" Neela blinked, listless.

Lenda could only shake her head and press her lips together as large tears beaded on the blanket.

"I should-a never thought I could stay in dis town. I know Jaroon took her because I can't feel her no more, Len, I can't feel my own baby . . ."

"I know, I know," she hushed and kissed her cheek, "I know he took Seetha. I know she's gone."

Neela let her eyelids fall. "If you weren't here with me in dis place I don't know what I'd do."

Lenda crawled around to the other side of the bed and squeezed herself in. She laid her forehead on Neela's shoulder and sobbed.

CHAPTER 12

*H*e could have murdered me if he wanted to, Granny. But he knew that taking Seetha would steal more than my life. He used to tell me that no man can cross him and get away with it. I took too many chances by staying here. He stole her from my own bed and I didn't even wake up.

I gave the police money and watched them write a report. I gave them all I have left and all they told me is that it's no crime for a man to take his own child. They didn't listen. I go every day and they still don't bother with me. They think I'm a mad woman.

Marasaw bustled with the news of Sugee Keetham's daughter's daughter who had gotten in trouble and whose baby had vanished in the middle of the night, stolen by Jaroon Begwan. *But how he can take her and her mother didn't know one thing? Wouldn't you feel de child lift up from beside you? . . . But what if you was fast asleep? . . . It's de same bed! How come de baby didn't cry out? . . . Isn't de man her daddy? Children know they fathers good-good!* Elderly women, the same ones who would scrimmage about town in defiance of their children's illusions of proper old-people behaviour, visited Neela every evening for weeks after the disappearance. They refused to enter her grandmother's house without a package of leftover stew or roti swaddled in napkins, sometimes even half-used bottles of cleaning supplies from under the sink. *Well, de girl looked sad last night, she was quiet-quiet,* they reported to the other ladies. *She still got her baby's things all over de house . . . Ow, poor Sugee and poor Sugee granddaughter, how can she sleep in dat bed? . . . She must put de baby's things away or they gon' make her go mad.*

Neela travelled to the capital city, hoping to discover where Jaroon could be—she knew it was suicide to try to track him on her own by returning to Nasee-Ki. But after she paid the government clerk to consult with other ministries and the airport, there was nothing, no file or trail with which to trace him. She stood on the flowered walkway that led into the Ministry of Citizenship, face toward the main street, where clunky cars and agile bicycles weaved scrappily between each other. Workers were dispersed around the government block in twos and threes, chatting and snacking, sitting on the edges of massive planters, oblivious to her brooding surveillance; the heat had bounced off the buildings and collided all morning long, gathering to a smoulder for noontime.

A soldier in the Ministry's entranceway lifted his standard-issue bayonet and circled its tip like a party noisemaker. "You can't loiter, honey," he called. "Builder Party property."

Neela flicked her hand at him and stepped from the block's luminous white concrete—she knew better than to rely on any authority's help, but the disappointment of the whole thing oppressed her nonetheless. Over the racket of a congested side street, she attempted to recall another detail, a forgotten fact of critical importance, something to snatch from her subconscious and tear back into the office with, *Yes, I remember he told me, de man said he was planning to* . . . But all that unfolded were wafting odours and sizzles from rundown restaurants and food stands owned by mister and missus call-name this, uncle and auntie call-name that.

Neela merged into the hungry lunchtime crowd snaking through hand-painted sidewalk signs that broadcast flashy, titillating messages—*Fried plantain and dumpling, get it while it's hot-hot-hot! Ice cream: guava and coconut swirl, refreshing! Rice and chicken or beef stew, spicy!* She was weak from hunger and prolonged, frantic exertion. Ever since the day she had lost Seetha, she had been desperate to recover those mysterious powers of hers once again—but now she understood their true fickleness, knew that their will to appear had little to do with her own. They refused to bless her with a usable gift to find her baby, no matter how she begged or how persistently her stomach ate into itself. She felt punished by and alienated from her powers, cursing their spiteful inconsistency, their cruel unwillingness to be harnessed at her time of greatest need.

She found the restaurant across the street from the national university, a tiny, shaded place that was heavy with the scent of fried dumplings. Students had crammed inside, sharing loud anecdotes and sopping up cheap meals on oil-soaked paper plates.

"I needed to see you in front of me," Karha said softly, reaching for Neela's hand across the table. In a different environment, people would have stared at these mismatched girls—*Eh-eh, what those two want with each other, pray, with them red and brown self? Don't they know what's happening in dis country nowadays?* But the patrons of such a humble eatery offered reprieve from that.

She closed her eyes. "I was foolish. I should-a left Marasaw long time. I knew he would-a come back to get me, I knew he would-a never let us be in peace, and still, I took de chance. I thought I would find a way, I thought something would-a come to me . . ."

"But I think he would-a follow you anywhere you went. Jaroon made plenty powerful friends, more than he had when we was in Eden. They say he's hooked up with these damn Builder Party people, they backing and protecting him now," Karha explained. "I don't think you could-a outrun him now. He can get anything he want and go anywhere now."

"But we can find some way to get back to Eden, right? He must return there sometime."

"Girl, you should hear de rumours. De government guarding him and de development closely, they getting fed up with how long it's taking to build de place. People say it's even harder to get out, and de soldiers gon' shoot any outsiders who try to get in. It's too dangerous. We got to find some other way."

Sorrowfully, Neela ran her fingertips across the patch of scars on Karha's arm; they had darkened and wrinkled. "How's it doing?"

Karha tapped the bumpy skin on her neck and collarbone, which would always feel numb, foreign. "Well, I rubbing it with leaf-oil like de women used to do back home. It's alright. I didn't forget you got your own wound to deal with." She lifted a few solitary grains of rice on a plastic fork and slid them into her mouth—the food had been purchased as an excuse to remain in the restaurant, but they had barely eaten.

"So what can we do now? If de government won't say where he is and de police won't move and we can't get back to Eden . . ."

"What about your brother, Neela? I wondering if he can try some-a his connections overseas. Maybe he might even know how to influence de people at Omega Global Ventures. You can get in touch with him?"

"I can't . . . I don't know where he is no more." She pursed her lips and gazed through the wide-open front of the restaurant. The university grounds appeared as ordered as the government block, studded with flowers in artful plantings that bore no resemblance to nature.

"But we can find out," Karha pressed. "I think he could help us. You told me he got a good position over there. Let's talk with your granny. You know how to get through to your mother, right?"

Yet when Neela didn't answer, cold and immobile and cheerless, Karha grew quiet and stared outside as well. She realized that it wouldn't be so simple for Neela to seek out Navi—that she would've done it already if she believed that she could.

Karha dug her fork into the plate in reflex, but when she suddenly recalled Seetha, how the child had screamed as they fled Eden, she dropped it in the food and left the meal untouched.

Since her exile from Nasee-Ki, Karha had been forced to attend the national university. "You must finish your degrees and stay right here with me from now on, I will care for you myself!" her father had decreed when she dragged her heavy feet through his door, grim and embattled. "Most red girls would die for de luxury you have!" She didn't explain why her resolve had broken and she had returned to that strict home, hiding evidence of burned skin and resigning herself to her father's techniques of cultivating dependence. Although she dutifully registered for the courses her father had instructed her to take, she preferred to spend her time in that tiny student restaurant and converse with the others—she was stunned to discover how much they knew about what was happening in Eden.

Instead of studying for her exams, she lurked through the corridors of the Ministry of Tourism to study Nasee-Ki's mercenary standing army; chronically procrastinating on her assignments, she searched for somebody who might have been in Eden after she and Neela had fled, someone who could inform her that the women were safe and the children were still learning. She tracked down a patient in the university's hospital and found him sickly, shrunken by a parasite into a skin-lined skeleton, shivering under a stained sheet and taking laboured pauses to swallow saliva. The man was a manual worker who had managed to escape the development by stowing away on a transport helicopter. Karha tucked a clean blanket behind his shoulder blades and sat beside his bed, whispering questions so the nurses wouldn't overhear.

He explained how a swell of soldiers had been sent to compel the resort construction forward, and how Jaroon had been granted new powers—the government had learned of the clout he had amongst Eden's inhabitants and gladly supported his rule for their own advantage. Workers were strictly guarded, rarely witnessing Jaroon or his close companions in person but certainly realizing his violent authority. What saddened Karha most was what had happened to her school. The man could not recall its presence; it had vanished after Jaroon's men burned it to the ground. No one had been left to fight for it.

Karha is trying to spread news all over the city, asking students to tell everyone about what happened. She's speaking to anybody she can find, but we can't go back to Eden and we still don't know where Jaroon is.

How could I let him take my child like that, out of my own bed? No matter what I try, nothing comes to me. I can't do anything to get her back. It's going to break me down, Granny. Drive me mad.

Neela shared another long visit with Baby, even though she had been ordered only to deliver food and scrub the outhouse. They sat together at the fold-out card table while Sally napped.

"You sure you don't want some?" Baby asked, holding a cup. "It's good to drink these things."

Neela sipped the lukewarm liquid hesitantly. It was syrupy and held a bitter undertaste. "What is it?"

"Cream soda. I mixed in some ginger root and spice here and there. It's not too tasty but it heals your insides."

Neela took an urgent gulp.

"Still nothing about Seetha, yeah? And your family ain't going to help you? Not even your brother?" Baby turned to observe some trinkets she had thrown in her bags from home, neatly lined up across a malformed cabinet in the corner of the room—miniature vases with colourful plastic flowers, carved birds made of red-purple wood, glossy white girls petting cartoonish puppies.

"I don't know what to think no more." Neela kept her eyes on the plastic striped tablecloth to dam her sneaking tears. "What can you tell me from your books, girl?"

Baby went over to the cabinet and slid its panel door carefully so as not to disturb the trinkets; they vibrated in place nonetheless. She retrieved a few books and opened one on the table, thumbing through its crackling translucent pages. She followed a sentence with her finger and mouthed the words to herself.

"Dis one says dat God sees things happening on earth . . . dat's good, right?" She smiled in satisfaction. She checked the spine of another book and cracked it down its dusty middle. "And dis one says if you behave good, good things will come to you." She moved to her last book. "I seeing here how God protect a man in his troubles, so dat ain't bad either . . ."

"How can you know real things from your books?"

"Well, I read them all, you know," she answered, a sense of accomplishment straightening her spine. "And when I was back home, I even went to services and prayers with my Auntie Mommy."

"But I don't know how dat gon' help you."

"What you mean? I always tell you good things from my books."

"Well, how I gon' know where to get help in dis damn town? And when will I see my child again? I don't understand what them books can do to help in my situation . . . or your situation . . ." Neela shook her head.

"You just got to read and think about them a little. It's hard to do, but you got to take your time and try . . ."

"But what I mean is dat I don't think they can help you understand what to do or what's happening to you. It's just words, talk. You know? Nice ideas dat can't truly do anything for you in de end."

Baby sulked and flicked her book's pages one by one, watching words and paragraphs and chapters breeze past. "But no one can understand nothing, then."

After sitting in silence for a while, Neela gathered herself together. "I sorry, Baby," she said, flattening her skirt. "I suppose it ain't for me. You right, I don't think I understand anything. I used to think I knew things, I thought I could do special things. But I know better now. I was foolish to think dat. I better go before Miss Leema frets on me again . . ."

Baby reached out to encourage her back to her chair.

Although her hand was cold and bony on Neela's wrist, it had the ability to comfort her disappointment. "What do you want me to say then?"

Neela looked at the girl's young face, how it was wounded.

"Tell me for true," Baby pressed.

"It's okay, Baby, don't worry with it."

"No, please tell me."

"I suppose . . . I suppose I want you to tell me what gon' happen to me now." She rubbed the scar on her shoulder. "It feels bad, Baby, real bad. I want you tell me dat some good spirit or something is watching over me and . . . and God don't want to punish me, he wants to give me and my baby blessings. And it will come to me soon, I will find some way to get her back again, to see her despite everything I done and de people I hurt, Lenda, Granny . . . my brother . . ." She closed her eyes tight. "I want you to say dat Seetha gon' remember me. I can't live if she forgets me, I can't live like dis . . ." She tightened her grip around Baby's hand.

"Ow, Neela." She came around the table to put her palm across Neela's forehead. It too was cool, the genuineness of its sympathy causing Neela's tears to fall again. "You really want know what I think?"

"Yes. Please."

"I don't know if it's possible dat Seetha can get a better life without her mother. My books don't say nothing about dat." She pulled Neela's head into her chest, the flowery pattern of her oversized housedress blurring in Neela's eyes. "But I do think Seetha gon' remember you. And you gon' always know her. Because mothers know they children and children know they mothers."

Baby tells me that good spirits must be helping Seetha. I don't have the faith to be so sure about those hidden things. It just feels like I'm being tortured.

They tell me to ask Navi for help. They think I'm staying away because of laziness or pride. But how can I ask him for anything? How can I ask any of you? I know none of you want to see me again. I caused you too much sadness and shame. I can't blame Navi for never wanting to come back here. I know he hates me.

I caused Seetha this. I think I deserve everything that has happened.

When people asked Neela how she was doing, she offered a bowing, noncommittal line, *I doing, I doing.* But if a neighbour probed more, she wasn't able to contain her contradicting interpretations—*He threaten to take de girl when I was in de bush, try to thief her even then to spite me! But what's de use in fretting now, they tell me. They say God knows de reason and they mus'ee right . . .* Neela started to speak like this to all of Marasaw, back and forth between bemoaning what Jaroon had done and grappling to find peace in it. As a child she had made hasty decisions and formed opinions with little reflection, but after Seetha was abducted at only three years of age, she couldn't latch herself to a fast belief. Instead, she swirled in mournful chaos, waffling between regrets and hopeful wishes for her baby, between dark malice against Jaroon and anxious prayers that she might see Seetha again.

She sought answers elsewhere. She attended the weekly Bible study at a local church, where many neighbours attended steadfast; she nodded to their exhortations, heartened devotees echoing the sentiment in a breathy, unified *yesss*. She visited the local temple and mosque as well. But although she had prayed and supped and meditated on holy words, she always returned to the silence of her grandmother's house dejected. *Seetha's gone and all you can do is talk to your damn self . . . but suppose one day she might come back and it gon' be alright . . . but how de man can do you dat, take your only joy left? . . . Maybe good spirits are watching Seetha . . . but what if she cries for her mother, who gon' answer?* The arguments battled each other in midnight dreams, her body gashed and bloodied between them. And every morning when she rose to do her work, her whispering mouth unwittingly planted these arguments throughout the town.

She still ached for a magical ability to arise prompt and mad within her, an advantage in her dire turn of events, but the power remained aloof. It seemed as if she couldn't do much of anything now, not even get her closest friend to forgive her. "I don't want to get blamed for making you miss your second degree!" she protested, when Lenda shoved her in front of the washboard.

Lenda thrust the hot iron in a passion. "Shut your mouth. Playing like you got loads-a time to argue with me!"

"You got to study!"

Lenda laughed crossly and cut her eye at the empty air. "Since when *you* telling *me* to study! You never did no school work! Too busy running around de place!" She went back to her ferocious ironing with even more determination.

A wave of water rocked and spilled on the floor when Neela slapped her hand against the wash basin. "I sorry, alright? I wish with all my heart you could know how I sorry I am!"

Muttering inaudibly to herself, Lenda focused upon the perfectly crisp shirt collar; it shone and smoked from being pressed over and over again.

"Please, hear me." Neela braced on the kitchen table and watched Lenda's back, how her elbow bent in and out mechanically and a cloud of steam lingered around her. "You was right, okay? I know I done you wrong. All these years I didn't really think about you. I went along my way and just, I don't know, assume you would want to follow." She turned to touch a wrinkled page from one of Lenda's textbooks, open on the table to crown a hill of articles. She followed the twists and turns of its creases with her thumb; the book had been studied so faithfully that its spine had split and innards of glue and stitching lay exposed. "I really didn't pay much mind to what you might-a wanted. Or needed."

Lenda placed the iron aside, tapered tip pointed up like a sinking ship. Her shoulders relaxed and she rested her hands on the opposite ends of the ironing board, stretching her arms straight, allowing her neck to fall low.

She wasn't the skinny girl with hair combed in beaded twists that Neela used to know. She was different, a woman now, mature and beautiful. "I want you to know how sorry I am for all I done to you. I need you so much. I think . . . I think I would truly die without you."

Lenda turned her head to the mangled mesh door that separated the house from the backyard—only broad shadows of banana leaves could be detected, shivering in the darkness, hiding in it as if they had done wrong. Water broke and ran along her cheeks, visible when it glinted in the candlelight on the way down.

Neela stepped forward and rested her forehead in the dip between Lenda's shoulders. "I don't deserve you," she sniffed, observing her own tears drop and darken patterns on Lenda's college uniform. "You been so good to me, so loyal. I never deserved friendship like dat." She curled her arms around Lenda's waist and locked her fingers together. "I can't expect you to run after me now and fix my mess. It ain't right no more."

Lenda tapped the shirt collar to feel if it had been scorched by the iron's heat, and pressed her head back to rest on Neela's. "I just don't know how it get like dis between us," she said, staring at the black ceiling, "like everything just falling apart."

"Oh Len," Neela choked, breathing Lenda's coconut-oil hair.

"You was my best friend. I ran after you because-a dat."

"But you still my best friend."

Lenda remembered how the two of them would linger outside in the dwindling light as children, ignoring the hunger growling in their bellies and the magnetic promise of dinner.

They would saunter along the main road, kicking their feet leisurely and hugging each other close although they should have gone home; heads rested together, the two would whisper wicked things about the other girls at school and giggle in conspiracy. *When she talks to de boys, you can see she thinks she's cute! But I does watch them, you know, not one-a them boys pay her any mind, you know* . . . As the sky got deep and speckled by stars and their breath rubbed against each other's skin, Lenda was secure in their intimacy, despite her mother's certain wrath at her disobedience. She simply pressed further into Neela's arms, warming herself in the cooling night air, and always found boldness to stay out later.

Their commitment had developed into a habit as they became women, time-ripened familiarity more unyielding than an emotional drive to love. Lenda had changed when Neela ran away from Marasaw, finally granted the space to grow up and into herself, yet the routine of their friendship had automatically reassembled upon her return. She wondered if it was foolhardy to renounce something so relentless and fundamental, regardless of how exasperating it could be—she pondered the courage Neela had given her back then, and decided that the consequences of losing her would be graver.

"You too." Lenda snorted softly, her eyes shutting. "But I got to say, you truly a mad woman, Neela. You gon' kill me, you know dat?"

Neela couldn't help but smile. She lifted her hands to Lenda's braids and stroked their smooth, rounded bumps. A silky, fragrant coconut residue varnished her fingertips.

"Alright, stop wasting time and concentrate on your washing. You got to collect more cash to go to de police dis week."

Money was especially scarce because Neela had been dedicating fewer hours to her steady job. She knew that Miss Leema was growing weary of her requests to start work in the afternoon, due to early police station visits and meetings with Karha in the city. More than that, she was increasingly battered by Miss Leema's open irritation toward her—the old woman undoubtedly received the other girls' reports of how Neela would talk with Baby for long stretches of time, coaching her to care for Sally as if she were a normal baby. Miss Leema would suspiciously scrunch her eyes the moment Neela passed through the property's filigree iron gates, uneasy that she was being corrupted against the missus and the family by Baby's tall tales.

"I got to tell you something," Neela said soberly in the shack's humid backroom after she had fetched lunch. As Baby bounced a grinning Sally on her hip, she bent into the blackened chair behind the door, aching and embattled like one of Marasaw's elders.

Baby allowed Sally to wriggle down her body and stamp around the floor. She sat on the bed, uneasy. "What happen?"

"Girl, things still ain't looking good for me here. It's starting to get worse. I know they ain't happy with me taking so much time to look for Seetha. You should see how Miss Leema does behave towards me. I don't think they gon' keep me here for too much longer . . ."

"But you always stay late to finish your work!" Baby

exclaimed. "And they can't tell you nothing, they would do de same thing if what happen to you were to happen to them!"

Neela chuckled sadly. "I don't think you wrong about dat, Baby, but things ain't so simple. I really gon' miss spending time with you and Sally," she said softly, face fallen to her lap.

Alarm flashed over Baby's features. "What? But . . . no, it not gon' happen, it can't happen like dat! They got to let you stay!"

"It's not just what they want to do. I myself don't think I can last too much longer." Neela bowed forward and rested a hand on Baby's stiffened leg, feeling the sharp edges of the girl's bones under thin layers of nightgown fabric and flesh. "I think I gon' go back to de old laundry work. It gon' be hard to make ends meet but I think it's de only thing I can do right now. It's impossible to hold on to any real job and keep dis search going at de same time. I thought it would be better to tell you now so you can prepare yourself . . ." Neela's small voice collapsed when Baby's leg muscle slackened beneath her hand, losing whatever strength it had had. "I don't want to do dis, child. I know we gon' miss each other bad. But I really don't know what other option I got. I'm so sorry."

Silent, Baby slowly shifted her leg away from Neela and pressed her knees together protectively. She rotated her head to look away and stared at a spot on the grainy plank floor, expression made of iron.

"No, please," Neela pleaded, approaching to sit next to Baby, "don't do dat to me. It gon' be okay, Baby, look. Look at your daughter, Sally, how nice de child's growing these days, and it's you taking care of her, all on your own now . . ." She twisted eagerly to locate Sally. The little girl's diapered bottom was pointed high to the sky and her arms were anchored around her calves; she was absorbed in discovery of the upside-down world that existed between her legs. "You don't worry. Things gon' be okay. I am so proud-a you, I see you come a long way. You doing so well these days and I know you and Sally gon' be fine . . ."

But Baby was stoic as a sculpture, utterly unresponsive. She had sunk into herself with a solid, angry chin.

"Baby, please answer me. I don't want to leave you dis way," Neela pressed, now too nervous to touch her. "Please tell me what you thinking. Say something to me." She waited, hoping for the slightest acknowledgment in the room's rising temperature, but Baby wouldn't budge—she hardly seemed to be breathing.

Unable to express her upset, Neela eventually slid to her feet and watched around the other end of the room. Even young energy couldn't survive in such heat—Sally had tired of exploration and slumped onto her pink play blanket in a half-dozing state, head against the rigid bed leg. Neela scooped the toddler up and delicately placed her on the mattress near the small of Baby's unyielding back. Concerned about being caught out of the house too long, she started to make her way out.

"It's my cousin."

Neela turned around. Baby hadn't moved.

"My cousin Davin. He's Sally's father."

She leaned against the door, quiet.

"Davin was my only friend," Baby explained. "I grow up with him and my Auntie Mommy and Uncle Byeo. They was my only family. My mommy died long time." She brushed her fingers over her damp forehead. "Davin's older than me but he was like my brother, we would get on so good. No one else would worry with me. None-a de girls in my class would even talk to me or eat with me at lunch. Especially de pretty ones. You know them kind-a girls?" She finally looked at Neela, countenance livened. "They not afraid-a nothing, no boy, no teacher, no big man calling out his car for them. They don't care who see, they hike up their school kilts and show de whole world their bare skin like grown women. And I notice how they loosen out their hair and let it fly free, just so. Auntie Mommy always made me plait my hair or clip it or put it in a bun, from since kindergarten. But I wanted to let my hair out, just like them bad girls."

Neela stepped closer. "Why didn't you say nothing about Davin before?"

"I don't know." Baby shrugged. She became suddenly broody and swung her view to the floor again. "I thought I could wait till later, but now . . . I never told no one nothing. I didn't know Sally was in my belly for a long time. Auntie Mommy was mad dat I was getting sick and I didn't get no blood, and then my stomach started to puff out. They told me I was pregnant. They thought I was hiding it from them but I didn't really know." Agitated, she scratched her ear and slapped her hand to the mattress. "I didn't know what Davin wanted. Everyone was asleep and I thought he was sneaking into my room to get me to watch television with him." She breathed out. "It happen plenty more times after dat."

"Is dat why you in dis shack?"

Baby affirmed it with only a slight bob of her head. "Auntie Mommy and Uncle Byeo pack my books and clothes and send me away. Uncle Byeo's cousin lives here with her family, she's your missus. They used to let me stay in de house, but when Sally was born they made us come out here."

Neela watched Baby, wondering if she apprehended the depth of calamity in what she revealed. "Your cousin," she ventured cautiously, "he force you?"

Baby paused to examine her fingernails, soon curling her fingers in a tight ball. "I used to pretend I was studying at break time, in de yard, with my head stuck in a book, you know," she answered with an embarrassed smile. "But I would always make sure I was close to them bad girls. They was my favourite out-a all de girls at school. They would collect in a circle and I could hear them talking about de senior boys—you should-a hear them, Neela. They would call dis one stupid and dat one ugly and de next one dirty. De senior boys! I could-a never understand how brazen they were, not afraid of nothing!" The memory dissolved and set into her tranquil face.

Neela stooped to the floor by Baby's feet, folding her knees up under her chin.

Hugging her arms over her chest, Baby laid her head on the pillow beside Sally, who was napping peacefully unaware. "I would always wish to be like them bad girls at my school," she whispered. "They weren't scared-a nobody, no boy, no matter who he was or what he tell them or how he push them. And they would-a never been scared to lose friends, even if they was going to lose their only friend in the whole world, it wouldn't really bother them. No, they pretty and smart and shameless. They would-a just skip off and make a new friend, easy-easy. Them bad girls would-a been able to handle Davin good, you know. They would-a just cuss him off with one bad piece-a cuss. He would-a truly meet his match."

For the first time, Neela felt free to quarrel with Miss Leema. She charged through the back of the house, straight into the kitchen. "What y'all been doing to dat poor girl is a sin!"

Miss Leema's initial surprise congealed into outrage at the prohibited backtalk. "How dare you, dat ain't your business! Eh-eh!"

"How dare dis family behave so wicked!" She conjured every hurt she had felt for Baby, watching the girl so depressed and alone that she relied on Neela's friendship to survive. "God gon' cast down fire for all de bad you people done de child and her baby!"

"And what right you have?" the old lady answered, even more astounded. "You think it's right to talk off your head about things you don't know?"

"I know everything, hear me?" Neela called out the kitchen entrance, where the other girls were eavesdropping and snickering with each other. "It ain't de girl's fault dat de boy forced himself on her! And it ain't right for them to cover it up by locking Baby away, punishing her just to save face . . ."

"Shut your filthy mouth, you little whore! Get out-a dis house right now and don't you ever think-a coming back for nothing!"

Neela was already halfway out, elbowing through the clump of stunned girls, hammering her feet on those rich mahogany floors.

"Don't let me see your face again or I gon' get de guard dogs on you!"

Even though it was the best outfit she owned, Neela went home and promptly burned her blouse-and-skirt uniform with the rest of the trash.

Neela continued to argue at the local police station, sending letters to the Ministry of Citizenship and scrimping money to meet Karha at the university. She didn't stop when the Ministry no longer sent replies, or when her too-common presence aggravated the policeman at the front desk—*You got to stop dis madness and go along your way! I sorry but dat's all I can say!* She remained fervent for answers, impatient for news that might reveal a sign of her child's return. But when many months had passed and no amount of bribes or stubbornness or anxiety had brought her closer to Seetha, silence threatened to settle inside of her.

I lost my only child, my only family left in dis world, and there ain't nothing I can do, why ain't there nothing I can do? She lamented at night in the same old cot, fingertips against her marred shoulder blade. Every part of her body—broadened hips, puffed belly, widened breasts—was an indication of Seetha's entrance into her life three years ago. As a wound inflicted the first time her child was almost stolen away, that scar was the only physical remnant of Neela's loss, the dark crevice hardly traceable outside. She kept herself in weightless sleep, wondering how she could fake normality and be so gapingly vacant without Seetha, how she was too shockingly inept to unearth her old magic as a guide now. *He took her and I didn't do nothing to stop it. There ain't nothing coming to help me, even to let me know if she's alive. It's my fault.* She touched the scar as she cleaned during the day and tossed in bed at night, to suffer the corporeal reminder of her child's disappearance, to make it into something more than mere neighbourhood rumours and useless arguments with authorities, to experience it on her flesh again and again.

Her hand had immediately drifted to that scar the evening a peculiar bird landed on the backyard porch, close to the bubbling wash. It was small, feathers fresh as the fruits of the marketplace, greens and blues and reds and yellows of the Nasee-Ki. Neela dropped the dripping bedsheet she was stringing on the clothesline, awaiting a moment to creep toward the bird. During her childhood years, hours of playing in the sun, wandering back roads and abandoned paths in the company of wild puppies, resting in long grass with her face to the sky, she hadn't seen such a beautiful thing pass through Marasaw.

It didn't deter her when Lenda called from inside the house. "You done yet? Come quick and fold these before they get mash up!"

The bird hopped a few paces and twitched its head, yet unprepared to fly off—Neela kept moving slow, stooped, noiseless. She watched in wonder; its ruffling feathers seemed to mock her as they shimmered through the colour spectrum. Her fingers finally glided from her shoulder blade.

"What are you doing!" Lenda flinched at the back door as Neela used her whole body to topple the wash bucket over the spot where the bird was perched. Scorching suds and fabric splashed out to soak the concrete and scald Neela's arms, but she didn't start; she simply glowered at the creature. It launched high above her head, reflexes too sharp for it to be affected by anything she tried to do.

"You mad?" Lenda exclaimed, scurrying around the boiling spill and cradling Neela's arms. "You burn youself! Why you do dat? Look at me!"

Neela didn't speak, but her eyes were fixed upward.

Lenda tugged at her shoulders. "Answer me, Neela! You mad?"

Neela remembered the rest as a trance, awake but floating in thickness, not enough presence to curse the aggravated tears behind her eyes. Lenda's fretting was far from her deadened senses—*So dis girl's ready to hurt herself and don't want give me an answer, dat's it?* She hardly experienced being dragged into the house, chill of cocoa butter on her scalded arms, relieving restriction of rags over blisters. *Carrying on like a mad woman now, what good it gon' serve to behave so? How it gon' make people help you, huh? It gon' bring de child back?* As Lenda led her upstairs, Neela could only gather enough awareness to focus on her shoulder scar beating hot blood at the memory of that bird—those exasperating rainbow wings, such careless, mystical beauty. *Tell me how dis nonsense gon' bring Seetha back!* Infuriated by the bird's appearance in her backyard, its autonomy and ability to go where it fancied, she couldn't stand to see it alive.

Whatever magic might have remained from her young life—whatever gifts that appeared when and how they pleased, to overtake her and those around her—had finally slipped from Neela for good.

⁓

Marasaw was soon granted a fresh batch of local gossip—the neighbours' curiosity was piqued the moment they saw a baggy-dressed, wild-haired girl shuffling down the road with a whimpering toddler at her side. *Can you show me where my friend lives, she's in her grandmother's house, you can tell me which one it is?* Neela returned home that breezy evening to find Baby peeping in through her back door amidst linens that fluttered and snapped like flags.

Sally whined until her mother let her wander and put her hands on everything in the strange new environment. "I come here to tell you something," Baby said, warning Sally to stay away from the cupboard doors. "I giving you Sally to keep."

"What nonsense you telling me, Baby?" Neela pressed her fingertips to her head. "Oh no. Do they know you gone? Where y'all gon' go?"

Baby scolded her child when she tried to climb up to the stove burner. "I told them I ain't coming back ever again, dat I got to see you and they can't do nothing to stop me. Miss Leema slap me and tell me to go along my way, and de missus say if you want me you can have me."

Neela groaned, collapsing her neck backward and gazing at the ceiling, exhausted. It seemed lower than usual, as if it were finally buckling down on her.

"It's alright, don't worry about me. I doing de right thing and now it gon' all work out 'cause I giving you Sally."

"I ain't taking de girl from you!"

Sally sulked when Baby attempted to tug a towel from her grasp. "But no! You got to, dat's why everything happen! You got to take Sally!"

"What one-a your cockeyed books tell you dat, Baby?"

"I read it last night and it make me understand everything! How come you get de job and find me and Sally and why poor Seetha disappear and your family can't help you and you lost your job and can't come to see me no more, I understand dat I got to be brave and bring Sally to you! Dat's why I get her in de first place!"

"You talking stupidness," Neela said.

"No, it's true!" she urged. "It say I must gird myself in strength and don't be frightened of de sword and de elements, de children of my loins gon' prosper in a new land! So Sally gon' got to be yours now dat Seetha gone, dat's why I come here, why I had her! For you!"

"Oh my goodness, Baby, no, you understand me?"

"You got to!"

"I ain't taking your child from you!"

"But you need her!" she shouted, flushing red with nervousness. "You need family more than me."

Baby unsteadily bent her knees to the floor and sat crosslegged in guarded quietness, observing Sally's reserved play in the wake of harsh adult voices.

Neela was silent too. When she slid her chair with a dull squeak and finally arose, she kneeled beside Baby and wrapped her in a close embrace. "Baby," she exhaled into the girl's frizzy hair. "Please don't tell nobody what I gon' tell you. Don't even say nothing to Lenda. I can't really ask my family for help. They don't want nothing to do with me. I wish I could find Navi. Maybe he could help, but I know he won't. Not after all dat happen between us. He hates me and to tell you de truth, I understand. And it don't seem like I got de power left to do nothing no more. I thought I had strength but I don't. I never told nobody about dis." She breathed out hard.

They held on to each other for a long time.

Baby and Sally lived with Neela after that—Neela instructed Baby on her housework, when to turn the fire down on the curry and how to scrub the laundry spotless. In between her studies, Lenda showed Baby how to iron and fold clothes to keep wrinkles out. "Dis is by far de most important part," she explained, watching the iron's steam. "If you don't do it right, de people don't care how clean you get their clothes . . ." It wasn't long before Baby turned into a capable helper.

As Neela had done for Seetha, she and Baby used every opportunity to teach Sally how to speak, encouraging her to spell and identify implements around the house, to number briefs and socks pitched into the wash basin. Neela insisted that Baby do her own learning every night as well; although she didn't attend a real school, Baby would transform into a dutiful pupil as Lenda tested techniques from her Principles of Instructing Adolescent Children course.

People in town say that Baby and Sally are slow, Neela wrote on the backyard porch, sitting on her grandmother's makeshift board-and-block bench while Lenda and Baby worked on math problems in the kitchen. *They say that's what happens when people are inbred and born in sin. But I don't believe it. Those girls are very smart. Lenda is teaching Baby everything and she's catching on fast. And you should see how Sally is a busybody and likes to touch everything . . .*

She was diverted by fluttering in the corner of her eye. A bird had landed on the clothesline, the same kind as the one she had tried to destroy with her blistering laundry—it still flaunted its colours, even in the feeble fire-lamp she used to write to her grandmother. But this time she felt no furious jealousy, no violent frustration at the bird's rare emergence. Only weariness. *I can't stop myself from looking for Seetha. I'll do anything for her. But what if nothing comes to me? Will I be without her, my only family in the world, forever?* She heard Lenda and Baby laughing inside the house, celebrating some hard-won arithmetic victory.

I know I can't lie to you. I don't have anything left inside of me that will help me find my Seetha. It's all gone now and I'm here, sick, foolish, dying. How could I explain it to Navi? I don't have a right to expect him to care. Neela brought her fingertips to the scar once more as the bird picked at tender flesh underneath its shiny green-blue feathers. *Those things aren't mine anymore.* She couldn't stand the thought of looking up to see the clothesline empty.

CHAPTER 13

Barefoot and tiptoeing, Baby crept into Neela's room—only she and Sally were home, and Sally was sound asleep in the other bedroom. She clicked the door shut behind her and knew exactly where to go. The night before, she had peeked in the doorframe's slice of light and seen Neela standing motionless, a single sheet balanced on her hands; her smile was sapped of vigour and she skimmed the words in front of her. Baby almost knocked on the door, stopping herself when Neela's face slumped and she clapped the sheet in half. She buried it hurriedly in a crate at the bottom of her closet, eager to disregard its existence yet incapable of actually throwing it away. Neela collapsed backward into bed, still in her work clothes. She hadn't gotten up to change by the time Baby finally abandoned the surveillance.

Digging through a mound of clothes, Baby excavated the crate, but wouldn't risk carrying it over to the bed; she rustled through it behind the shield of the closet's open door instead. *From long time,* she thought to herself, *I could sneak good.* She wiped moisture from her top lip and passed sweaty fingers over her shorts, not wanting to leave handprints behind.

The crate had been stuffed with letters penned in Neela's hand. She thumbed through them and felt another kick of guilt, particularly since they were all addressed to Neela's grandmother. The letters were dated at the top, the earliest ones hidden more than a year ago and the latest only yesterday. She realized that the many nights she had seen Neela stay awake to write were not as they had appeared—her letters never made it to the post office. Yet after Neela had started whispering cryptic regrets about what had happened between her and her family, after her constant insistence that she had done too much wrong and was already dead in their eyes, Baby could hardly be surprised.

Familiar names sparked on each page, Nasee-Ki and Lenda and Karha and Sally; Baby might have wanted to drape herself over a pillow and decipher the connected story they told, but there was something more important to do. She found what she needed on a slip tucked deep in the crate's corner. In her mounting paranoia she thought she heard feet, a stranger coming to catch her transgression, shuffling over the stairs irregularly—stopping and starting, two steps up, one step down. Her stomach burned with nervousness although she had become well acquainted with the groaning of this old house. She shoved the scrap of paper into her pocket and madly rearranged the letters to imitate randomness. She muffled the closet door's snap and slipped away from the bedroom.

~~~~~

Neela pedalled as fast as she could manage while balancing her mountains of laundry. Although she had done it night after night, the effort still planted stinging pepper in her calves and shins. She released her grip on the handlebars to tuck tickling strands of hair away from her cheeks, but had to slap her hands right back to avoid losing balance altogether. *Blasted bicycle,* she growled to herself, resenting the fact that she had to ride with such cumbersome burdens. She rolled beside the trench to rest, with a throbbing leg as a kickstand, envisioning herself dumping everything—bicycle and laundry together— into the muddy water for good. In fact, she wanted to abandon more than that; she'd rip out her too-long hair, kick her sandals off, even toss her makeshift cleaning uniform into the trench. The neighbours would be subject to great trauma witnessing her rebirth, unable to avert their eyes from her naked, bald and free march. *Well, dis is it, de girl lost her mind, what I tell you, it finally happened* . . . Neela would stare straight into their faces and laugh loud with a big open mouth. *And now she's laughing us! Mad for true!*

Neela pedalled to her grandmother's house and dumped armfuls of clothes on the porch, holding her breath so she wouldn't have to inhale their stale, grubby filth. She decided not to have dinner—Lenda would fret at her rejection of the precious fish stew, red goop whisked and spiced in breaks between textbooks, but Neela rarely had an appetite at night. All she ever wanted to do was slink into her bed and be at peace in her sleeplessness, picturing her daughter with a hand on that pulsing scar, envisioning her strong and cheerful and smiling. No laundry or ironing, no pitying friends, no attempts at strained chatter. Just imaginings of Seetha's far-off face in the darkness.

But there was no hope of that, not with the muttering that rumbled low in the backyard. She stepped lightly so no one would notice her steal upstairs, but her feet stuck at the first step. There was something different about this conversation. She twisted her neck at the murmur of an unfamiliar voice, deep and inhibited; the other, familiar voices let out nervy giggles in response.

He sat on the warped wood bench, Lenda and Baby opposite him with courteously crossed legs. The cutting whiteness of his suit blended into bedsheets on the clothesline and reflected the moon's gleam. All three of them looked to Neela as she propped the screen door with her foot.

"Hi, Neela," Navi said. They watched each other, expressionless. She noticed that he held a glass of Baby's special cream soda.

Lenda dropped her head and Baby closed her eyes; before words could emerge from Neela's mouth, her body had propelled her away.

"Wait!" Baby pleaded, scurrying to catch up before Neela made it down the front porch. "Don't go! It's not his fault, it's mine!"

Neela stopped near the dirty laundry's stink.

Baby attempted to smooth the wrinkles from her dress, instinctively making herself more presentable. "It was me,

I asked him to come. I know I shouldn't have done it. I didn't mean to make you mad . . ."

Neela was all of a sudden dizzy in the windless weather. "Baby, why would you do dat?" she asked, as words jumbled in her mouth. She pressed against the railing to prevent herself from toppling down the stairs.

"And I know I shouldn't have gone into your private things, I just wanted his address." She wiped gathering tears and sucked an anxious breath. "And I shouldn't have sent him no letter without telling you but I wanted to do it so bad, I know you wouldn't let me, but from all you tell me . . . I know he would come back if I could just explain everything dat happen . . ."

Neela fought nausea and held her head to the sky.

Baby sniffled, unsuccessfully steeling herself against the temptation to cry.

"Come on, don't get upset, I ain't really angry at you. I know you didn't mean no harm, but you just don't understand these things . . ."

"I know I don't understand," Baby moaned and buried her face in her hands. "I don't understand nothing!"

"Baby. Please, stop now."

Lenda crept to the doorway with Navi close behind, neither of them venturing to step onto the porch. Neela set herself toward the street, both hands steadied on the railing, monitoring the sparkling of dust on the road.

"Navi?" Baby squeaked through her sobs. "I'm very sorry. I didn't tell her you was coming."

"It's alright," he mumbled.

Lenda cleared her throat definitively. "Okay, come with me, Baby, alright? Let's go upstairs. It's late. Leave it alone now."

Baby followed Lenda, but she looked back at Neela—how pale and tired she was, how her shoulders had shrunk and curled into themselves like the corners of aged paper. The thought that she could lose her only friend to despair and helplessness, the only support she had left in the world, made her breath wobble and fail inside her chest. "Will you help us?" she whispered, trembling, unsure of whom to look to. "We can't find Seetha and we don't know what to do now."

Navi lowered his head, conscious of his recently born habit of wearing socks and shoes everywhere. No longer did he reside in a rented apartment. Soon after a promotion to regional director, he had purchased an impressive townhouse overseas in his home city, one rectangle that slotted into a select string of rectangles surrounding an unbefitting garden in the heart of downtown. Yet even in his new home, his feet were shrouded by fabric and leather. Returning to Marasaw gave him a rare glimpse of his stubby toes. "I didn't even know you had a baby. You didn't say anything to us."

The sound of her brother's voice, after everything that had happened, stole Neela's words away. She couldn't respond.

Navi noticed her feeble respiration, how the air barely provoked her gaunt frame to move against the backdrop of the street—she seemed different to him, lessened in a way that ran deeper than her physical state. The fear she had once instilled in him was remote, unconnected to the dispirited woman in front of him now.

"It's been . . . very hard," Baby tenuously responded. "I don't really think she wanted to hide it from you." They all stood where they were and listened to Baby's fading sniffles, the coarse howling of a neighbour's dog across the way, the serenading insects. "You gon' help us, Navi?"

He nodded back. Neela didn't see him do it, but Baby figured that she knew he had.

In a fitful sleep that night, Neela saw herself as a child—young Navi, dressed in his old elementary school uniform, calculated a compound sum in front of an auditorium of captive adults. *Twelve hundred thousand minus eight hundred and sixty-seven* . . . He was the only contestant in this competition; she glanced around the place in alarm, eager to find a face that wasn't washed by blankness, eyes that were not shackled to the stage. Her heart galloped in terror that her brother would win the contest . . . *four hundred and thirty-five by ninety-three divided by* . . . She found herself twisting in her seat, yanking the ends of her own pigtails. Soon, the room began to warp around her.

When she could no longer stand Navi's numerical drone, she leaped to her feet. "Stop it!" she screamed. "Stop it! Stop it!"

Navi glanced to her in the back edge of the auditorium and hardened his body. He began to calculate more resolutely, more frantically. *Nine hundred and forty-seven! By six thousand five hundred and eighty-four!* he shouted.

She staggered out of the aisle and rushed toward the stage, feet uncontrollable and tripping over each other with every step.

"No more!" Her anger and fear transformed into tremendous desperation. "I can't take it no more! Please, Navi, no more!"

Two million! By four hundred! And fifty-five thousand!

Fingers clawed in attack, Neela flew onto the stage with a singular desire to smother her brother's endless sum. *Five hundred! And ninety-three thousand!* Yet before she could assault him, she stumbled and crashed to the floor.

"Stop, Navi, stop it!" she cried, writhing at his oiled elementary school shoes, fists against her temples. "Please, no more, no more!"

But he wouldn't pause, not even to pity her in her agony. The whole auditorium, cumbersome and lethargic, started to double over on itself; it folded again and again, gaining momentum with every rotation, soon arcing into the strained shape of a giant, swirling hole. She couldn't save herself from its powerful swing and jarring tremors, from being mercilessly shaken into its black centre. The sensation of falling woke her with a start.

Baby was across the hallway in the other bedroom, on an uncomfortable mattress. Sally snored at the far end of the room in her little cot, barricaded in position by a mass of pillows. Tonight, Baby was awake and restless and all too conscious of Navi's extraordinary presence on the living-room couch. She slipped her hand under her nightgown and traced the path of the stretch marks that had formed when she was pregnant, imagining them as rivers spread across the landscape of her stomach.

She shot up and jerked her nightgown down when the bedroom door creaked open. "What happen?"

Neela crouched beside the bed, messy hair creating an outlandish shadow above her head. "I want to know what you told him," she whispered, so as not to wake Sally. Baby noticed that her voice was edged. "What did you write to him about?"

"I just . . . I told him about Seetha and how we been looking all over de place for her. I only said what I know, I didn't tell him nothing dat . . ."

"Did he tell my grandmother anything? What about my mother?" Neela gripped Baby's bony elbow and shoved in closer, cornering her. "Did he say anything to them?"

Baby tried to ease back but Neela pinched her arm and made her wince. She was startled by the odd aggression and her muscles began to tremble. "Well, I really don't . . . don't know for sure . . ."

"You have to know, Baby! Tell me de truth! He told them, yes? They know and you can't watch me in me eye and lie about it!"

"But I ain't lying, I promise . . . I only told him . . ."

Sally let out a yelp and kicked at her fortress of pillows— she coughed and whined in the throes of a dream. They froze until her snores bucked and revved up, rattling strong once again. Neela was haloed by light trickling into the room through the space between the wall and the ceiling, and Baby saw her tightness wither away.

Neela slumped on her heels and rubbed her old scar. "Oh no," she breathed, dejected, "I shouldn't-a . . . I didn't mean to frighten you . . ."

Baby hugged her stomach to soothe her tremors. "It's alright, it's alright . . ."

Neela nodded remorsefully, sluggishly stretching herself up in exhaustion. Before she could get to her feet, Baby found a handful of her nightgown and guided her to sit on the bed.

"Wait." She leaned close to Neela's ear. "I was trying to tell you dat I told Navi not to say nothing about what happen to your granny or your mommy. I don't think he told anybody."

"You did? How did you know to say dat?"

Baby shrugged and softly rested her temple on Neela's shoulder, never uncharitable with her trust for very long. "I see you. I know plenty about shame."

The thick smell of saltfish seeped upstairs, snaking through wood and mosquito netting and fabric to draw Neela's eyelids open. Sun had elbowed between the curtain's threads and she squinted into light, rubbing her milky eyes, trying to decipher movements downstairs. She knew that Lenda had come by before her Saturday morning Aspiring Educators debate group meeting at the college. She pictured Lenda hunched over the stove as fish bubbled in a riotous jump-up with tomato and onion; Lenda would be wearing that faded denim dress, her weekend uniform—its front already freckled in beads of oil, despite her every attempt to remain at a safe distance from the pot. Sampling a chunk of saltfish, Lenda would be reflecting on Neela's poor choices, why this fleshy white-pink cut of fish tasted too salty, too fishy. *After all dis time in dis damn town,* she'd carry on, *dat girl still can't handle herself in de market . . .*

Baby would be playing with Sally, both in wrinkled night-gowns and manoeuvring the pointed toes of shabby dolls, their hair sticking up every which way. Lenda would stoop to spoon some steaming hot stew into Baby's mouth and cause her to blow heavy breaths after each chew; Baby would nod in false approval, as if she could actually taste the food. Neela smiled at the image of the girl's expression as she bravely disguised her watering eyes and scorched tongue, combatting the urge to spit the saltfish on the floor with a barbaric hack. But Neela frowned as her mind swerved in a different direction—she found that she couldn't picture where Navi was or what he was doing.

In fact, he had gotten up early that morning, head beating from jet lag and spine warped from his grandmother's prehistoric couch. He had stumbled around the living room to find his pants and shirt and eased out of the front door to lean against the porch's railing. Every time he came back, the town seemed so much smaller than he remembered—he scrutinized the road, the shacklike houses, the distant hills, once again needing to reconcile perception with memories. Night insects were flipping and humming, making final preparations for their approaching daylight rest. Marasaw was a ghost town in every direction; he sensed no movement beyond the swatting ears of a gang of donkeys near the trench, asserting their turf in a groggy trance.

Borrowing a pair of stretched flip-flops, Navi lumbered along the roadside to catch what was left of the nighttime breeze. He was reminded of how brazen the sun was here in contrast to overseas, already threatening to smoulder big and thick and near the horizon. He crossed the road to kick into the grassy yard of his old high school, slapping at prickling burrs fastened to his pant legs and swatting mosquitoes that circled his head.

Compared to the imposing regal high schools abroad, forged of brick and stone and marble, this wooden one appeared like a broken shed. But he could recall how exhilarating it had been to step in for the first time—Marasaw High School was one of the biggest buildings he had ever been inside back then, and its yard had seemed to spill in abundance for miles around. He remembered how accomplished he had felt ascending those front planks, dressed in a crisp new uniform, too old for shorts; he had swelled with pride at the opportunity to perspire in tweed pants. He had loved how his textbooks collapsed heavily in his knapsack. They had dragged solid at the small of his back, as if trying to persuade him to run home, to return to elementary school and protect himself in its familiarity. But he wouldn't have any of it.

I see it different than you—he remembered what Baby had revealed to him in her bubble script. The sight of the envelope's blue and white airmail bands and forwarding marks had hardened him, turned him righteous against the outsider that his grandmother had carelessly offered his old student apartment mailing address to. Navi knew how they judged him now—they thought him rich and naive, they were convinced he would send money to any fool who claimed that his grandmother was their *good-good* friend. But when he slipped out the weathered paper and was faced with the peculiarly articulate writings of a child, he was suddenly bewildered. *You don't know who I am. But Neela tell me all sort of things about when you were at home in Marasaw. She told me not to say nothing to anyone, but I know I can speak to you. You know all about it anyhow.*

Navi's first impulse was to crumple the letter in a ball and spin it down the metal corridor of the garbage chute, but it embodied such profound sincerity that he kept reading. *I understand why you got mad at each other and why you both ran away from home. You must think Neela was only trying to get you mad. You thought she wanted to ruin you . . .* This examination of his childhood, dissected and recast by a stranger's hand, stunned him more than it angered him; he slid to the cold floor of his echoing kitchen. *But I read about life in my books and I see things very different. You two don't understand it because you're brother and sister. Brothers and sisters don't understand things like that. But I think you got each other so upset because you were close in your spirits. So close that you didn't like it and didn't know what to do with it.*

Baby had pleaded with him, begged him to come home and to reveal the contents of her letter to no one. He could hardly process the details she had exposed—that his sister had given birth to a child he knew nothing of, had hidden Seetha's existence for three years and then said nothing to her family about the abduction. But the amazement he found in Baby's bluntness ran further than the facts of this outrageous situation. *You might not believe me, but Neela isn't the same any more. Something happened to her when Seetha disappeared. She changed. You might worry but I don't think she could hurt you anymore. She's too hurt herself. She would never ask you, but I know she needs you. Please believe me, Navi, I know you can help her . . .*

Against his better judgment, he decided to do what this child asked of him even though he didn't know her real name—she had signed the letter *Baby* and drawn a lopsided heart beside it. Her words were compellingly unhindered, her intimate knowledge and bold-faced entreating so convincing. But Navi was certain that he would come to regret his decision to return.

⁓

Navi spent his time in Marasaw searching for and meeting with as many government officials in the capital city as he could, bribing as many policemen as he could afford. He retraced the steps Neela had made over the last several months, believing that his new-found influence in the Ministry of Foreign Investment would bless him with success where she had received none. He was optimistic about his new leads—businessmen, politicians, and combinations of both whom he keenly pursued. Yet as the week sifted and shrank to the final afternoon of his visit, Navi and Neela left the city with nothing. They had spent a hectic day buying news of Jaroon, but they were no closer to finding Seetha than before.

A moody silence clouded their minds along the overcrowded ferry ride back to their hometown; neither bothered to protest when other passengers rushed through the dock and pushed past them to claim the good seats. Accompanied by sounds of the obsolete motor's indigestion, they watched the city contract into a line scratched on the horizon, weathered buildings coloured in a limited number of miserable browns. Wet wind lashed against their skin and settled upon their lips as the ferry surfed the river's swings without flair. When it stopped in its rusty creaks and shudders, they managed to silently agree upon going the rest of the way home on foot; they ignored appeals from eager taxi drivers, cars parked in a clump so tight that it was a mystery how they would depart the docks without a scratch—*Cousin, brother, uncle, I can take you home quick and give you a good rate, just for today* . . . Navi noticed that his steps were more motivated than Neela's. He had to pause many times for his sister to catch up as he scanned the road, hands balled in his pockets, nodding tense hellos to curious neighbours. The slow drip of disappointment and disparagement hadn't seeped into his bones the same way it had long done into hers.

Neela froze near a patch of rogue mango trees. People had picked the tempting fruit as far up as they could reach, leaving the highest mangoes to loosen their grip and splatter rotten on the ground—the whole side of the road was stained by mal-formed yellow ovals. "Why you come back, Navi?" she asked.

He turned and saw that she was shaking with rage. "What?"

"You come to laugh at me? Laugh at what a mess I get myself in? Dat I let my own baby get taken like a stupid fool and can't do a thing about it, huh?"

Navi felt the sun wallop his neck, lashing intense as a

switch. "Oh, this is . . . ," he huffed, incredulous. "What's wrong with you now, Neela?"

"Well you get your wish," she spat, kicking a dried mango seed at him, indifferent to who might be watching their exchange from nearby porches and front yards. "Go ahead and laugh at me, Navi. You know I ain't as good as you. You a big man. Alright? You done prove you better than me, so go along your way and leave me be . . ."

"Shut up!" He skittered in a fervour and kicked the seed back with a clumsy swing of his leg. It smacked her ankle bone and attempted to roll off and hide. "Just shut up!"

"Oh, you want fight me now?" She stepped forward rigidly. "Say what you want say to me. Come on."

"You always, Neela! Always! I shouldn't-a come back here for true! You still so . . . stupid and . . . and wicked!"

"So there, then, you say it, you think I stupid, smarty-boy! Eh? You got your big-up fancy education and now you know everything! And I know nothing!"

Waves of heat radiating from the street only stoked his bitterness. "You bring your own mess on yourself, you know! You ain't got no sense, you never did . . ."

"Dat's right, say what you think . . ."

" . . . and I come all dis way after all you done to me, how you get on so bad with me! I trying to help you find your own child, and look how you thanking me . . ."

" . . . alright, I see what it is now . . ."

" . . . you only behaving like a damn fool! I should-a known it would happen and I shouldn't-a worry myself to come back to dis damn town! I only wasting my time and energy on you!"

Neela pointed into his face. "No. Don't lie. Don't you play like you come back to help me out-a de goodness of your heart. I know you just been waiting to see me bust apart and fail, you been waiting long time to see all dis happen . . ."

"What de hell are you talking about?"

"You just waiting to tell Granny and Mommy everything, how I so careless, how my baby gone, you only want to make me a fool in front-a them . . ."

"Well I'd be telling them de truth, don't you think!" he shouted. "Eh?"

She hurled herself around and stomped hard, mindlessly smashing fruit under her sandals. This caused nearby birds to flap their wings, to warn that they might be forced to search for a more peaceful part of town.

"Why you running away, Neela?" he screamed. "Since when you scared to fight me?"

Her body congealed in midstep.

"Why don't you get me? You know to hurt me good, right?" She hardened her spine straight and he marched forward. "Use your tricks against me, nah! Remember? Do it like you done it to me before!"

She didn't face him when he reached the spot where she stood, under the patchy shade of a wilting palm.

"Come on!" he egged, against her loosened, frazzled ponytail. He poked at her shoulder blade like a child, now fully assured by her hollow silence that she no longer had the ability to carry out her old threats. It hit him all at once—the childhood town he couldn't shake off, the resonance of his empty house, his congested body, untouched by the only woman he had ever loved. "You hear me? Why you don't show me dat you hate me, Neela! Don't you love to do dat? Even when I was far away you was scheming to hurt me, nah? I know you, anything dat would make me happy, you was ready to rob from me." He poked harder, almost shoving; her body jerked with each strike. "What, too weak now? Show me you want me dead! Come on, big woman, show me you want me dead!"

She slapped her palms to her face and crashed down on her knees in soundless despair, shaking him out of his fit. Blushing with embarrassment, he stumbled back a few steps and gazed about, only now aware of the scene Marasaw might have been privy to. He lifted his fingers to his temples and soon crumpled to the road himself, pants scuffed and soiled by wormy mangos.

"I don't know no more," she whimpered into her hands. "I don't know what's wrong with me. I don't know why I can't do nothing to find my baby, nothing's coming to me and I don't know why . . . you right, I'm only a fool, always been, and I lost her, Navi, I lost her and I can't live without her . . ."

He used his cuff to wipe sweat dripping along the angles of his nose, leaving a remnant of salt that burned his lips. "I shouldn't have said those things . . . it ain't your fault she's gone," he answered hoarsely, mumbling to himself.

Neela sagged cross-legged in the dirt, still facing away from her brother, observing the stitching of her stained skirt. She disregarded an army of ants that had gathered near her sandal to claim some decaying fruit for themselves. "I shouldn't-a done all those things. I shouldn't-a been against you so bad . . . I thought I would always be strong but it's gone from me now . . ."

"I was against you too." He nudged that dried mango seed with his toe and it finally cracked into two rough, ashen pieces. "I don't really know why it was like dat."

The shadow of the palm gradually altered itself, lengthening across the ground to protect a new clump of spoiled mangoes, and leaving the old ones to bake in their own sugars. It eventually slunk from Neela to cover Navi as he slouched with forearms slung across his knees, forehead dead-weight against them. Sounds of Neela getting up unsteadily, grunting and forming uncertain steps toward home, were hardly noticeable to his ears; all he could sense was the tickling, loud-quiet drone of insect wings. He quickly grew accustomed to the stink of decomposition laced with his own body odour and allowed mosquitoes to nourish themselves at his expense.

Baby saw Neela's filthy, brooding state and knew it would be unwise to probe about the day's progress or Karha's efforts at the university. She allowed Neela to return to her eternal loads of laundry in peace and tried to forge some sort of normality, but the house was tense and hushed. Only when it became dark outside did Navi totter up the stoop, just as haggard and gloomy as his sister, heading straight to the kitchen to pour some of Baby's bitter pink drink. Somehow, he had developed a taste for it.

Weakened by another immobile, sticky evening, Navi wrenched off his shirt and tie and stayed on the front porch in his sweaty undershirt, the same way he used to as a child doing math around the house. He tried not to concentrate on the endless sensation of water oozing from his pores—he had never noticed himself sweating in this slow-leaching way when he was living in Marasaw. It disturbed him.

"Oh, you don't have to do dat," he said feebly when Baby stirred behind him, gathering his clothes from the sandy wood boards.

She shook off the dust with a few firm flaps. "But they so pretty. I don't want them to get more dirty." Daintily, she draped his shirt and tie over her arm and tucked them close to her chest. "You hungry?" she asked, uncertain whether he was in a speaking mood.

"No thanks."

"But Lenda made stew dis afternoon."

"Lenda makes a lot of stew." He placed his hand against his stomach and blew into his cheeks. "I think I might die of stew."

Baby cupped her mouth and giggled deviously. "You different than I thought." She passed her hand over his silk tie; it was slick and cool, tender under her skin. Catching her own affection, she buried her hand into her skirt's square pocket. "I didn't know you was so nice."

Navi could only smile uncomfortably for a short moment and bring the glass to his eyes, following tiny bubbles on their journey from the bottom.

"I got dis for you." She handed Navi a tattered little book

from her pocket, warm from being cloaked in fabric all day. The chestnut cover was so worn that its faux-leather texture had been smoothed down and its faux-gold-leaf title had long ago flaked away. "When I ain't feeling too right, I turn to my books. Dis one is my favourite."

He bent it open it with one thumb. "What's it about?"

"Lots of things. But I know you gon' like it. You can take it with you tomorrow."

Navi flipped randomly and read some lines on a yellowed page. "I can't take your favourite book from you, Baby."

She got distracted by Sally's shouts inside the house. "Bring it when you come again, dat's all," she answered, nodding at him in assurance that he would surely return to Marasaw. Before entering the house, she bounced over to kiss him on his cheek and cup her hand around his ear. "I know you won't give up," she whispered.

He went through as much of that little book as he could before his sight wore thin in the dull candlelight. The electricity had already been cut, as it was every night across the country. He lay on the couch and closed his scorched lids—words trailed across them, overlapping and blending into each other.

What shall the corrupt man do but be led to destruction by riches, Baby's book warned. He straightened the sheet bunched at his ankles, tucking it around his neck even though he was sweating. *He shall fear losing his ill-gained wealth, only to forget to fear losing his life* . . . Baby had shown him the only photograph Neela had of Seetha, taken just after she had returned to Marasaw from the bush. He pinched his eyes until they prickled, attempting to redraw the child's image and compare it to Neela's face. But he was concerned when he couldn't conjure details of what his sister looked like. With so many years spent ignoring and stepping around Neela, he had never formed much of a mental picture of her. *His prosperity will become his own undoing and corruption shall dig his grave.* Despite cautioning himself that he had an early flight to catch, he remained sleepless, disquieted. He still couldn't resolve what his sister was now, this woman who would inexplicably foil him, brandishing her bull-like autonomy, volatile and reckless. Now, all of a sudden, in a noiseless upheaval, she needed him.

He wasn't aware that Neela was also awake upstairs. An old memory had snuck into her head—she saw her grandmother, so bright and content, leading her and Navi to Mr. Jenhard's house for another overseas phone call. Neela would peer over her brother's shoulder, eagerly watching Granny punch strings of numbers on the dial pad and promising herself that she would memorize the pattern. But all she could concentrate on was how to trick Navi away from the headset and claim it as her own, assuming that he was calculating similar moves. *Mommy, guess what I did today at school,* she would rehearse in her mind, young enough to believe that she could make her exaggerations sound true, *My teacher told me that I got de highest mark in de spelling test and dat I might win de spelling award at de end of de year . . .* Only tonight did she realize how they had stood by the phone, too prepared to push and shove when Granny passed the receiver down—Neela would be behind Navi, arms inadvertently around his waist, both of his hands grasped tightly around hers in anticipation. In the moment's relentless rivalry, they hadn't noticed that they were clinging to each other for dear life.

"Navi?" Neela whispered into the dark living room. "You awake?"

"Yeah."

She crept in and eased onto the old coffee table. It groaned with her weight. "Can't sleep?"

He propped himself up halfway on his elbows. "You can't either, it seems." He coughed dryly.

She could make out only his outline in the feeble grey moonlight that crawled through the living-room window. "You need anything? I can go to de kitchen. What you want?"

"No no, I'm okay." He punched his pillow on the armrest and put his head on it, looking up into the shadows of her face. "We didn't really get anywhere this week," he said. His voice was slowed by fatigue. "I wish I knew what else we could've done. But I don't."

"I don't know either. But . . . thank you for trying." She rubbed the surface of the coffee table, surprised that she didn't get snagged on a splinter.

"It's alright." Navi smoothed the sheet over the bump of his legs. "You should probably try to sleep. I'll be leaving early."

Neela heard the uneasiness in his voice and suddenly reached for his hand, gripping and releasing it and shuffling back to her bedroom in one straight movement. She knew that if she didn't do it quickly, she might be tempted to cling to him with the little she had left in her. This time, on purpose.

CHAPTER 14

The assistant held out a pen, tapping a line on the document with her glossy orange fingernail—she was clearly annoyed but bound by contract to hide it under a pall of seriousness. "Sir, you have to sign dis line too," she said, professional only for the sake of the manager who examined the type over her shoulder. "Please." Her eyelashes fluttered as if she could hardly trap the rude comment inside her mouth.

"Oh, sorry . . . sorry," Navi stuttered. He scratched his signature and wrenched around to observe the massive wall clock. It was only eight in the morning and the bank hadn't officially opened, but he couldn't stop peering through the glass, over the second-floor railing, directly to the lobby's majestic patterned floor. Bored hired soldiers, dwarfed by their machine guns, were still the only ones moving down there.

"And how would you like de withdrawal, sir?" the manager asked, slipping the document into an envelope to be sealed away—it happened so fast that Navi saw the sheet in front of him and by the next second it was cradled in the arms of another assistant heading out the door.

Navi pulled a folded note from his suit jacket and slid it across the desk.

"And I take it you have somewhere to store de bills?"

Navi nodded distractedly.

"And one of our armed escorts will accompany you?"

The manager wasn't pleased when Navi shook his head. "It won't be necessary."

"But your government colleagues called to say dat there would be need of one, and naturally with such a large amount of money, it only makes proper sense, given de state of de nation these days . . ."

Navi's stern expression quickly cut the man off.

"Certainly," the manager replied humbly, leaving the office with light feet.

Although the national bank was one of the few public buildings in the capital city that was air-conditioned, it didn't help Navi feel more comfortable. He reached to liberate himself from his necktie's repressive knot in reflex, but his fingers slid away—it was too early in the morning to be loosening ties. Forcing an exhale and blinking hard to erase the blur of sleep, he scratched stubble on his cheeks and took note of the clock once again; he recalled the plane's descent over water and beach and bush only a few hours ago. Sparse luggage in his hand, he had felt vicious intolerance against the airport staff's play-acting, their make-believe stamping and scanning and scrutiny. He knew that his sister couldn't know he had come back home, that he was only a ferry ride away from Marasaw.

After finishing Baby's book that he had taken with him overseas, Navi had decided to launch a campaign of selective research. Some of Omega Global Venture's worldwide endeavours enjoyed the sheen of success; by digging up the right examples, he could supply his Ministry with a plausible argument for partnering with the corporation. That was not difficult. It was the courting process that concerned him, the wooing of bureaucrats and politicians to assemble high-end support to secure an investment in the Eden Development; he would have to string a web of promises for each of them over hard liquor. Navi had observed the other regional directors at the Ministry of Foreign Investment getting their own dubious pet projects approved with effortless skill. Less observant eyes might have construed their comfort with gentle bribery as a kind of nonchalance, but he knew it was utter brilliance. He would study his colleagues, scrutinizing their calculated demeanour and tactics in order to perfect his own. Yet even in his ambition, he was bathed in acidic worries, once again lying wakeful for many nights—no matter how he measured his plans, they were more daring, more costly, than what he had seen the others get away with.

Opportunity to recant had disappeared when he invited the Minister out to dinner. Feigning a great deal of solicitude, he had let his hand hover over the glass of the Minister's wife, refusing to allow the waiter to pour the wine. *No no, my dear, it's entirely my pleasure . . .* He had draped a napkin over his arm and winked, grinning at her delight; he had eased the bottle's mouth up tantalizingly slowly, allowing the liquid to trickle on a bit after she asked him to stop. Referring to his home country with a fondness he had never possessed, he had managed to dazzle his dinner guests, painting the wonders and dangers of the interior as if he had actually seen them himself. When the Minister's wife thanked him with a clumsy and flirtatious embrace—*Lovely evening, we had a lovely time with you, Mr. Keetham, I hope we will soon see you again*—Navi had known it wouldn't be long before his plans blossomed. He had only hoped that she was too tipsy to notice how his muscles were quaking.

He used the tip of his dress shoe to nudge a deflated duffle bag closer to the bank assistant's feet; she drew her high heels back and openly scorned it underneath her desk. "Tell your people to bring everything to de back entrance," he instructed, now having difficulty breathing. He had rarely known such apprehension in his life, and decided to leave right away.

The unmarked building was hidden amongst larger structures that populated the government block. Its lobby was comparatively modest and lacked the typically garish adornment of political service, but it was heavily secured. Navi prepared himself for interrogation—his hand was already firm against the wallet in his pocket, more than equipped to pass gifts as necessary. But an assemblage of soldiers swarmed at the entrance, wordlessly forming a buffer around him and swerving toward an ominous pair of steel doors. He had no choice; he was suspended in a bubble of camouflage uniforms, walking up the building's spine with rumbles of army boots bouncing about the stairwell.

When they emerged at the top floor and Navi was brought into a colossal office, he didn't wait for a greeting to stride forward and place a cheque on the coffee table's granite surface. "Dis is an instalment for de New Builders Party," he said, "de first of many investments from my Ministry." He plunked the duffle bag, heavy and cumbersome with bricks of foreign cash, on top. "And de rest is for Mr. Begwan. Untraceable bills."

A Builder Party representative was sitting in front of him, frowning and nameless; he was certainly younger and more handsome than Navi had imagined, perhaps due to the transmission of his voice across waters. His business suit was similar to Navi's—black, formal, important—and the man combed his hair into a smooth conservative wave to match. Such particulars wouldn't have typically made an impression on Navi, but today he was overtaken by details. "You and your colleagues cannot turn away from dis now," he said. "It will not be good for anybody. Especially not you. Do you understand?"

Navi noted that, unlike his exterior form, the man's cold candour had been accurately conveyed over the telephone. "De money is already here. If I make up my mind to finish dis deal, they won't back out." Almost winded by intimidation, he drove unhelpful reactions into the deep end of his belly.

The man zipped the duffle bag half open and closed it again, as if disgusted by its contents; he leaned back and planted elbows on his armrests. Navi wished that he could emulate such detached moves, but he wouldn't dare attempt it. "What are these conditions you want, Mr. Keetham?"

"De little girl. And Mr. Begwan will not bother my sister again. Never. No matter where she is or what she's doing. Or I will shut dis deal down in an instant."

"But how can you expect me to ensure something like dat?" The man let a smirk coil his mouth for a brief moment. "What can I do to control him?"

"You'd better find a way," he answered. "Or dat Eden hellhole you Builder Party people dug will never be built and you'll have to deal with it on your own. My sources at the university have been very diligent in watching de party. They say you're already close to bankruptcy, that you've squandered de people's money and have gotten nowhere. They're ready to unite de whole city and lead de way in burning dis block to de ground. Do you think your party will really be able to handle de whole country against you? A handful, yes, but thousands? All of de people will finally have a common enemy. They'll stop fighting each other and turn against you. Tell me, how are you planning to deal with a multimillion fallout with Omega?" He pointed at the soldiers standing erect along the spacious office wall, causing a few to glance at him. Their uneasy eyes looked humorous and adolescent, like boys playing a prolonged game of dress-up. "You think your party will know how to handle these army boys when they rethink their allegiances? They'll want blood. You can't afford to let dat Jaroon-fool ruin your only chance of completing de development."

The man came forward in his chair; Navi didn't know how to interpret his blank facial expression. "And how do I know *your* government won't fall through, now? Hum? Who are you to de party?"

"I'm nothing to your party. I'm nothing to de Ministry of Foreign Investment either. My involvement has nothing to do with any of you people. I want de girl. And I want dat bastard gone." Navi flicked his head to the duffle bag, now sagging and spilling its fat over the edge of the table. "Believe me, I would use that money to kill him if I could."

"Now those are bold words, Mr. Keetham," the man replied. "Especially for dis party at dis time. Are you sure you want to claim them as your own?"

But Navi wouldn't force himself to lie, not even for self-preservation, not even in front of these party people, certainly loyal supporters of Jaroon. "Yes, I do. Make sure all your colleagues know dat. Do you accept my offer, or not?"

For the first time since he had entered the expansive office, the man's smile faded in over his mouth. He set his sight on the broad view of the city gleaming bold into his office window—the capital's streets were already streaming with people and bicycles and cars. "You may not believe me"—he reduced his voice—"but there are others who share your sentiments. In de party and beyond." Standing, the man brushed the front of his pant legs flat and signalled for one of the soldiers to claim the duffle bag.

Navi's eyes trailed him as he scrutinized the cheque, authorized by the Minister of Foreign Investment's blotchy signature stamp. The man casually stepped toward the window. "I'm curious to hear your thoughts on Jaroon Begwan," Navi said.

The man hunched as if stumbling upon a familiar face in the streets below. "In my opinion, dat man is nothing but a petty hustler. But I have come to learn dat he can maintain a bargain when de benefits to him are made obvious." Thoughtfully, the man folded the cheque twice and slotted it into his jacket pocket, a mirror of the pocket it had first emerged from in Navi's suit. "To tell you the truth, I don't care if Mr. Begwan rots to death in dat bush."

It was pitch black in both directions along the road, no moon or stars or backyard fires to assure Neela and Navi that they were within range of Marasaw's inhabitants. They walked far past the edge of town, late into a damp and lonely evening. Weighty drops of rain had completed their course and a persistent mist saturated the air, preventing nighttime winds from passing through. They had left their grand-mother's house side by side; as the road narrowed and became increasingly foreign, they moved closer. Their fore-arms were soon pressed together and they were bothered by the feel of each other's quickened breathing.

"I don't hear no bugs," Neela said. "I can't hear nothing no more." It was as if the insects along this strange part of the road were apprehensive, too anxious to call to the sky, unable to act on their instincts. But Neela understood that she was merely projecting her fretfulness to the environment around her. Mist had gathered on her skin to the point that it began to drip from her chin; she passed her sleeve over her face and licked the dew.

Although he knew he wouldn't be able to see much of anything, Navi peered in front and behind. "It's just de rain. Dat's all."

"You think they really gon' come?" She tried to disguise her quivering voice, as this was not the time to let weakness escape. "What if they break their promise to you?" Nevertheless, her whole body trembled—her jittery voice was only one of its radiating symptoms. She had to concentrate to gulp down the forming lump.

"They'll come. They will," Navi said, measured and low. He didn't know of any other way to quell his sister's fears but to conceal his own. His feet throbbed and he pressed his toes into the bottoms of his shoes. "I still don't think it was a good idea for you to come, Neela."

He had tried to convince her to stay home with Lenda, Karha and Baby, but even after the warnings, she wouldn't entertain the idea. She had stepped stiffly into her sandals and pulled on a jacket, mouth wrinkled small and obstinate, ignoring the loop they had formed around her, their pleading. The truth was, Navi had only attempted to talk her out of it from a mild sense of brotherly duty—he could hardly blame her for being unable to survive the night in that house.

She jolted and tucked closer to him when two lights appeared, sneaking over a dip in the road ahead. "Oh no," she whispered. "It's them?"

"Come dis way." He put his arm around her and they stepped backwards until the tall field grass brushed their calves. As the headlights intensified, they could distinguish the shape of an approaching army jeep with a grunting engine. It slowed down, drove past the place where they stood and lurched to a squealing stop.

They watched the jeep idle and vibrate and steam angrily into the air. Navi tugged Neela's arm as she started forward. "Wait, not yet."

The jeep's back door swung open, crashing metal against metal, and a soldier leaped down—he emerged from a cloud of exhaust shirtless and damp, a large wrapped bundle laid across his arms. Neela's heart jumped and immediately plummeted. *Oh God* . . . The bundle was compact, completely covered by an oversized white sheet. Navi let go of her and put on a cocky swagger toward the vehicle. *Please, Lord, oh please* . . .

But she could no longer contain herself—she rushed past her brother with outstretched arms. "She's mine! Please, give her to me! Please!"

Navi latched onto her waist to prevent her from clinging to the soldier. "Give us de girl," he said, struggling to hold her. "Give her now!"

Neela swatted her brother away and fastened onto the bundle, hauling hard. "Please, give her to me. I need her, oh God, my baby!"

The soldier allowed her to snatch it and she cradled it tightly, rocking and hushing. *Please, please* . . . Yet it was heavy and lifeless in her hands, warm but frighteningly inanimate.

Oh please, God . . . She buried her head in the folds of the fabric. *Let her answer me, please.*

Navi glowered and spoke strongly so those inside the jeep could heed his warning too. "You make sure you tell Jaroon and his fools not to come back to dis town or I will make certain . . ." His voice was snuffed by the soldier's rifle, its barrel pointed squarely into his face.

"Run."

Navi didn't move.

"Now!" the soldier barked.

He scrambled to his sister. "Go, Neela!" he pressed, colliding into her and trying to drag her away.

She could barely see the soldier's gun through the darkness and tears and she let out a gasp, still stooped over her motionless bundle. She had made it only a few steps along the road when a fire-red shot cracked loud and pierced through the fog. "Navi!" Her ears stung and she cowered, eyes wide and grappling around. "No, Navi!"

"I'm alright! Go!"

Cruel laughter and more shots blasted as they ran, clumsy and frantic, crouching over and clinging to what they had come for. Neither would dare to look behind. *Seetha? Baby?* Neela squeezed her eyes shut and put her lips against the bundle to exhale into it; she concentrated on her bumbling stride, one foot barely making it in front of the other. *Please answer me, answer, baby, tell me you're alive* . . . She continued breathing into the sheet and prayed that she could instill new life into her child.

Just one word, one noise, babylove, please, anything. I need to know you with me. You see me, child, you see what a fool I am. You know how much I truly need you, dat I know I ain't nothing on my own, you is all I got and I can't live without you, how I nothing but ash and bone and pain without you . . .

And it came, the sound that made her want to plummet to her knees and release her body to the earth in bottomless hurt and immeasurable relief—those muffled whimperings of a child under the swath of fabric. *Oh Seetha! Oh Lord, my baby!*

Even as the air left her lungs faster than it could enter, Neela couldn't control the overflow of her mouth—*Seetha, my baby Seetha, how mommy miss you so bad, how I die without you, oh God, you know I die without dis girl . . .* The closer they got to the unmarked boundary of their hometown, the more that overflow began to transform on its own, quite unexpectedly, quite unnoticed.

Oh Seetha, Seetha baby, my little darling, my love, you with me, you with me, Navi, you hear her? My baby Seetha and my brother Navi, oh God, my love, my Seetha, my Navi . . .

~

She felt her limbs dangling. After such a long, lonely journey lying on the floor of a jeep, the shots and shouts, the sensation of being cradled hard and rushed indoors, the jerky ascent on creaking stairs, were bewildering. Her body was rested upon a soft place and she pressed her hand against the fabric over her face, moisture from her breath forming a cocoon of heat. She listened to shocked whispers and watched shadows gather close. Their voices were hazily familiar, something she had heard in the background of her dreams during the many months she was away. *Oh God, she's alright? Pull de sheet off, bring some water . . . You think she's alright, Neela? You think de child's hungry? . . . Oh God, she mus'-ee hungry bad . . . Ow, poor thing, quick nah, pull dat sheet off-a her . . .*

Her skin was struck by cool, dry air; the soft white haze was slipped away and sharp light penetrated her squinted eyes. A group of strained faces floated above her, first with covered mouths and complete silence, then with widening eyes. They dissolved into stunned tears. *Oh Neela, oh, de girl grow so beautiful all dis time, look at her, look, she is you, de girl is you, oh Navi, thank you Navi, thank you Lord, oh God . . .* She began to weep too as they brushed against her cheeks, neck, forehead, pleading with her not to cry even as they sobbed into each other's shoulders, backs, hair; they pulled at each other's arms and pointed at the child and began to smile and laugh and hold each other, howling a muddle of disordered phrases. *Dis day come, yes, it come, it's answered prayer, Seetha-baby, look at de child, Neela-girl, Navi-boy, she come home . . .* Only now was she able to separate them in her vision—a man with eyes fixed on her, a faint dumbfounded smile, bending close to stroke her hair; a child straining to carry another puzzled child, hardly smaller than the one holding her; two grown women clinging to a different grown woman, the one she recognized most of all.

Seetha raised her hand to Neela. *Oh baby, it's me, yes, it's me . . .* The child was gathered up—she had wished for this embrace when she was originally lifted from it, when she saw the old house and town's landscape careen away, too confused and shaken to cry. Surrounded by strangers, Seetha had understood that she was far from home; she had been whisked from car to boat to plane, taken to a man who insisted he was *Daddy* and a series of women who would sloppily call themselves *auntie*. Regardless of who they had claimed to be, she had found no relief in their mindless consolation, no comfort in their dismissive, preoccupied care.

Seetha had been alone amongst them all. As her father fetched her from the city to Eden to a nameless collection of towns and back again, he would attempt to appease her embittered face, her sense of cruel disruption. But it was still her mother's arms that she wished for and mourned, no matter how he held and rubbed and bounced her. Her mother's arms had been an enduring sanctuary, wrapped in flesh and breasts and heartbeat, founded deep inside the Nasee-Ki's breathing bush. They became the child's singular desire.

Seetha's loneliness and longing had twisted the course of events, had been the force behind her journey back to Neela—it was her desire to return to her mother that had prompted broken people to collide and converge, to rage and retrieve her from her father. She would not comprehend her untamed power until years later, and she would never know that the power had been planted in her by Neela's loss of it. Still, she would get her wish to have her mother, and she would have the rest of them from then on, Navi and Lenda and Karha and Baby and Sally, to crowd and reassure her; she would eventually have even more, when her grandmother and great-grandmother were added as well. Marasaw's sun and rain would stream down on her and she would sprout over the years in the thicket of her family, sheltered and bright, vivid green like the rainforest's leaves.

But to begin, Seetha would be with her mother once again, and she would soon fall asleep in her embrace.

ACKNOWLEDGMENTS

Working with Michael Schellenberg, Associate Publisher at Knopf Canada, has been a great honour. Thank you for taking this book on. My thanks go to Ron Eckel, Associate Rights Director, all of the kind people at Knopf and Gena Gorrell, the skilled copyeditor who pored over this novel.

Suzanne Brandreth at The Cooke Agency has helped me in so many ways. Thank you, Suzanne; your generosity and persistence have made a huge impact upon me.

Many thanks to the Toronto Arts Council for the writing grant that helped me start this book.

To my dear family and friends, thank you for being a support network and an inspiration. To David Hunter, my best friend and partner, thank you for always encouraging me.

And most of my thanks go to God, who makes incredible things happen. I'd be foolish to attribute this wonderful opportunity to anyone else.

Andrea Gunraj is a community outreach worker for METRAC (www.metrac.org), which promotes the rights of women and children to live free from violence and the threat of violence. Her parents emigrated from Guyana, a region whose culture and politics have infused Gunraj's writing. She and her husband live in Toronto.

A NOTE ABOUT THE TYPE

The Sudden Disappearance of Seetha has been set in Granjon, a modern recutting of a typeface derived from the classic letterforms of Claude Garamond (1480-1561). It is named in honour of Robert Granjon, a successful French publisher, punch cutter and founder who lived during the sixteenth century and was a contemporary of Garamond.

BOOK DESIGN BY CS RICHARDSON